Unbreakable Bonds

An Angela Panther Novel

Carolyn Ridder Aspenson

Booktrope Editions
Seattle, WA 2014

Cover Design by Tatiana Vila

This is a work of fiction. Names, characters, places, brands, media, and incidents are either the product of the author's imagination or are used fictitiously. Any resemblance to similarly named places or to persons living or deceased is unintentional.

PRINT ISBN 978-1-62015-353-6

EPUB ISBN 978-1-62015-378-9

Library of Congress Control Number: 2014905166

PRAISE FOR
UNBREAKABLE BONDS
AN ANGELA PANTHER NOVEL

"I laughed and I cried...and laughed...and cried...throughout the entire book! This book was so real (yes even with the heroine seeing her mother's ghost) and the emotion in it will stay with me for a long, long time!"

—*JOE COOL REVIEW*

"*Unbreakable Bonds* is just as captivating as *Unfinished Business*. Angela and her sarcastically funny Ghost Mom are a perfect puzzle solving team - you won't want to put this down until you know how it all ends!"

—*KATE LUCNIK*

"*Unbreakable Bonds* is a fantastic follow up to *Unfinished Business*. To see the story develop in this way is exciting! I can't wait for the next book in the series!"

—*KARYN CLOUGH*

"*Unbreakable Bonds* finds Angela searching for the gift she never wanted, while tackling the everyday issues of being a wife, mother, friend and daughter. What follows is a personal journey full of grief and comic relief as Angela handles the turmoil of life after death, without losing her wit and charm. "

—*ERIN HARTMAN*

For my mother, Rita D. Palanca

And my father, Richard L. Ridder

If only we'd have had more time together.

RIP

CHAPTER ONE

THE SUN'S BLISTERING HOT RAYS beat down and singed my skin. Rays so hot even the shaded woods and sunscreen didn't stop the burning. I sprinted, sucking in big gulps of air. I needed shelter, and chastised myself for parking my car two miles away. I knew I couldn't keep this pace for two more miles.

Pebbles and rocks pelted me like hail during a Georgia winter storm. They bounced off my head, pinged me on my arms and legs. It would have been funny if it didn't hurt.

Out of energy, I sought shelter under an oak tree. I pressed my back against it and the bark pierced my skin, but it hurt less than the rocks. I bent over, hands on my knees, and drew in air, hoping to catch my breath when another rock clipped me on my right knee. "Knock it off," I yelled.

Another rock dropped through the tree's branches and smacked my head. I rubbed the spot and felt a bump beginning to form. "Ouch, that hurt."

Another rock the size of a small lemon plopped down at my feet, but at least it didn't make contact with my battered body. I picked it up and tossed it between my hands. "This ain't gonna work. I can't hear you, let alone see you. My psychic juju's out of whack so unless you can spell with these rocks, you're screwed. *Capiche*?"

The rocks stopped but only for a short time.

"Thank God." I hit 'play' on my iPhone and ran. Halfway through the first song, another rock smacked me on the head. My face tightened and through pressed lips I said, "Enough already. I can't help you. If I could, don't you think I would, just to stop the darn rock attack?"

A small tree branch cracked me on the arm. "Now that's just rude." One by one, rocks battered my legs. I doubled my pace, feeling the tiredness in my legs kick in. "Boy, you're a testy one, huh?"

The rocks hit me at breakneck speed and no matter how fast I ran I couldn't escape them.

I knew it took copious amounts of energy for ghosts to move objects. Usually they wore out quickly and had to disappear to recoup that energy, so I egged the ghost on, hoping to tire it out enough to make it go away.

My heart pounded. I picked up my pace. "Is that all you got? Come on, Casper. Bring it." I thrust out my chest and sprinted for a full minute, jumping over tree stumps and thrown rocks. I relished my ability to conquer an unseen competitor, and did my best Rocky Balboa imitation, hands in the air and cheering—until I tripped and face-planted it into a pile of animal poop. "Crap."

I pulled off my tee shirt, exposing my workout bra, wiped my face with the shirt and waited. The rocks stopped. I'd worn out the ghost but it one-upped me with the face-plant. "Touché," I said, and sulked the rest of the way to my car.

I'd lost the ability to hear and see ghosts after my father died six months ago but that hadn't stopped them from trying to connect. I understood the desperate need for closure, for a final chance to say I love you or ask for forgiveness. I needed something similar because when I lost my father and my gift, I also lost my connection to my mother, whose spirit had been a constant in my life for almost a year.

All of my efforts to fix my gift had failed, and when a ghost tried to connect, it just left both the ghost and me frustrated and annoyed.

*   *   *

On the drive home I called my best friend Mel and told her about the face-plant. "So I had another one," I said.

"Did you see it?"

"Nope."

"Hear it?"

"Nope."

"What did it do?"

"Attacked me."

"What? How?" She asked.

"Threw rocks at me."

She giggled. "Ticked it off, huh?"

"Maybe just a little."

"Uh huh."

"My entire body will be purple by this time tomorrow."

"Could be worse," she said.

"It is."

"Oh, crap."

"Exactly."

"Huh?" she asked.

"Crap."

"Speak English, please."

"Says the Asian."

"Born and raised in New Jersey, baby. Tell me what happened."

So I did.

I held the phone away from my ear while she laughed. "You done?" I whined.

"You just made my crappy day better." She busted out laughing at her own joke.

"Are you at Fowler Park?" Mel asked.

"Nope. The bike trail at Central Park."

"I hate that place."

"You hate running, not the place."

"You're right."

"If you ran more often, you'd probably beat me once in a while."

"I just let you win."

"Uh huh."

"I don't want you to feel bad," she said.

I laughed. "You and Nick up for dinner tonight? I'm thinking Mexican."

She let out a loud sigh. "Nick's gotta work."

"Again? How many Saturdays in a row is that now?"

"Six."

Mel had reason to complain about Nick's work schedule. After my mother died, he worked every weekend for several months. Mel had been frustrated then, too.

"That sucks."

"Yup."

"Is everything okay at his job?"

Another loud sigh. "Heck if I know. We barely talk anymore."

"What?"

Mel backpedaled. "It's not a biggie. Don't worry about it."

"Um, hello. Best friend code? You tell me everything and I tell you everything, remember?"

"Not when one best friend just lost both parents. You've got enough on your plate."

"I didn't just lose them," I said. "And there's always room on my plate for your stuff, too."

"Fine. I'll tell you, but not on the phone. The walls have ears. How about Starbucks, tomorrow morning? Say eight o'clock?"

"Sounds great."

"Okay. See you then."

"I'm worried. Are you okay?"

"Not really, but we'll talk tomorrow."

That was Mel's way of telling me to drop the subject, so I did.

"Okay. Call or text if you need me."

"Always do."

I wrinkled my nose. I smelled feces and rolled down my windows for the rest of the drive home. When I got there, I walked into the kitchen and smacked right into my husband, Jake.

He scrunched up his face and backed away. "Good God woman, you smell like crap."

"Literally or figuratively?"

"Literally."

"There's a reason for that."

*   *   *

I woke up at three a.m. drenched from night sweats. After a quick, cold shower, I was wide awake and cranky, so I grabbed my phone and brand new bifocals and went to the den. My Pit-Greyhound mix Gracie followed.

I'd been waking up soaked for a few months and was probably in the throes of peri-menopause but wasn't ready to fully admit it.

I sent Mel a text, something I always did when I couldn't sleep. "Woke up soaked again. Stupid Eve. I hate her. Hope you're okay." I firmly believed that Eve was responsible for all women's ailments, from periods, to childbirth, to sagging breasts. Had she not taken the first bite of that apple, I was sure men would be popping out kids and wearing tampons. I hated Eve.

I powered on the TV and clicked through the channels until Mark Harmon and his NCIS crew appeared. I texted Mel again and complained, but she didn't respond. She was probably sleeping. Cold, I wrapped my mother's old plaid blanket around me and snuggled into the crook of the chair, Gracie at my feet. Tiredness eventually kicked in and my eyes struggled to stay open, until they finally gave in to sleep.

Something crashed to the floor and jolted me from my slumber. I switched on the light, scanned the room and that's when I saw it—a rock, the size of a lemon, sitting on the floor in front of the TV console. "Well I'll be damned."

Gracie, awake and on high alert, sniffed the air. Her ears dropped and she moved closer to me, both signs of fear. I rubbed her head, comforting us both. "What's wrong, Gracie girl?"

I did a quick ghost check, running down the list of common signs of paranormal activity. Though the room had been chilly, the temperature returned to normal. No unusual smells, no sense of being watched, nothing touching me and no creepy sounds, but my gut told me something was up. I hoped it was my mother, but Gracie knew Ma both dead and alive and wouldn't be scared of her. Just in case, I said, "Ma," but got no reply, not that I thought I would.

I stiffened. The idea of an unknown ghost in my house made me uncomfortable. My house, my turf, and I didn't like having it invaded. I sent Mel another text, hoping my desperation would somehow transmit through the cell towers and wake her. "THERE'S A GHOST IN MY DEN! WAKE UP!"

She didn't reply so I clicked off the TV, threw the blanket down and bolted up the stairs, with Gracie at my heels. I jumped in bed and snuggled up next to Jake. He moved closer, spooning his body around mine, and let his hands wander.

"Oh, yeah." Jake considered snuggling foreplay. Jake considered breathing foreplay, too.

"There's a ghost in the den," I whispered.

"Uh huh." His hands wandered lower.

"I could feel it, Jake."

"Uh huh."

I pushed his hands away and sat up. "Jake, there's a ghost in the den!"

He opened his eyes. "I heard you, Ang. What do you want me to do, go down and beat it with a baseball bat?"

"Yes, please."

He sat up and turned on the nightstand light. "Okay, go to the garage and get Josh's old bat."

I punched him in the arm. "Not funny."

"Good grief," he said and crawled out of bed. "Be right back."

"My hero." I lay back down and pulled the covers up to my chin. Gracie jumped onto the bed, turned in circles and finally settled next to me, right on top of Jake's pillow. I laughed, knowing how he hated that.

A minute later Jake was back. "Great," he said, pushing the dog off of the bed. "Now my pillow is going to smell like dog ass."

"Well?" I asked, keeping the covers up near my chin.

He climbed back into bed, scooted up close to me, and assured me the coast was clear, and then went back to letting his hands wander. I wasn't so sure but exhaustion replaced fear, and my eyes once again lost their battle with sleep. Poor Jake didn't get lucky because I was out within seconds.

* * *

Mel was sitting at our regular Starbucks table, twisting her wedding ring around her finger, waiting for me. Her hair, pulled up in a ponytail, looked less stellar than usual. She had both drinks on the table, as always.

I set my purse down and sat across from my friend. "Sorry I'm late. Rough night."

"I read." She handed me my coffee.

"Thanks. Next one's on me."

"Baristas already know that. So what happened?"

"I finally fell asleep on the chair in the den and all of a sudden I heard something hit the wood floor, and it was a freaking rock. I ran upstairs, got Jake, and made him check. He said everything was fine, but it's not like he can see ghosts anyway. I felt bad for waking him up, though."

"Did he try to get lucky?"

"Do bears crap in the woods?"

She laughed and I saw a slight glimmer in her mostly bloodshot eyes. "Wouldn't a more appropriate question be, does Angela face-plant it into bear crap in the woods?"

"Touché."

"Sorry I wasn't up," she said through a yawn. "I took two Ambien and was out before nine." She took the lid off her coffee, swirled the cup in circles and took a drink. "Nick is cheating on me."

My chin dropped. "Shut the front door."

"If I'm lyin', I'm dyin'."

"How do you know?"

"A woman knows when her husband's pounding someone else's punanni pavement."

Pounding someone else's punanni pavement?

Mel's marriage wasn't perfect, but it seemed solid. Sure, she complained about the same things most women did—he worked too much, burped too much, passed too much gas, that kind of stuff, but pounding someone else's punanni pavement was a serious accusation. "You can't be right, Mel."

"He's banging his new assistant."

"But *how* do you know?"

"His work schedule, for starters. It's practically twenty-four seven like it was after your mom died."

"Maybe they've got a big project or something. Working late doesn't always equate to an affair."

"It did before, after your mom died."

Before? "What?"

She pulled her hair out of its ponytail and ran her hand through the long, black strands. "Nick made me promise not to say anything but I should have known not to listen. He just didn't want to look bad because he knew he'd do it again."

My skin tingled. I couldn't believe there'd been a first time, let alone a second. "How'd you find out about the first time? I can't believe you never told me."

"Your mother had just died. I wasn't going to drop a bomb like that on you."

I was shocked. Nick didn't seem like the kind of guy who'd cheat on his wife. "Did he actually admit to it then?"

She nodded. "Yup. When I told him I knew he was doing it, he did."

"What made you think he was cheating?"

"Typical cheating signs. Working late, smelling freshly showered when he got home, no interest in sex." She stared into her cup. "Stuff like that."

"Wow."

"Yup."

I couldn't think of anything more to say.

"I'm divorcing him."

"I'm sorry." I covered her hand with mine. "Are you sure that's what you want?"

"My kids will be heartbroken, but I can't live with someone who's unfaithful. I just can't." She pulled her hand from mine and stared at her wedding ring.

"So what happens now?"

"I need proof of the affair. I don't want my kids to blame me. I want them to know the truth."

"They're young, Mel. They're not going to blame you."

"I know they won't now, but I want something in writing so when they're older they can see it if need be."

That made sense, so I nodded.

"Can you help me?"

"Abso-freaking-lutely. We'll nail his ass to the wall."

"We're gonna need your mom."

My heart sank. "Fran? For what?"

"For spying, you know, like she did with your kids."

My mother did help keep an eye on my daughter Emily during a rough time but that was when I could see and hear her. "You know I can't communicate with her."

"But you're still connected to that world somehow, and that has to mean something. You haven't completely lost your gift if ghosts are still trying to contact you. That could have been her yesterday, and last night, and the countless other times stuff has happened."

"I know, but I can't hear or see them and those are important pieces to be missing, you know? Besides, it didn't feel like Fran throwing those rocks at me, and last night Gracie was scared. She wouldn't be scared of my mother."

"Well then for the sake of me and all of the ghosts trying to communicate with you, you need to get your gift back, pronto."

"Easier said than done."

"Maybe Linda can help?"

I'd been working with Linda, my psychic counselor, ever since my mother returned from the dead. Linda helped me work through the kinks of my gift and assured me I wasn't crazy. Lately we'd focused on fixing my gift, but so far nothing we tried worked.

Mel picked up her phone and poked the screen with her index finger.

"What are you doing?"

"Calling Linda."

Oh boy. She was determined and Mel in *determined* mode was scary. It ranked second to Mel in *don't screw with my kids* mode, which was feared worldwide. "Don't bother. I'm seeing her tomorrow."

Her eyes stayed glued to her phone.

"Mel?"

She looked up. "I'm sorry. Think she'll do it?"

"Do what?"

"Talk to Fran." She touched her neck with her fingers. "Didn't I just say that?"

"Nope."

"Oh." She tilted her head and gave me a half smile. "Sorry. My brain is working faster than my mouth."

"That's a first."

"Har dee har har."

"And I doubt she will. She said she wouldn't talk to my mother until she thought I was ready."

"But this isn't for you."

"I'm not sure that'll matter."

"Can you at least ask?"

"Of course."

"Thanks," she said.

"Do you think Nick knows you know?"

She rolled her eyes, which wasn't as annoying as when my daughter did it. "That would require him to talk to me so, no."

"What a tool."

"I prefer cheating rat bastard."

"Good one." I sipped my coffee. "I bet we can dig up some dirt on Nick without my mother."

Mel raised her eyebrows. "Go on."

I grabbed my phone and searched the Internet for *how to catch your spouse cheating.*

Mel moved her chair over to my side of the table. She looked at my phone. "You know I've done that, right?"

I nodded. "I figured, but look, there's all kinds of phone apps and stuff you could put on his phone." I swiped my phone's screen between different websites.

She shook her head. "Too risky. I don't wanna do that. We need to follow him, find out where he's banging his assistant."

I put down my phone. "Uh, he knows our cars."

"Yeah but if we're careful, he won't see them."

"I'm not sure that's a good idea."

"Well, other than using your mother, it's the only one I can think of."

"Lemme think about it for a bit, okay? I don't want to rush into doing anything that could make things worse for you."

She leaned back in her chair and folded her arms across her chest. "I've got nothing but time."

"Are you keeping track of money and stuff?"

She nodded. "Yeah, for the most part. I'm writing down anything and everything. I researched divorce laws in Georgia. It's a no-fault state—which I think is a bunch of crap, but if I have proof, I think I'll have a better chance of getting what I want from him."

"You're probably right."

Mel rubbed her forehead and exhaled deeply. "I can't believe this is happening."

I rubbed her arm. "Me neither. I'm so sorry."

"Fran could get me what I need, you know?"

"I know."

"We gotta get your gift back, and not just for me, but for you, too. I know how much you miss your parents."

She was right about that. "I know. I'm doing all I can, but so far it's not working."

"Well, maybe Linda will have a solution."

I didn't think she would, but I didn't say that to Mel. Right now she needed to stay as positive as possible. I drank the last of my coffee. "Do you want a refill?"

"Nah. I need to run to the grocery store and get home. The kids will be up soon."

I walked her to her car. "I'm here for you, you know."

We hugged. "I know."

I cried on my drive home. In the past few years my life had been a rollercoaster ride full of loops and twists and stomach-shocking hills, and I couldn't catch my breath. I longed for the consistency of the mundane, of my old life, but deep down, I knew that life was gone forever.

*   *   *

I pulled into our cul-de-sac and saw Jake mowing the lawn, and my kids, Josh and Emily, arguing next to the driveway. I debated turning around and driving away but Jake waved and I blew that thought. I wouldn't have gotten far anyway because as much as my family drove me insane, they were mine and I loved them—most of the time, anyway.

I parked in the garage, got out of the car and stepped between my kids. "Can't you at least pretend to get along?" I yelled over the sound of the mower.

Emily's face was red. "Josh is gettin' all up in my business and like, it's pissing me off." Her hands moved to the flow of her frustration.

I gave my seventeen-year-old, smart-mouthed daughter the stink eye. "Language, Emily."

She cowered, her shoulders sinking. "Well, he is."

"What exactly does that mean, *getting all up in your business*?" I asked.

"He was reading my Facebook posts."

Josh pushed his chest out and held his chin up. "Was not."

Emily narrowed her eyes at her brother. "Was too."

"Was not."

I glowered at my husband mowing the lawn in blissful oblivion. I hated lawn work, but would have traded that for dealing with my kids in a heartbeat. "You have two thousand Facebook friends, Emily, and you don't even know two hundred people."

"So."

"So you don't care if strangers see your posts, but you throw a hissy fit if your brother does?"

Josh smirked and puffed his chest out further.

"Yeah," she said, completely unaware of how ridiculous that sounded.

"Then don't leave your Facebook open on the iPad, stupid." Josh said, mimicking his sister's whine.

It was Josh's turn to get the stink eye.

"Shut up, loser," Emily said.

I threw my hands in the air. "All right. Guess what time it is." Every time my kids argued, I made them hug. It reminded them of their familial connection and made them feel silly—a win-win in my opinion. "It's hug time! Oh yeah!" I hummed, bouncing from foot to foot.

Both kids wrinkled their noses and flinched. "No, Mom. Please," they said in unison. At least they'd agreed on something.

"Too late." I wiggled my eyebrows and laughed. "Ya'll forced me to do it, now go ahead. I'm waiting." I gently pushed on both of their backs, urging them to come together. They groaned but acquiesced. Emily stuck her finger in her mouth and gagged.

I held back a giggle and said, "That doesn't count. Do it again."

Josh balked. "Mama, come on. I did it."

"Emily gagged. It doesn't count."

"Why'd you have to do that?" He asked her, and then just barely wrapped his arms around her in another hug.

They both made gagging faces. "Wow, so dramatic." I made a gagging face for them.

"Mom," Emily said, her voice strained. "You need to teach him to, like, keep his hands off of stuff that doesn't belong to him."

"It's the family iPad," he said.

Josh had a point, but more importantly, Emily was guilty of her own complaint. She touched my stuff on a daily basis and it made me so mad I'd practically grown horns. "Pot calling the kettle black there, Em."

She rolled her eyes—my biggest Emily pet peeve. "I don't touch other peoples stuff, Mom."

I picked my jaw up off the ground. If I couldn't find something I just had to look in her bedroom. I could usually find it buried under piles of clothes. "Oh no, you did not just say that."

She eye-rolled me again and the vein in my forehead throbbed. I pressed on it just in case it tried to pop out.

"That's different, Mom. Like, just make him stop, please." She bounced on the tips of her toes.

I shook my head. Her ability to separate herself from her own wrongdoing was fascinating. "There is a solution to the problem, you know."

She stuck her tongue out at her brother. "See, I told you Mom would, like, side with me."

He curled his upper lip at her.

"Emily," I said. "Mothers don't take sides. We review the situation and make a fair and educated decision based on the evidence presented."

"So you're gonna, like, tell him to stop sticking his nose in my business, right?"

"Nope. I'm gonna tell you to delete your Facebook account, Em. Problem solved."

Josh double fist-pumped the air. "Yes!"

Emily threw her hands up and stomped into the house saying, "He's totally your favorite."

I turned to Josh and nodded. "That went well."

Josh laughed. "Yup."

* * *

Emily stayed in her room until she had to leave for work a few hours later. After dinner, Jake and Josh bonded over video games, so I had some much-needed alone time. Linda had given me a month-long homework assignment—to practice meditating. I'd tried several times, but my brain couldn't chill out. Instead of repeating calm, relaxing chats, I'd sing entire versions of 1980s pop rock songs, something at which I excelled. Since Linda and I had an appointment in a few days, I wanted to give the meditation one last shot.

It was a beautiful night. The sky was clear and stars shone like a *Lite Brite* board filled with only white pegs, so I sat in a chair on our deck, closed my eyes and tried to relax. Male crickets chirped their mating songs as male frogs croaked for the same reason. I pictured crickets and frogs having sex. A bird sang and I sang back, though less in tune than my feathered partner. I thought about birds having sex, but only until I realized they didn't actually perform the act, at which point I just felt stupid.

The breeze picked up, ruffling the leaves on the trees. It almost sounded like a whispered, *Ah Madone*—my mother's favorite expression. I stilled and listened closely. "Ma? Are you here?" A frog croaked. "Got a frog in your throat?" I laughed at my own joke. "Come on, Ma, that was funny."

I heard nothing but silence. I sat again and contemplated another meditation attempt but knew it was hopeless. I was tired, so I gave up and went to bed.

Face washed, hair brushed and Elmo pajamas on—I knew how to dress sexy for bed—I did another Internet search on catching cheaters. Every site said the same thing. Get phone records, credit card receipts, bank statements, and the like. I did a search for *how to follow someone in a car and not get caught* and came across a private investigator site full of tips and tricks to catch cheating spouses. The site said the most important tool was record keeping. Everything from who the spouse claimed to see, where they went, what times they were gone, etc. I copied and pasted some of the information into a text to Mel. She sent a return text asking if I would be willing to follow him soon.

"Sure. Will call you tomorrow."

* * *

That night I dreamed my mom and I were standing in the kitchen of my childhood home. She was making my favorite Italian cookies, *pizzelles*, and looked like she did before cancer ravaged her body, full-figured with a tiny waist. I looked like the nine-year-old Angela, buckteeth and pigtails and not even remotely attractive.

"Why are you gone, Ma?" I asked, picking at a cookie.

"Ah Madone. I'm not gone. Just 'cause you can't see me don't mean I'm gone," she said.

"Dad's dead."

"I know."

"It hurts," I said.

"I know."

"I need you, Ma. It's hard without you."

"You gotta do the work."

"But how? I don't know how." I handed her a Barbie with its head missing. "I can't fix her by myself."

She said, "I know. I got it covered," and then she shimmered away.

CHAPTER TWO

GRACIE WOKE ME UP AT FIVE A.M. Half awake, I shuffled downstairs to let her out, turned on the coffee and got her breakfast. While she ate, I shuffled back upstairs and dressed for the gym. I came back down, poured myself a cup of caffeinated heaven and sat at the kitchen counter. I took a sip of coffee, inhaling the smooth, bold delight. When I put the cup down, I noticed a rock sitting right next to it. "Good grief."

I examined the rock and then rolled it back and forth along the granite counter. Someone was trying hard to get my attention, but for the life of me, I couldn't figure out who. The rocks just didn't make sense. I stared at the ceiling. "I need a little help here," I said, but got nothing in return. I sighed and rolled the rock to the other side of the counter. "You're not helpful."

I finished my coffee and headed to the gym where I worked out harder than I had in weeks. During the ride home I was on an endorphin high and regretted not hitting the gym sooner. I blasted the radio and sang along at the top of my lungs to Air Supply—a 1980s ballad duo. It wasn't exactly rock, but I rocked it regardless.

Jake and Josh were eating breakfast when I returned.

"Is Em up?" I must have been talking to ghosts because neither of them answered. "Is Emily up yet?"

Still nothing. "Bueller?" Music from the 1980s wasn't my only specialty. I was the queen of movie trivia from that time, too. I had no recollection of when Christopher Columbus discovered America, but I could recite entire scenes from every John Hughes movie made that decade, verbatim. My brain was a wonderful, mysterious thing.

"Bueller?" I repeated, but it still didn't work. "Jake, I'm leaving you for another woman."

"No, you're not." He caught my eye and grinned playfully.

Of course he heard that.

Josh shook his head and muttered, "Gross, Mama."

"Seriously? You heard that, but didn't hear me ask twice about Emily?"

"I heard you," Jake said.

Josh said, "Me, too."

I flicked my hand in the air like Ma used to. "Then why didn't you answer?"

"I figured he would," Jake said, pointing at our son.

"She wasn't asking me, Dad." Josh said, shaking his head.

"I give up," I growled, went upstairs and knocked on Emily's door.

"I'm up."

"Can I come in?"

"Sure."

She was sitting at her desk, putting on make up. Her green work apron sat on top of a pile of clothes on her bed. I cringed at the sight of the pile, but hard as it was, ignored it. "What time do you have to be at work?"

"Eight."

"What time do you get off?"

"Four."

Emily was a teenager of few words, unless of course she was complaining or whining. Having a normal conversation with her was like trying to milk a bull. Actually, milking a bull was probably easier. "Got any plans for the night?"

"Hangin' out with Hayden." She used her fingers to open her left eye wide and drew a line on her lower inner eyelid with black eyeliner.

"Cool. She's coming here, I assume?"

"No. We're going to a movie."

I picked up a bottle of perfume and smelled it. "Oh, hadn't realized you'd asked to do that."

Emily rolled her eyes. I pretended to ignore it, but rubbed the vein in my forehead just in case it tried to pop out. "Mom, can I, like, go to Hayden's after work and, like, go to a movie?"

"Who's, like, driving?"

"Mom."

"Whose mom?"

She rolled her eyes again.

"Honey, you know how Georgia law works. You can't have her in the car with you yet. We've discussed this before."

"Like, I know, Mom. She's gonna drive. I promise."

"Was that, like, hard?"

"What?"

"Telling me who's, like, going to drive?"

Blank stare. Loved that one. She used it so rarely and I enjoyed the change from the eye roll.

"Okay, you can go but remember your curfew is, like, eleven p.m."

Third eye roll. My patience was astounding. I wanted to beat my chest with my fists to brag about my strength, but didn't want to appear a braggart.

"I know, Mom. You've only told me that, like, a billion times."

"And I'm sure I'll tell you, like, a billion more, because, like, that's what moms do."

She shook her head. "Fine. Can I finish getting dressed now, please?"

"Like, totally."

"You're funny, Mom."

"It's a gift," I said and got up to leave. Walking out, I saw a shadow move near her bed, but when I turned my head, it was gone.

I got ready for my appointment with Linda and as I headed downstairs, I saw three small rocks sitting on the hallway bookcase. "Seriously," I muttered. "I'm over the rocks. Try something else."

Jake was working in his basement office, and Josh was at the kitchen table, reading a lacrosse magazine. I showed him the rocks. "Are you leaving these lying around the house, Little Man?"

"Nope."

"You sure? I keep finding them."

He flipped a page in the magazine. "Not mine."

"Maybe one of your friends brought them in?"

"We're twelve, Mama. We don't play with rocks."

I grabbed the French bread loaf from the breadbox and cut two slices for a sandwich. "Oh, sorry. I forgot how mature you are now. You shoot aliens on the X-Box instead."

"I'm growing up. It's part of life."

"No fair using my sayings back on me, Josh."

He laughed. "Going somewhere?"

"Yup, to see Linda."

"Cool, tell her I said hi."

"I will. I'm sure she'd love to see you again sometime, too."

Like me, Josh had the gift, but he only saw my mother. And like me, when Dad died, his gift died, too. I took him to see Linda a few times, but because I wanted his life to be as normal as possible, I didn't push it when he said he didn't want to go back.

"Maybe someday."

"I'll let her know."

"And don't worry, Mama. You're gonna be talking to Grandma again real soon."

I put the bread away. "Why do you say that?"

"Just a feeling."

"Something you wanna talk about, Little Man?"

"Nope."

My pulse quickened. "Have you seen Grandma?"

"Nope."

I trusted him to tell me the truth. "Okay, just asking, 'cause what you said seems a little strange to me." I grabbed some ham and cheese from the fridge and made my sandwich.

"I dreamed about her. And Grandpa, too," he said.

"Oh yeah? Me too, at least about Grandma. What'd you dream?" I grabbed an orange and peeled it.

"I dreamed Grandma and me were in a kitchen and she was making cookies. She told me her mom used to make them all the time. She said you loved them. Pizza cookies or something like that."

"Pizzelles. So, did you two talk or anything?"

"Yup." He flipped another page in the magazine.

"Well, what'd she say?"

"Just that she was trying really hard and you'd better be grateful."

I didn't think Ma was talking about the cookies. "That's Grandma for ya, always bragging."

"Yup."

I glanced at the sandwich and the orange, deciding which to eat first and chose the sandwich. I took a bite, and chewed before speaking. "So what'd you dream about Grandpa?"

"We were sitting outside on a deck. Well, it wasn't really a deck 'cause it was cement, and Grandpa had a ball and threw it into a bunch of trees and then told me to get it."

I stilled. "Was it dark?"

"Yup."

"Did you get the ball?"

"Yup."

"Were you scared?"

"At first, but then I wasn't."

"You're a brave kid."

"It was 'cause of Grandpa. He told me not to be scared. He said I could do it, and he wouldn't let anything bad happen because he had my six." He flipped another page in the magazine.

"Was that the whole dream?"

"Pretty much."

"That's a nice dream."

"Oh, then he said he liked playing with electrical stuff."

"Really? That's odd. Grandpa wasn't much of a handyman."

He shrugged. "That's what he said."

We talked a little more about his plans for the day as I finished my sandwich. Before leaving, I kissed him goodbye, grateful he was still young enough to not be completely grossed out by his mother. "Make wise choices today."

"Always do, Mama."

He was right. He did.

In the car I thought about his dreams. It wasn't a coincidence that Ma showed up making cookies in both of our dreams. "I'm trying, Ma. I really am. And I'm sure you are, too."

Josh's dream about my father wasn't just a dream. It was too similar to a regular event of my childhood. My dad and I would often sit on the back porch at night. He'd throw the ball and tell me to get it, but it was dark, and I was scared. My father was former military, and "I've got your six," or anything referencing having someone's six is a popular military expression meaning, "I've got your back." My father used that expression often. I didn't know the significance of replaying that scene with Josh in a dream, but I knew it meant something.

I hated not being able to understand the signs of the dead, especially the ones from my parents. When I first began communicating with the dead, I fought it and now I kicked myself for that. Maybe if I'd accepted it sooner, it wouldn't have disappeared.

Knowing the odds were stacked against me, I asked my dad for help anyway. "Can you gimme a hint about Josh's dream, Dad? And the reference to electrical stuff? I'm at a loss for that one, too."

Dad kept quiet.

*   *   *

Linda was waiting for me in the front lobby of her office. We said our hellos and then walked into her spiritual room. Before she sat, she grabbed two bottles of water from her mini-fridge and tossed one to me. I sat and guzzled the water.

"Thirsty?"

"I'm pretending it's wine."

"Nervous?"

"Me? Absolutely not." I tapped my fingers on the table. Linda looked at me and I shrugged. "What?"

She raised her eyebrows.

"Okay, so maybe I'm a little nervous."

"Why? This is old hat for you."

"Just ready to get back to talking to the dead, I guess." It was still strange to hear myself say stuff like that.

After my gift disappeared I was desperate to connect with my parents. I hadn't needed to mourn my mother since her spirit was ever-present, but when my father died and took my gift with him, I got hit with a double whammy—the loss of both parents. I teetered on the edge of sanity, but Linda kept me from falling. We worked diligently to fix what was broken, trying everything from chanting to hypnosis. I hounded her to make contact for me, but she refused. She said my spirit guides nixed the idea. Not knowing them personally, I objected to their involvement, but Linda wouldn't budge. Since I didn't really have any other choice, I acquiesced.

I fidgeted in the chair, but stopped when Linda raised her eyebrows again. "Sorry." I tapped my foot, knowing she couldn't see through the table, or hoping she couldn't. After all, she did have a psychic gift.

Linda took out her lighter, lit the candles on the table, and then shut off the lights. Serene music played from small speakers near the ceiling. She was in *psychic mode*. I was in *get 'er done* mode. I caught myself tapping my fingers on the table again and quickly folded my hands together.

"You need to relax," she said.

"You know that's not a word in my vocabulary."

"That's part of the problem. Breathe." She showed me how to breathe in and out slowly, like I'd never done it before.

I mimicked a woman in labor and she laughed. "I've spent a month breathing and centering and saying all of that Namaste crap and it's not helping. I just want to talk to my parents." That sounded snarky. "Sorry. I'm just frustrated."

She blew out the candles and flipped on the lights. "I understand, but let's just cut to the chase." She sat back in her chair and folder her arms across her chest. "Repeat what you just said."

I was pretty sure where this was going and knew the direction wasn't in my favor. "Which part?"

"I think you know."

I rolled my lips together. "I want to talk to my parents?"

She nodded. "Exactly."

"So?"

"So the universe is teaching you a lesson and until you get it, you're not going to have that opportunity."

"What's fair about that?"

"Nothing, actually. Your gift isn't about you. It's about helping others, and until you're ready to do that—truly ready—you're not going to get it back."

"But I do want to help others."

She took a drink of water. "Saying it doesn't make it true."

I stiffened. "It is true. I want to help others, but I also want to talk to my parents. Why can't I want both? Why can't I have both?"

"You can, but it's what's more important that's the problem. You want to talk to your parents, and if that means you have to talk to other spirits, you will, but helping others should be more important than helping yourself."

"You make me sound selfish."

She tilted her head and raised her left hand. "If the shoe fits."

"So what you're saying is that I'm pretty much screwed."

She leaned into the table. "You've been given something special— something truly amazing, but it's not about you, and you have to understand that. And I think you will. In fact, I think you're getting close. Things are happening more and more, aren't they?"

I hated how she did that, knew things I didn't tell her. "You spying on me or something?"

She tapped her temple with two fingers. "Psychic, remember?"

"So what you're saying is that once I stop being a spoiled brat I'll get my gift back?"

She nodded. "Pretty much."

I ran my hand through my hair. "Cheese and rice, I'm doomed."

She shook her head. "No, you're not. Right there you just said, *I'll get my gift back*, instead of, *I'll be able to talk to my parents*. That's progress, Angela. Baby steps."

I updated her on the rock incidents and the dream about my mother.

"See? Progress."

"I need to speed up that progress, Linda. Mel thinks her husband is cheating on her and she wants Ma to help her find out for sure."

"Think about your dream, Angela. Your mom knows."

"How do you mean?"

"The Barbie Doll is Mel. Pay attention to your surroundings. She's communicating with you."

"She may be, but I'm not smart enough to understand."

"Yes, you are. Go with your gut. It knows. You just have to stop trying so hard."

"Do you think we could talk to my mother? You know, for Mel, since it's not really about me?"

"I'd be happy to make an appointment with Mel, if that's what she wants."

"Can I come?"

She shook her head. "Baby steps."

"Fine."

"It's going to be, eventually." She pulled out her appointment book. "When can you come see me again?"

I pulled out my phone and checked my calendar. "Can I just call you? Would that be okay?"

She closed her book. "Absolutely. And Angela, it's all going to work out, so don't worry, okay?"

"I wish I could believe that."

She touched her two fingers to her head again. "Psychic, remember?"

That didn't make me feel a whole lot better.

*   *   *

I texted Mel from the parking lot. "Done with Linda. Starbucks in twenty?"

"Yup."

We sat at our regular table outside of Starbucks and drank our coffee. Mel's hair was disheveled, her eyes puffy and red. I glanced at her finger, and her wedding ring was gone. I filled her in on my conversation with Linda.

"You're not selfish," she said.

"You're my best friend. You're supposed to say that."

"Good point. Stop being selfish, dammit."

I squinted and shook my head. "Didn't work."

"Are you constipated?"

"Uh, no. Why?"

"You just made your constipated face."

"That was my concentrating face."

She shook her head. "Nope, it was your constipated face."

I took my phone out of my purse, put it in camera mode, and used it as a mirror. I made my concentrating face. "Lovely. When I try to look smart, I look like I'm pushing out a brick."

She snorted. "Not a brick, maybe a charcoal briquette or two."

"Thanks. That's so much better."

"That's what I'm here for." She bit her bottom lip. "So, should I make an appointment with Linda?"

I played with my mother's gold cross hanging from my neck. I wasn't sure. I wanted Ma to help, but I wanted to be there when they connected. Mel was wrong. I was selfish. "If that's what you want." I sounded like a twelve-year-old not getting her way.

Mel shifted in her seat. "I won't if you don't want me to."

"I want you to find out the truth about Nick and if that means Ma helps you, then yes, I want you to."

"You're lying."

"Am not."

"Are too."

We were both acting like twelve-year-olds. I handed her my cell phone. "Make the appointment, seriously."

She handed it back. "We'll follow him on our own and figure out another way to contact Fran."

I handed her the phone again. "I've tried. The only thing I can think of is a Ouija Board."

Mel leaned back in her chair, waved her hands in front of her chest and shook her head. "Um, no thanks."

"Why not?"

"Because that idea sucks, that's why."

"I didn't say it was a good idea."

"It's not."

"You got something better?"

Her shoulders slumped. "Just following him, but we're already planning that."

"Then a Ouija Board it is."

Her face grew white, which was impressive for an Asian woman. "Those things are satanic."

"They are not."

"Uh, yeah, they are."

"How do you know?"

"Because I used one once."

That was news to me. "When have you used a Ouija Board?"

"I was twelve, and I still have nightmares about it." She breathed in through her nose and out through her mouth like a woman in labor. "Can't do that again. Not ever."

I scooted my chair closer and leaned on the table. "What happened?"

"We contacted a demon and it said it was going to burn my house down. I was so scared I ran through the house screaming, a *fire! A fire!* My mom called the fire department and two fire trucks, three police cars, and an ambulance came. When my mother found out why I did that, she made me apologize to all of them individually. Then she called our priest and made me tell him what I'd done. My penance was one hundred Hail Marys. He had to perform a cleansing on the house and my mom made me go to confession twice a week for a year, just in case."

I spit out my coffee. "Knowing your mother, she still hasn't forgiven you, either."

She took a big gulp of her drink. "She hasn't. Those things are satanic, Angela. Trust me."

"I guess you don't really want to know the truth then."

"That's not fair."

"I'm going to get one. Maybe I'll tell you what my mom says."

"Ugh," she said.

"You really think my mother would let a demon come through before her? *My mom?*"

She propped her elbow on the table and put her cheek in her hand. "You've got a point."

I stood and rubbed my hands together. "Good. Let's do this. It'll be fun, and God knows we both need some fun in our lives. Let's go, scaredy cat."

She guzzled the last of her drink. "Fine. I'll drive." She stood. "I hate you."

"Think you can stop shaking enough to steer?"

"Bite me."

"My, aren't you the testy one?"

She growled at me.

"That's scary."

I texted Jake and let him know I was running errands.

"First we're stopping at Nick's work," Mel said.

"Why?"

"To see if his car is there."

"It's the middle of the work day. I'm sure it is."

"Never hurts to check."

We got in Mel's car and drove the fifteen minutes to Nick's office. The parking lot was full, so we went row by row looking for Nick's car.

Mel stopped in the third row and ducked down in her seat. "Crap, there he is."

"Where?"

"Over there," she said, pointing out the front window.

I looked and saw Nick and a tall blond woman walking down the row in front of us. "Oh, crap!" I ducked in my seat, too. "You know, ducking really isn't going to help. He knows your car."

She cleared her throat. "I don't care. Just stay down."

We sat there for a few minutes, trying to get as small as humanly possible, in a car Nick's not only seen, but also driven, for four years. I peeked out the window to see if he was gone. "Okay, he's gone."

Mel sat upright. "Did you get a look at who was with him?"

"Tall blond. Long hair. A little on the heavy side."

"Oh. That's the Executive Vice President, Marla something or other. He's not sleeping with her."

I raised an eyebrow. "How do you know?"

"She's in a relationship."

"So is Nick."

"With a woman."

"Oh."

She nodded, and put the car in drive. "Yup."

We headed to Target.

*   *   *

Neither Target nor Walmart had Ouija boards. "This sucks. I swear I've got some seriously bad juju going on. Nothing's going my way lately." I opened my mouth and moved my jaw around in circles, trying to loosen its tightness.

Mel put her arm around me as we walked to her car. "You're not fat anymore."

"There is that."

After my dad died I stopped exercising and ate myself from a size four to a size ten. Jake never said a thing, and I was in denial, but one day I looked in the mirror, realized I was becoming wider than my height, and went on a strict diet and exercise regimen. That actually helped me through my grief a lot more than ice cream and cupcakes. I eat them now, but not the whole gallon or dozen in a day like before.

"How can they not have Ouija Boards?" I asked.

"Probably because they're satanic."

"Oh geez. They are not."

"Have you ever used one?"

"No."

"Then how do you know?" she asked.

"I don't, but what I do know is that you're a wuss."

She nodded. "Yup."

"I ain't afraid of no ghost," I said.

Mel raised her hand and jumped up and down. "Oh, pick me! I know this one! Pick me!

I tilted my head at her. "Go ahead."

"Ray Parker Jr., Ghostbusters theme. Like you didn't abuse that one when you first started seeing ghosts."

"Yeah, I kind of did, didn't I?"

She pinched her fingers into an inch sign. "Just a little. And tell me, were you scared the other night when you felt someone in your den?"

"That's different."

"How?"

"Oh fine. It's not different."

"Say it."

"Say what?"

"Say why it's not different, Angela-I-ain't-afraid-of-no-ghosts-Panther."

"No."

"I wanna hear you say it."

"Why? Because you wanna be right?"

"I already am."

"Then I don't need to say it," I said, jutting my chin out.

"Humor me."

"Fine." I covered my mouth and mumbled. "Ididn'tknowwhothe-ghostwas."

She clapped and giggled. "That makes me happy."

I scrunched my eyebrows. "What? That I was afraid?"

"That you made my point."

"You're a pain in the butt."

"That's something at which I excel, too."

"It was at night, Mel. Everything's scarier at night."

"Seriously? That's what you're goin' with?"

"It's true. I read it on the Internet."

"Oh geesh, what are you, five? Scary things can happen during the day too."

"I know. I see a lot of scary things happening right now." I pointed to a woman walking through the Walmart parking lot wearing flesh-colored spandex leggings, a see-through white mesh top and a black bra. I'm all for personal style, but flesh colored spandex and white mesh were questionable.

She smirked. "Oh my." She squinted. "Is she wearing pants?"

I squinted, too. "You know, I'm not sure. I thought she had on flesh-colored leggings, but maybe not."

"Nobody should ever wear flesh colored spandex."

I laughed. "Let's check Goodwill. If they don't have it we'll figure something else out."

"We ought to ask your mom for some help, just in case."

"Good point."

Mel lifted her hands to the sky. "Fran, it'd be great if you'd help us find a Ouija Board. Actually, we can skip the demon-finder altogether if you'd just show up on your own. 'Kay-thanks-bye." She looked at me. "Think she heard me?

"The people inside Walmart heard you."

She touched a finger to her chin. "Was I loud?"

It was my turn to make the inch sign with my fingers. "Maybe just a little."

She turned red. "Whoops."

"Ma," I said, lifting my head to the sky. "This isn't about me, so I'm not being selfish. We either need the Ouija Board or like Mel said, you can pop on down for a chat, 'k? A sign to know you're listening would be awesome, too."

We stood and waited, but nothing happened.

I shrugged. "Well, we tried." And then a rock flew out of nowhere and smacked me on the knee. I kicked it. "Oh my Gawd. Enough with the rocks."

"Wow. That's pretty cool."

"What? Getting hit by a rock?"

"Uh, yeah."

"That's because you're not the one getting bruised."

"Ang, you just asked your mom for a sign and a rock pelted you. Don't you get it?"

"Not so much. No."

"The rock is the sign, Ang."

That didn't make sense. "Why would Ma throw rocks at me?"

"Because she can?"

There was that.

"All I'm saying is it doesn't seem like much of a coincidence," Mel said.

My temples throbbed so I rubbed them, hoping to stop a possible migraine. "But what would rocks have to do with my mother?" And then it hit me. Not a rock, the reason. "Hole-eee crap. Rocks. My cousin, Roxanne. Ma and my Auntie Rita always called her Rox for short."

"There's your sign." We high-fived.

I race-walked to Mel's car. "I'm calling my cousin."

Mel race-walked, too. "Put it on speaker."

Mel turned on the car, putting the air conditioner on high as I called my cousin.

"Hello?" Roxanne said.

"Put it on speaker," Mel said.

I ignored her.

"Roxanne? It's Angela."

"Put it on speaker."

I held up my index finger.

"Oh, hi Angela. How are you?"

Mel poked me in the arm. "Speaker phone."

"I'm doing good Rox, how are you?" I clicked the speaker button on my phone. "Hey, I'm in the car and I've got you on speaker phone, okay?"

"Oh, sure."

"I'm sorry I haven't called in awhile. Life gets busy, you know?"

"Oh, I know. It's busy here, too. John is traveling a lot and we're remodeling our kitchen, but I've been meaning to call you. I had the weirdest dream about your mother the other night and wanted to tell you about it."

I looked at Mel. She whispered, "Yes," and we high-fived again.
"You did? What was it?" I asked my cousin.

"Oh gosh, it's been a few days now. Lemme think." She went silent for a second. "Let's see. It wasn't like a normal dream so I think your ma was trying to give me a message."

"I bet Ma would do that."

"Yeah, knowing your mom, I think you're right. Let's see, we were sitting at the kitchen table in Grandma's kitchen, your ma and me. You remember Grandma's house in the Heights?"

My grandparents lived in a suburb of Chicago called Chicago Heights. I spent many days and nights at that kitchen table and could still picture the floral print plastic tablecloth with the napkin holder and matching salt and pepper shakers in the middle. "Like I was just there yesterday."

"Oh, good. I wasn't sure because you were so young and all."

"So what happened in the dream?"

"Well, lemme see. We were sitting at the table and Auntie Francie says to me, she says, "Ah Madone, I'm there. You tell her for me. Tell her it's her fault she can't see me and to stop the nagging 'cause I'm leaving signs all over the place." So I says to her...I says, 'Who can't see you, Auntie Francie?' And she says, 'My Angela. You tell her to pay attention because we got stuff to do, her and me.' Then she took a pizzelle cookie—you know, those pinwheel-like cookies Grandma used to make, and she says, 'Ah Madone, how I love a good pizzelle,' and ate it. And then I woke up. It was the strangest thing. I think it was really your ma though, Angela. You know, like a visit."

I had never told my cousin about my gift. "I don't think it was just a dream either, Rox. I think Ma was trying to get a message to me. I ask her for them all the time."

Mel's mouth made the shape of the letter o and her eyes widened. I thought she might wet herself.

"Did she say anything else?" I asked.

"Nope. Like I said, I woke up."

Mel whispered for me to hurry up, so I cut the conversation short and told my cousin I'd call again soon. "Gawd you're a pain in the butt, Mel."

"We need that Ouija Board."

"Have a change of heart, did you?"

"If it's the only way to talk to Fran so I can get on with my life, then yeah, I guess I did."

My pulse raced. It struck me that Mel might get on with her life somewhere other than here, somewhere away from me. "Do you think you'll stay here?"

She squished her eyebrows together. "Do I think I'll stay here? Of course, where would I go?"

Relief washed over me. I'd already lost enough important people in my life and I didn't want my best friend to leave me, too. "Back to New Jersey? To be closer to your parents?"

"Good God, no." She pretended to stick her finger down her throat and gagged.

"You love New Jersey."

"I love *visiting* New Jersey, not living there, though I do kind of like having someone else pump my gas." She winked at me.

"That's not all you're gonna need pumped." I snapped my fingers and said, "Oh snap!"

"Seriously. If I don't get out of this marriage soon I'm gonna need to buy stock in a battery company."

"TMI, Mel."

"I have needs. I'm not suffering from peri-menopause and a reduced sex drive like, ahem." She pointed at me.

"I'm not peri-menopausal and even sex addicts don't have your sex drive. You ho."

She laughed, a strong, from the belly kind of laugh. "Whatever, Queen of Denial. And I'm not a ho yet, but once I'm divorced I will be. I'll need to make up for this lost time."

I wrinkled my nose. "Nice."

She laughed. "Me love you long time," She said, quoting a line from the 1980s movie *Full Metal Jacket*.

"Excuse me, I'm the 1980s trivia queen, not you."

She shook her head and laughed again. "And you can keep the crown. I dunno how you keep all that garbage in your head anyway."

I shrugged. "It's a gift."

"Wish you'd have lost that gift instead of the talking to the dead one."

"Touché."

We found a Ouija Board at Goodwill, and Mel panicked about demons the entire drive back to my car.

"Where and when do you plan to do this?" she asked.

"Your house, of course. Tomorrow morning okay?"

"Oh hell no. You are not bringing that demon transporter into my home."

I laughed. "I was kidding, Mel. Tomorrow morning at my house unless you're too chicken?"

She clucked and said, "Who'll be there? I don't wanna bring demons in if Josh's there. Emily's kind of already a demon, so I'm not too worried about her."

"I'll tell her you said that."

She laughed. "Kidding. Sort of."

"Jake's leaving for New York and Emily has to work in the morning. I'll tell Josh we're going to watch chick flicks in the basement. He won't come down there then and the demons won't even know he's home."

"I hope not. I love Josh."

"Me, too," I said.

"I'll text you when I'm heading over."

I got out of the car. "Have fun with your battery operated friend tonight."

"I plan to."

"Ew."

"You started it," she said and then added, "I might do a little following tonight, feel like tagging along?"

I leaned my head back and rubbed my forehead. "We're gonna be so busted."

"We'll see," she said. "He said he's got a meeting at the office until about eight tonight. I checked his email and saw the calendar request from his boss so I'm pretty sure that's not a lie. I'll pick you up at 7:15 and we'll wait for him. Wear black."

"Wear black?"

"Yeah, in case we gotta get out of the car or something."

"Good grief."

"See you later."

I waved and smiled but inside my stomach churned and I thought I might be sick.

CHAPTER THREE

I DIDN'T TELL JAKE ABOUT MEL AND NICK, so instead of telling him Mel and I were planning to follow her husband, I said we were going to a movie. I hated lying, but Jake and Nick were friends, and until I was reasonably comfortable with the facts, I didn't want to put my husband in an awkward position. I wasn't entirely sure that was the truth either, but it was the best excuse I could give myself.

Mel sent a text. "In the driveway."

I kissed Jake goodbye.

"Isn't she coming in to say hi?" He asked.

"Nope. She wants to stop and grab some candy at the gas station before the movie starts. It's cheaper there."

"Good idea. What're you seeing again?"

Crap. I had no idea what was even out, let alone what was playing at about eight o'clock. Lying wasn't my specialty and I hated digging an even deeper hole. "You know, I don't even know. Mel just needed to get out so I told her I'd do whatever. Didn't even think to ask."

He lifted the side of his mouth. "Huh. Usually you're all about the plan." He grabbed my waist and pulled me close to him. "I like this more spontaneous, go-with-the-flow woman you're becoming." His hands wandered to my backside and he pinched. I jumped.

"It's just a movie, honey," I said, twisting myself out of his hold. "Gotta go. Love you."

"Love you, too."

In the car, I smacked Mel on the arm.

"Ouch, what's that for?"

"For making me lie to my husband, that's what," I said, my bottom lip stuck out like a toddler. "I'm going to hell for that, you know, and it's your fault."

"Meh, don't worry. I'll be there right after you."

"Great. So I'm going to hell because of you, and I'm gonna die first. Thanks for that, best friend."

She laughed. "What did you tell him?"

"That we're going to a movie. Then he asked which one and I had to lie and say I didn't know, that you'd picked and I'd forgotten. Or something like that. Heck, I can't even remember what the lie was now. Great. I'm definitely going to hell." I scowled and folded my arms across my chest. "I hate you."

"Just tell him we didn't go to the movie and ended up at my house, watching *When Harry Met Sally*. God knows you can recite every line from that movie anyway, so he'll never know it's a lie."

"How did you get so good at making stuff up?" I asked.

"I'm married to a cheating rat bastard, remember? Not only can I lie like him now, but my lie detector is better than the kind cops use." She pointed to her head. "I could make millions with this thing."

It was sad and funny and I couldn't help but laugh. "Sorry."

She laughed, too. "Don't be. It's so pathetic that it's funny."

We drove out of my neighborhood. "So, what's the plan?" I knew I'd regret asking, but I figured I'd better be prepared.

"We're gonna go to his office and wait for him to leave and see where he goes. He told me the meeting would last until at least eleven o'clock but the email meeting request said it would only last about a half an hour. He's planning to go somewhere after, probably to his ho's house to get laid."

My stomach flipped. How she could speak so casually about her husband sleeping with another woman was beyond my comprehension. "Don't you feel sick? He's not even my husband and I want to puke."

She shrugged. "I've had more time to come to terms with this than you, I guess."

"I guess."

A few minutes later we pulled into the parking lot at Nick's office. The building, a five-story multi-office structure, was partially lit, with most offices dark. The lot was about fifteen rows deep, and there were only ten cars there. Mel pulled up next to Nick's car. "He's still here," she whispered.

"Why are you whispering?" I whispered back.

She smacked her forehead with her palm. "Because I'm an idiot."

I giggled. "Not all of the time."

"Thanks," she said. "I'm going to text him and see when he plans to get home."

Nick responded immediately. Mel showed me his text. "Meeting is supposed to end around eleven. I'll be home straight after."

"Liar, liar pants on fire," I said.

"That remains to be seen, but I'm guessing you're right."

"We can't stay parked next to his car, Mel. He'll see us."

"His office is on the other side of the building so he can't see us from the window, but you're right." She pulled through the space in front of us and drove toward the exit. She parked at the opposite end of the lot, facing the exit, shut off the car and switched off the lights. "I feel like Kris Munroe."

I recognized the name, but it took me a second to place it. "Kris Munroe? Of *Charlie's Angels*?" I asked.

She nodded. "It was on in the 1980s, you should have got that."

"You're right. I'll work on it. And uh, you're Asian and she's blond. I think I would be a better fit for Kris. You're more of a Sabrina, but less smart."

"You did not just say that."

I nodded. "Did so."

"Fine. They're old now anyway. I'm more like Lucy Liu from the movie version actually. And she's Asian, so shut it."

"Then I'm Cameron Diaz, without the plastic surgery."

She scrutinized my face. "Probably could benefit from a little, if you ask me."

I cringed. "Ouch."

She smiled. "We're even."

I hit the home button on my phone, lighting up the screen to check the time. It was five minutes after eight. "Maybe he wasn't lying? It's past eight already." I angled my phone toward her to show her the time.

"It's five minutes past, Ang. I wouldn't count on going home just yet." As if Nick had read her mind, he walked out just after she finished her sentence. He wasn't alone but the only people with him were men. "Duck," Mel said, crouching down in the car seat.

I followed suit.

The men stood next to Nick's car for what seemed like an eternity. When Nick finally got in his car, he left in the middle of the other three cars, and turned right out of the lot. His house was the other direction.

Mel and I exchanged headshakes.

"Coming straight home, my ass," she said. She flipped on her lights and pulled out shortly after the last car.

"Oh, yeah. No one's gonna notice that, Alex Munday," I said, referencing Lucy Liu's character in the *Charlie's Angel's* movies.

"Hush," Mel said. "I'm busy being stealth-like."

I busted out laughing.

Nick made a few turns and ended up at the apartments behind a local outdoor mall. We stayed back behind the entrance, watched him enter through the electronic gate and turn left. Once the coast was clear, Mel pulled up to the gate.

"What're you gonna do? You don't know where he's going, or who lives here," I said.

"I'm pretty sure he's not here to visit a buddy. We'll just drive around and look for his car. She stretched to look behind the iron gate. "These are the townhouse style apartments. Looks like there are only four to a parking area. It should be easy to find him."

"If we can get past the gate."

"We can," she said and opened her window. She pressed a button and someone answered.

"Yes?" A voice from the speaker box said.

"Hi, I'm here to deliver a pizza but the customer isn't answering. Can you let me in?"

A second passed and the buzzer went off, opening the gate.

"Wow, you really could be a Charlie's Angel."

"Funny."

Mel drove around until we spotted Nick's car. She passed it and pulled into a parking space five buildings away. She was right, there were only four townhomes attached together with parking spaces for them. We didn't know which townhouse Nick was in, but from the direction he'd turned, we had an idea where to look. I stopped Mel before she got out. "Wait. What's the plan?"

"You and your plans," she said. "The plan is to get out and walk behind the buildings and see if we can hear anything. It's beautiful out. Maybe the ho's got her windows open or something."

Eep. I shivered. I didn't like that plan. "So we're just gonna walk around and peer into people's homes? We can get arrested for that, Mel."

She pushed up the sleeves on her black spandex jacket. "Only if we get caught. Who's the chicken now? Come on, let's go." She got out of the car.

"Demons might not be real but the cops are, and I don't see anything wrong with being afraid of them," I said, but got out of the car anyway because best friends risk getting arrested for each other. "If I get busted, I'm giving you up, too."

"If you get busted, I'll turn myself in," she said and tilted her head toward the back of the townhomes. "Now, let's go."

We tiptoed behind the building, checking for open windows and lit rooms. Most of the townhouses still had lights on, probably because it wasn't even nine o'clock at night.

I pasted a smile on my face, pretending I was out for a leisurely night walk, in the dark, behind stranger's homes, wearing black, instead of actually spying into said strangers homes looking for my best friend's cheating rat bastard husband. My heart beat as if I were running a marathon.

"Wait," Mel said. "I think it's that one." She pointed to the last townhouse of the second set of units even though Nick hadn't parked in that one's lot.

"How do you know?" I rubbed my arms even though I was sweating.

"She pointed to the patio. "Because that's the cooler I got him for Christmas last year. Bastard."

On the patio sat an Atlanta Braves cooler with *biggest fan ever* inscribed on it. Mel had it specially inscribed for Nick. I knew because I was with her when she did it. Bastard. We creeped closer to the patio, Mel a few feet ahead of me, head up and shoulders back. The blinds were closed, but the patio door was slightly ajar, and we could hear muffled voices, though we couldn't make out the words. I glanced at Mel and could have sworn I saw steam coming from her ears. I grabbed her arm and pulled her back. "We should go, Mel. It's not like we can see or hear anything anyway."

She shook me off. "Gimme a sec, okay?" She walked up onto the patio, and I wiped the sweat from my brow. I tried to stand still but couldn't stop shaking. I stayed back behind the half fence separating the unit from the one next to it. That unit was totally dark so I assumed no one was home to notice me, freak out and either call the police, or beat me with a baseball bat. Just thinking that made me shake more.

Seconds later I heard a door slide open and Mel sprinted past me. "Go! Go! Go!" She yelled.

I broke into a sprint and passed her before we got to the end of the units. I slowed rounding the corner, and Mel passed me again. She jumped over something a few feet in front of me. The townhome units were dark and with no outside lighting, it was hard to see the ground. I looked down, but it was too late. My foot hit something hard and solid, sending me flying through the air. I tried to turn and land on my side but was too slow. I hit the ground with a thump and landed on something furry and wiggly. It grunted like a pig and then darted out from underneath me with a squeal, but not before it sprayed me.

The putrid smell of burning tires and long-rotted eggs engulfed me. I tried to wipe the wetness off of my face but that only made it worse. I stood and said the f-word.

Mel ran back. "What the—" she broke off mid sentence and backed away, laughing. "Holy mother of God. You got skunked." She continued to back up as I stood there gagging at the smell.

Mel covered her mouth, gagged and giggled. "Come on," she finally said. "Let's get you in the car."

We got to the car and Mel opened all of the windows, including the sunroof. "First I face-plant it into a pile of wildlife poop and then I'm skunked. My life sucks."

Mel snorted. "Just get in, Stinky. I promise we'll fix this." She busted out laughing.

I started to run my hand through my hair but stopped, thinking it would just make my hair smell worse. "I'm glad someone finds this funny."

"You will too, someday. Now come on, get in."

"I can't. The smell will be there forever."

She rocked on her tiptoes. "Well, we don't really have any other option now, do we?"

I scanned the area—for what I didn't know, but hoping something magical would happen and I'd be fresh smelling and clean. Nothing magical happened and I was about to puke so I got in her car and told her to get me home quickly. "Maybe the smell won't stick that way," I said.

Between gagging and laughing, Mel told me I stunk like a pig. "Or, I mean, a skunk."

"Hardy har har," I said. "Think Jake will want to get lucky tonight?"

"Probably. His pheromones will love your new perfume."

"It is rather attractive, almost passionate," I said.

"Definitely has depth and staying power, like a good perfume should." She busted out laughing again.

I laughed, too. "You so owe me for this one," I said. "I'm serious. Anything I want, you owe me. What the heck am I gonna tell Jake? Frick, I'm totally busted."

Mel glanced at me and tried to speak but ended up doing her gag/laugh thing again. If I didn't love her, I would have pummeled her. We got to my house and she shut off the car. "I'll go in for you," she said.

I nodded. "Probably best."

Seconds later she was outside with Jake and Gracie. Gracie approached me and then dropped her ears and ran back in the house. "Thanks, Gracie. I'll remember that the next time you roll in something dead," I said.

Jake and Mel stayed their distance. "Wow," he said, suppressing a laugh. "How the hell did this happen?"

I pointed to Mel. "This one's on you, my friend. And someone please get me a glass of wine and a few towels. I'm gonna change in the garage and hit the shower."

They both shook their heads. "I don't think coming in is a good idea," Jake said. He typed something into his phone. "Do we have baking soda?"

I nodded. "In the pantry."

"Okay," he said. "What about hydrogen peroxide? We need that and dish soap."

"I thought tomato juice got rid of the smell," Mel said. "Mix it with a little vodka and you can lick it off her, Jake." She bent over laughing.

"I think I'll pass," he said.

I whistled to get their attention. "Peroxide's upstairs in the hall closet. There should be three bottles. Luckily it was on sale a few weeks ago and I stocked up. Dish soap is under the sink where it always is. Not that you'd know that," I said, looking at my husband.

He gave me the stink eye, which I found funny considering I was the smelly one. "Be right back," he said, and then added, "I'm getting the towels and your bathing suit. You can clean up out here and then come in."

I caught Mel's eye, even though she'd been trying not to look directly at me. She shrugged, pressed her lips together and then cracked up all over again. "I'm so sorry, Angela. I'm not laughing at you."

It was my turn to give someone the stink eye.

"I mean, I am laughing at you, but I feel bad about it. I didn't mean for this to happen. You gotta know that."

I nodded. "I know. What did you tell Jake?"

She shook her head. "Nothing yet."

"Chicken."

"I'll tell him whatever you want, I promise."

"Only one option, Mel. The truth."

Her shoulders drooped and her expression sagged. "Okay."

"Hold on," I shook my head. "Don't tell him yet. I've got this."

Jake came out with my supplies. He went around to the side of the house and turned on the hose and brought it to the driveway while I changed. I tossed my clothes toward Mel, but she backed away. "Can you go inside and get a garbage bag for those?" I asked her.

She nodded.

It took me about an hour to get rid of the smell and I wasn't sure if it was still on me or just stuck in my nose hairs, but Jake and Mel both assured me I was fresh as a daisy. Just in case, Mel sprayed me with Febreze. Jake laughed and said it was *stinking hilarious*. "So what happened?" he asked.

"I'll tell you inside," I said. "Mel, thanks for helping. I'll call you tomorrow."

"I'm really sorry," she said, laughing.

"No worries," I said and mouthed, "You totally owe me."

We walked to her car and even with the windows open, it stunk. "Crap." She sniffed her clothes. "I think I stink a little, too."

"Come back in the garage," Jake said. "I'll get you some towels and stuff and you can wash up here, too. Ang, can you get her something to wear home? I'll spray her car with Lysol and Febreze. Maybe that will help, at least for the short term."

"You're an awesome husband, Jake," Mel said. "Wish Nick was more like you."

He laughed. "Nick's not a bad guy, but few can be as amazing as me."

I stuck my finger down my throat.

It took Mel about half the time to wash the skunk smell off her, probably because she wasn't the one who nearly planted the stinker like a pancake.

After Mel left, I told Jake we'd decided to go for a walk through her neighborhood instead of go to the movies. I told him I'd run into the skunk a few streets up from Mel's and that she'd gone home to get the car and drive me here. I said I didn't think I should bring the skunk smell into her house. I was getting pretty good at being dishonest and I didn't like it one bit.

*   *   *

The next morning Jake woke me before he left. "I fed the dog so you can sleep in." He sniffed me—yes, he really did, and then nuzzled his face into my neck. "Hmm. You smell good."

"Gee, thanks. But if you want me to sleep in, you gotta stop nuzzling me and leave," I said, pretending to push him away.

He kissed me. "You're right and I gotta go. Love you."

I blew him a kiss. "Love you, too."

I lay there for a few minutes, trying to fall back asleep, but my mind wandered and I couldn't. I smelled myself, making sure I didn't stink, but my nose was still filled with residual skunk smell. I tossed and turned, flopping around on the bed so much that Gracie jumped up and pawed at me. "I'm okay girl, just can't get comfy, I guess." She licked my face, turned in a few circles and nestled in on top of Jake's pillow.

I grabbed my phone and Googled *common causes for sleeplessness in women*. That was a humungous mistake. It directed me straight to a site listing symptoms of peri-menopause.

I covered my eyes. "No, I don't wanna look," I said. Gracie lifted her head and glanced in my direction, then snuggled back into Jake's pillow.

Of the ten symptoms listed, I figured I had two, tops. Sleeplessness. Check. Hot flashes. Check. Low libido. Sometimes, if I was cranky or

Jake ticked me off, so half check. Irregular periods. If irregular meant every six months or so, check. Mood swings. Well heck, I always had those. No check. Vaginal dryness. I invoked my Fifth Amendment rights on that one. Weight gain. My parents recently died so I had an excuse, and took a pass on checking yes. Tender breasts. Yikes. I thought that was a caffeine thing, but I gave that one a check, too. Migraines. Uh oh. Check. Check. Check. Though that could have been because I have kids. Urinary incontinence. Dear God, that was gonna happen? I pulled the covers over my head and wallowed in self-pity. Seconds later I was hot, so I pushed the covers off and snuggled up next to my dog as I continued to torture myself searching Google.

Five whole checks. If that stuff was true then I was screwed. One site said a good indicator of menopause was the age your mother went through it. Huh. I hadn't a clue. I set the phone down and pouted some more.

I flipped the cross on my necklace and my eyes filled with tears. There was so much I didn't know. What key medical history had I forgotten? What family history was now lost forever because I'd never taken the time to ask or just simply forgot?

Desperate for answers, I broke the cardinal rule of psychic mediums — never talk to the dead in the bedroom. Linda said mediums were most vulnerable when tired, and the bedroom was a sacred place meant for sleep and sex. Talking to my parents there could open a portal for uninvited spirits, but desperation and hormonal issues beat out rational thinking. "Ma," I said out loud. "I've got some questions and would appreciate it if you, and Dad, you too, would answer. When did you go through menopause?" I sat silent and then said, "Dad, which house were you born in again? I'd like to show the kids some day."

Questions poured from my brain and I blurted them out like an auctioneer calling out bids. No one responded and I bawled like a baby. "Why can't I hear you? Why can't I see you?"

Gracie shifted on Jake's pillow and licked my face. I was in the throes of a major self-pity meltdown when Mel texted.

"How's the smell?"

I didn't let on that she'd interrupted my pity party. Some things were better kept private. "Can't tell. I think my nose is permanently damaged."

"Clean it out with peroxide and a Q-tip. Might help. Did anything happen with the Ouija Board?"

"Yup."

"Oh my God. What?"

"It spoke to me."

"Hole-eee crap. What did it say?"

"It said *Mel is a total sucker*."

"You suck."

"Not according to Jake."

"Hardee har har. You're all jokes now, but when that thing starts projectiling pea soup at you don't think I'll save your sorry butt."

"Inanimate objects can't puke, Mel."

"You sure about that?"

"One hundred percent," I wrote.

"You have any weed?"

"Excuse me?"

"Weed. You know, pot. Do you have any?" She wrote back.

"Uh, no. Drug free, remember?"

"Maybe Emily's got some hidden in her room. Can you check?"

"EMILY DOES NOT SMOKE WEED." I used all capitals to stress my point.

"AND I'M A VIRGIN."

"And pigs fly."

"Fine. Emily doesn't smoke weed. Forget I asked."

"Why would you ask in the first place?"

"Not to smoke. For protection."

"Huh?"

"I was researching protection from evil spirits and read that you should cleanse your house with sage, but I didn't think you'd have a big rolled thing of sage just lying around, so I thought maybe we could use a joint. You know, if Emily had one. Which she doesn't because she doesn't smoke pot."

"You want me to cleanse my house with a doobie?"

"Cannabis and sage are both herbs," she wrote.

"Speechless."

"I figured it was the next best thing."

"Linda gave me sage last year. I'll sage when you get here."

"Thank God. Pot stinks."

"And I don't have any."

"I know, because Emily doesn't smoke pot."

"Exactly."

"Uh huh."

I ignored that. "She's working this morning. Come over whenever."

"Picking up a nose plug and cupcakes and heading over."

"It's six in the morning."

"Oh. Staying in bed for another hour, and then getting a nose plug and cupcakes, and heading over," she texted.

"Yum. Cupcakes. Red velvet for me, please."

"Duh."

"Don't forget your cross and garlic."

"Garlic is for vampires. You need holy water for evil spirits," she wrote.

"Then bring that."

"I've got tap or Mountain Springs. Take your pick."

"Bring the Mountain Springs. I have tap here."

I heard Emily leave for work so I got up, splashed cold water on my face, put on my robe, and headed downstairs. I was grateful Mel had unknowingly cut my pity party short. Nothing good ever came from me feeling sorry for myself.

Josh was already up and talking to his not-real friends on his X-Box. "Hey, Little Man, little early to be on that thing."

"I'm playing with my friends in London and it's afternoon there."

"Fine, but I don't want you on it all day. You know how I feel about that."

"Mama, I won't end up a violent criminal. Promise."

"I never said that. I said you get irritable if you're on it for too long."

"I won't be."

"Okay. Mel's coming over to watch chick flicks in a bit. We're gonna be in the basement."

"Guess I won't be coming down there."

I tousled his hair. "I miss the Josh that loved to watch chick flicks with me."

"I was four."

"You used to let me paint your toenails then, too."

"Because I was four."

"I can paint your toenails later if you'd like."

"Mama, stop."

"You're no fun."

"Is Mel bringing cupcakes?"

"Of course."

"I call a chocolate."

"Didn't say she was bringing one for you."

"She always does," he said, and then stuck his tongue out at me.

I stuck mine out back and shook my head. "Good point."

I reheated a cup of day-old coffee, checked the counter for rocks (just in case), let the dog out and, coffee in hand, went back upstairs to get dressed.

Mel sent a text saying she'd be late. "Nick had a flat this morning. He's changing it now."

"Are you helping him?"

"Heck no. He parked behind my side of the garage instead of pulling into his side. Don't ask me why."

"Does your car smell?"

"Not that I can tell. I showered again when I got home, too. Be there soon."

"K."

I held my coffee cup up toward the ceiling. "If that was you Ma, good job."

About an hour later, Mel showed up with Starbucks coffees and a half dozen cupcakes. She put the cupcakes down and sniffed me. "Hmm. You smell good."

I backed away from her. "Gee, thanks, but don't ever do that again please."

"I just wanted to make sure."

"I'm pretty sure Josh would have noticed if I reeked."

"Well I wouldn't have been a true friend if I didn't check."

"And I wouldn't have been a true friend had I not followed your husband with you, and been skunked in the process."

"Yeah, you definitely win the friend of the year award for that one." She held out a cupcake and smiled. "Here's your prize."

"How sweet of you." I took the cupcake and set it on the table, then grabbed a chocolate cupcake and took it to Josh.

"She brought you two. You can have one now, but wait on the other one, please."

"I will." He took a bite and yelled, "Thanks, Mel."

"You're welcome, buddy," she yelled back.

I sat at the kitchen table. "Way to sugar up my kid before breakfast."

She sat across from me and her eyes narrowed. "Why's he up so early?"

"He wanted to play on his X-Box with his friends in London."

"You know they're not friends if he's never personally met them, right?"

I flicked my hand in the air. "Preaching to the choir."

We both picked the frosting off my cupcake. "Tire fixed?" I asked.

"Yup." She pulled her leg up and tucked it underneath her.

"Anything else new?"

"Nope."

"Ready to do this?"

"Nope. You?" she asked.

I shook my head and bit my bottom lip.

"What's wrong?"

"Been thinking about the pizzelle cookies."

"Liar. You're scared," she said.

"A little, but the cookies did cross my mind."

"Why? Are they good? Do they have chocolate in them?"

I shook my head. "They're Italian. Flat, waffle-like cookies. Ma and my grandma used to make them. Haven't had one in years, and probably never will again, either." I let out a big breath and stared at my cupcake.

Mel tilted her head. "You okay?"

"Josh had a dream about Ma and the cookies, too."

She raised an eyebrow. "And?"

"He said Ma said she was trying hard and I'd better be grateful."

"Trying hard at what?" Mel asked, then broke off a piece of cupcake and ate it.

"I don't think she said."

"That's not helpful."

"I know."

"I wish you'd dream about her."

I smiled. "Actually, I did."

"And now you tell me? What'd she say?"

"She said I had to do the work."

"Huh? Work for what, I wonder."

"I told her my dad was dead and it hurt, and I needed her, so probably it's about that."

"Wow."

I wiped my eyes.

"I'm sorry," she said and placed her hand on top of mine.

"'S okay. I'm good. It comes and goes. One day I'm fine and the next I'm not. I guess it's my new normal."

"It's going to get better."

"It already has." I gave her a half-hearted smile and then said, "Oh, and I gave her a Barbie Doll with its head missing. Told her it needed help. Pretty sure the doll is supposed to be you."

"Me? How'd you figure that?"

"Well, it wasn't the big boobs or the blond hair, but since I told her it needed help and you have the Nick thing going on, I just assume it was supposed to be you."

"Barbie isn't Asian."

"Figuratively speaking."

"I know." She laughed. "What did Fran say?"

"That she had it covered."

Mel's lips curled and her eyes lit up. "The flat tire."

"That's what I'm thinking."

"God, I love your mother."

"I know." I got up and grabbed the Ouija Board from the top of the refrigerator.

"You sure you're up for this?" she asked.

I nodded. "I'm worried about you though."

"Me, too." She made the sign of the cross. "Lord, help me."

"I'm pretty sure you're beyond help." I giggled.

"Thanks for your support."

"Anytime."

I told Josh we were going to the basement to watch chick flicks. He curled his lip and wrinkled his nose. "Better you than me."

"He's becoming his dad," Mel said.

"Stop depressing me."

"Hey, at least his dad isn't Nick."

I held my index finger up and nodded once. "Good point."

* * *

We walked into the basement and stopped dead in our tracks. My eyes widened and my mouth dropped. "What the hell?" Then I dropped the f-bomb. Twice.

"Oh, boy," Mel said, her hand covering her mouth. "You said the f-word. Someone's gonna get a big ol' can of Angela whoop-ass."

The basement looked like a Chuck E Cheese party room someone forgot to clean. Empty bags of chips, soda cans, and two pizza boxes with leftover pizza from God knows when littered the floor. Opened DVD cases and DVDs were lying everywhere. The couch pillows sat propped up against the front of the couch with piles of blankets near them. I smelled pee. I inhaled through my nose twice just to make sure and almost gagged. The stench was so strong it overrode the skunk. My heart raced and I started to sweat. The vein in my forehead pulsed. Messiness to an anal-retentive and slightly obsessive-compulsive person like me could cause a heart attack. I dropped to my knees and breathed in deep breaths. "Cheese and rice, we've got rats now, I know it."

"Which one?" Mel asked.

"Guess," I said between deep breaths.

"How many girls?"

"Four. Over a week ago."

She walked over to a pizza box and picked up a piece of molded, pepperoni pizza. It was disgusting but was probably even nasty before it molded. "Over a week ago? Pizza sure molds fast. Who knew?"

I stood and walked over to the pizza box and closed it. "I cannot believe she thought it was okay to leave the basement like this. I hope one day she has two daughters."

"Twins," Mel said.

"Then when she's forty-five, I hope she has another one."

"Now that's just cruel."

I picked up the garbage and put it all on the mahogany coffee table. Mel folded the blankets and picked up the pillows and put them all on the couch. We moved the DVDs and their cases into one big pile. I didn't worry about scratching them and would probably regret that later. "Do you smell pee?" I asked.

She rubbed the back of her neck. "I was afraid to mention that."

I got on my hands and knees and sniffed around the floor for pee. I couldn't find any but I knew it was there, somewhere. My nose never lied. It had superpowers ever since being pregnant with Josh. "I know there's pee here somewhere," I said. "Come sniff with me."

"Heck no," Mel said. "And darn it, I left my phone upstairs. This is a prime Kodak moment right now."

"Har. Har," I said and sniffed another section of the floor. "It's the only way to tell for sure."

She pushed garbage off the couch and sat. "Add that to my list of reasons for not having a pet."

"I didn't say the pee was Gracie's," I said, only half kidding.

"No way."

"You never know."

"I'm glad my kids are younger," she said.

"Your time is coming, and trust me, I'll be the first one to laugh my butt off when you're down on the ground sniffing for pee."

"Idea," she said. "Let's skip the demon-rousing and Google boarding schools."

"Nice try."

We sat on the floor in front of the table. Mel ran her finger across the small space not covered with trash and blew the dust my direction. "Clean down here lately?"

"About thirty seconds ago."

"You missed."

"If you want, I'll go grab a dust cloth and you can dust until your heart's fulfilled."

She smirked. "I'd much rather do that than conjure up demons."

I lifted my eyes toward the ceiling and sang, "Ma, Mel keeps calling you a demon."

Mel swatted my arm. "I did not. Fran, don't listen to her." She made the sign of the cross again.

"Stop that. You're not really Catholic anyway."

"Am so."

"Yeah? Maybe by birth, but not in practice."

"Once a Catholic, always a Catholic."

"Really?"

"Yup. It never goes away, ever."

I raised an eyebrow and smirked. "Uh huh. So, tell me, when'd you last go to confession?"

Her forehead wrinkled and she tilted her head like a dog. "Um."

"Tick tock. Tick tock." I tapped my wrist where a watch would have been if I wore one.

She held up her hand and said, "Gimme a minute. I'll remember."

I laughed. "I don't think you've been since we met, Mel. Imagine how long it would take you to confess now."

"I'd be there for months."

"Years."

She sighed. "You're right. I'm screwed."

"Not lately."

"Touché."

I pulled the Ouija Board out of the box. Mel shivered. I laughed.

"So what do we do?" she asked.

I flipped the box over. "Not sure. There aren't any directions. What'd you do when you did it?"

"Uh, I was twelve, remember?"

"Yeah, probably that's too far back in the past for you to recall."

"Funny."

She picked up the pointer and examined it. "What's this thing called again?"

"Pointer thingy?"

"You're a wealth of knowledge."

I held up the box and pretended to dump out the empty contents. "Not much to work with."

"Great. So what should we do? I say just forget the whole thing. Without directions, we have no idea what can happen."

I shook my head. "You're not getting out of this that easily."

Her shoulders slumped. "Was worth a try."

I placed the pointer thing on the board. "I guess we just put our hands on it and start talking."

"We should say a prayer first, you know, for protection," Mel said.

"Go ahead."

"Why me? It's your Ouija Board."

"Because you're the practicing Catholic. Duh."

"That was a cheap shot."

"But true."

"Fine." She closed her eyes. "Heavenly Father, please keep us safe from harm and protect us from evil. Oh, and I'm sorry for all of the recent inappropriate thoughts about Ryan Reynolds. I'll get to the rest of my sins later. Amen."

I gave her the stink eye. "You're having X-rated thoughts about Ryan Reynolds? You know he's my imaginary boyfriend."

"Not in my imagination, he's not."

"So rude." I put the pointer on the board. "You ready?"

She sat on her hands. "Nope. My hands are cold. Gotta warm them up first."

"Too bad. Put your hands on the pointer."

"I gotta pee."

"Now?"

She shrugged. "Fine, I'll wait. But you know this could end badly. What if it curses me and I can't have another orgasm or something?"

"Good Lord." I rubbed my hand over my face. "Can we just do this?"

She nodded. "But if something happens, I'm blaming you."

I had no idea what to do, so I just started talking. "We're trying to contact my mother, Fran Richter. Are you there, Ma? It's me, Angela."

Mel laughed.

"What?"

Are you trying to contact your mom or Judy Blume, because I think she's still alive."

It took me a second but I figured it out. "Oh geez."

We tried again. "Hello, this is Angela Panther. I'm trying to contact my mother, Fran Richter."

Nothing happened.

"Fran Richter. Hello? Come on, Ma."

The pointer moved.

I raised my eyes to Mel, but kept my hands on the pointer. "Is that you moving it?"

Her eyes widened. "Oh God. Oh God. Oh God."

Obviously not. "Keep your hands on the pointer, Mel."

"Oh God. Oh God. Oh God. We're gonna die."

"Hush, drama queen."

"I'm about to die or be rendered orgasm-less. I'm allowed to scream."

The pointer stopped on the word yes.

"Is this Fran? We don't want to talk to anyone but Fran, unless you're my dad. We'll talk to him, too. And my Auntie Rita, but no one else."

"Geesh, Ang, pick one."

"Shush." I focused on the pointer. "Ma, if it's you, what kind of candy did I steal from you as a teen?"

The pointer moved.

"Are you pushing it?" Mel asked.

I shook my head.

"It's a ghost. Frick. It's a ghost." Her body shook.

"Don't wet yourself," I said, holding in a laugh.

"I told you I had to pee."

"Oh geez."

The pointer moved to the letter H.

"H," she said.

It moved to the E.

"E."

"Yes, I can see that, Mel."

"Oh, sorry."

It spelled out Hershey and Mel squealed. "It's Fran!"

"Hold on, I need to verify. I don't wanna be duped."

"Yeah, demons do that," she said.

I ignored her. "Okay, Ma, if it's you, then tell me how many people in our family almost drowned."

Mel mouthed, "How many?"

I held my finger to my mouth. "Shush."

The pointer moved all the way around in a full circle and then down to the number zero.

"Zero, Ang. It's on zero. Is that right?"

I shook my head.

"Holy crap. It's a demon." Mel's hands flew off the pointer thingy and she backed away from the table.

"Put your hands back. I don't wanna lose the connection."

The pointer moved and spelled out the name Lisa.

Mel's mouth formed the shape of an O. "Who's Lisa? Is she a demon?"

I shrugged. "How should I know?"

"You know dead people."

"I knew a few dead people, briefly."

"Did you know a Lisa?"

"Not that I recall, no."

"Crap."

I turned my attention back to the Ouija Board. "Lisa. Hi Lisa," I said.

The pointer didn't move.

"Way to be polite," Mel said.

"I know, right?"

"Lisa, I'm trying to contact my mother, do you think you can help me?"

The pointer shot up to the word no.

Mel pulled her head back. "How rude."

I nodded. "Okay, then, why are you here?"

The pointer moved back to the middle and then landed on the W.

"W," Mel said.

"I can read, Mel."

"Oh, sorry."

It moved to the A.

"What do you think it's gonna spell?" Mel asked.

"Heck if I know. I'm not psychic."

"Well you sort of were."

"I could talk to dead people, I couldn't read their minds."

"Did they really have minds anyway? I mean, technically speaking."

"I don't know. I couldn't see inside of them."

"But you saw through them, so..."

"Are we really having this conversation? Right now?"

She shrugged. "I was just asking."

"I know but we need to focus."

She nodded, and the pointer moved to the R. "R."

"N," I said.

"I."

"N."

"G." Mel's hands shot off the pointer like it was on fire, and her eyes grew as wide as Asian eyes could. Which, by the way, wasn't much. "Holy crap. It's a warning."

"No, it *spelled* warning."

"Same thing in my book."

I placed my hands back on the pointer. "Put your hands back on it, too."

She shook her head and sat on her hands. "No way. I'm done."

"Do you want to find out about Nick?"

She shook her head. "No thanks, I'm good."

"Oh geez. Just one more time, it'll be quick."

She huffed, but did it, and her hands trembled on the pointer.

I laughed, and then focused all of my energy on the pointer. "Lisa, can you find my mother for me?"

The pointer shot across the Ouija Board from one letter to another. I looked at Mel and she shook her head as if to say she wasn't moving it. I mouthed, *me neither*, and then watched as it spelled out the word penis.

"Seriously?" I asked.

"Maybe Lisa's horny? She wouldn't be the only one," Mel said.

I shook my head, and the pointer moved to the word no and stayed there.

Mel's chin trembled and she pulled her hands away from the pointer. "That's it. I'm done now. We tried. Too bad, so sad." She stood up and bolted upstairs and the basement door slammed shut.

"Bwok! Bwok!" I yelled.

"Bite me!" She yelled back.

I said goodbye to Lisa and told her to vamoose, just in case. I wasn't worried about her warning, figuring it was only nonsense or a ghost joke I didn't get. I put the board back in the box and shoved it under the couch for the time being. I surveyed the mess Emily and her friends made and scowled. "She's so grounded for this," I said out loud. I flipped off the basement light and scurried to the stairs. On the first step something pierced my foot so I flipped the stair light on to see what it was. There, smack in the middle of the stair, sat a rock. "You've got to be kidding." I grabbed the rock and huffed my way up the stairs.

"Interesting," Mel said when I showed her the rock.

"Uh huh."

"What do you think it means?"

"Heck if I know, that's why I'm showing it to you."

She shrugged. "She's not my dead mother."

"Good point."

We sat at the kitchen table and picked at cupcakes. This time I picked at a vanilla one and Mel, confetti. I licked the frosting off the entire cupcake and then took a bite of the top. "Ohmygosh," I mumbled with the cupcake top stuffed in my mouth. "Thisissogood."

She pursed her lips, picked up her cupcake and then tossed it back onto the table. "You're having a cupcake-gasm." She picked her cupcake up again and gave it the once-over. "And this cupcake is doing nothing for me. Oh my God! I'm not even gonna have cupcake-gasms anymore either." She dropped her head onto the table and banged it twice. "Ouch," she said, sitting upright again and rubbing her head.

I laughed so hard I spit cupcake juice in her face. She picked a piece out of her eye. I flicked a piece off of her chin. "My bad."

"This is serious. Nick and I haven't had sex since the cell phone was invented. What if that's the last time?"

"It's not."

"How do you know?"

"Because I know. You're a beautiful, funny, amazing woman, and some guy is going to want to make you happy in every way possible."

"But what if that can't happen? What if I'm not able to, you know?"

I put my elbows on the table and rested my head on them. I knew Mel was getting to something so instead of trying to pull it out of her, I cut to the chase. "Tell me."

She pulled her hair back into a ponytail. "What if I'm alone the rest of my life?"

I placed my hand on hers and squeezed. "You won't be. I may not be psychic but like I said, I can absolutely promise you that. You'll find love again and have the best sex of your life, too."

"Screw love. It's too complicated. I'll stick to just sex."

I mimicked my mother. "Ah Madone."

"It's true."

I took a sip of my coffee. "Coffee's cold. Want yours reheated?"

She handed me her cup. "Sure."

I took the lids off and put them in the microwave. I knew people said not to reheat coffee with cream but it hadn't killed me yet. "Do you want fresh cream?"

"Yes, please."

I grabbed the cream from the refrigerator and something behind me made a loud popping sound. I jumped and the cream container slipped from my hands and crashed to the floor. "What was that?"

Mel pointed to the microwave. "Uh, it's on fire."

"Shoot." I grabbed the paper towel roll and used it to poke the button to open the microwave. It stopped sparking. The inside was brown. "What the hell was that?"

"Looks like your microwave blew up," Mel said.

I furrowed my brow, and frowned. "Thanks. I couldn't tell."

I took out the coffees and poured them down the sink. "I think it's time for homemade coffee."

She nodded. "Me, too."

I turned on the light above the coffee pot and it went pop, like the microwave. "Seriously?"

"Maybe you have a blown circuit?"

I picked up the creamer container and set it on the counter. Mel got up and grabbed the paper towels and wiped up the floor.

"The box is in the basement," I said.

"Ain't no way in hell I'm going back down there. Lisa could be down there with some ghost penis or something."

I shook my head and muttered, "Good grief." I went to the basement and checked the breaker box but nothing was flipped.

Back upstairs, I whined to Mel. "That microwave was practically brand new."

"I'll go shopping with you if you'd like."

"Shopping sucks."

She hated that I hated shopping. "I don't know why we're best friends."

"Yin and yang," I said and then grabbed a piece of paper and a pen from the kitchen desk and wrote *out of order* on it and taped it to the microwave.

"Who do you think will try it first?"

"That's a tough call. None of them read my notes, Jake included. Think I should put masking tape across it, too?"

She nodded. "Probably a good idea."

I made fresh coffee and gave Mel a cup.

"We need to talk about the warning," she said.

"Penis isn't a warning, Mel. It's a word."

"Why the heck did she spell out penis anyway?"

"How should I know? You're the horny one. You tell me."

"You've got a point."

I noticed Mel's eyes were puffy and I wanted to kick myself for not noticing sooner. "You know what we need to do," I said. "We need to sit here and eat our cupcakes until we're ready to throw up and laugh about stupid stuff, like we did before both of our lives got on the crazy train. That's what we need to do."

"Damn straight." She held up a cupcake and took a bite. "Screw the crazy train."

I held up a cupcake, too. "Yeah, screw the crazy train." I took a big bite and let pieces drop from my mouth.

So we ate cupcakes, drank coffee and laughed until we cried. Sometimes there was nothing more healing than laughing with your best friend.

CHAPTER FOUR

EMILY CALLED LATER THAT DAY and asked if she could stay the night at Hayden's. I hadn't mentioned the basement, and knew she'd hate the serious case of Angela whoop-ass she'd get when she got home the next day.

Not in the mood for cooking, I gave Josh the decision of what to pick up. He picked Chick-fil-A. I got a shake and chicken nuggets. Not a smart move on my part but I figured I'd run it off later. We sat at the kitchen table, drank our shakes, and ate our chicken nuggets.

"Grandpa did that."

"Huh?"

He pointed to the microwave. "That. Grandpa did it."

"What makes you think that, Little Man?"

"My dream, Mama. Remember? He said he likes electrical stuff."

"I don't think that's what he meant."

"I bet he did. If I could blow stuff up, I would, and you always say I'm like Grandpa."

I nodded. "You've got a point." I eyed the microwave.

He gobbled his dinner down in less than three minutes and retreated back into his not-quite-a-man-yet cave.

I cleaned up the kitchen and thought about the microwave. "Dad? Are you here?" I waited for a shift in temperature or a slight tap on my shoulder, but nothing happened. "Sure wish you were around."

I plopped down on the couch, excited to not only have the room to myself, but also to have complete, utter control of the TV. That hadn't happened since I married Jake. I flipped through the channels and stopped on one with a commercial for popcorn. I could almost smell the butter from the TV. Suddenly craving the buttery artery-clogger, I headed into the kitchen to nuke a bag. I grabbed a bag and ripped off the plastic but when I went to put it in the microwave, the sign stopped me. "Well, crap." I tossed the popcorn bag back into the drawer and grabbed a bag of cookies instead. I made a mental note to suck it up and go shopping for a new microwave soon.

I poured myself a glass of Diet Coke and plopped back on the couch. I flipped through the channels, searching for something entertaining. The TV, a monstrous flat screen I'd bought for Jake last year, and the surround sound system he'd installed made the house shake so I turned it down.

I'd flipped through all of the regular channels and finally settled on some show about mountain lions, but when a baby was killed, I switched to a cheesy ghost hunter show. I understood the circle of life but I didn't need to see it in action.

Even before my psychic gift kicked in, I never thought ghost hunter shows were real. This one was ridiculously cheesy, too. The smarmy host spent more time flexing his oversized biceps than ghost hunting.

This episode's location was a hotel in the south rumored to be where a woman who was stood up on her wedding day decided to kill herself by drowning in a bathtub. Seemed to me there were easier ways to do it but maybe back then there weren't. A psychic medium attempted to contact the woman. I had a feeling the medium was a scam and watched to see.

The medium's head rocked back and forth like one of those bobble heads my mother got Josh for Christmas a few years back. He told the host he was receiving a message from the jilted bride. "She's coming through strong now," he said.

The host did a quick pose for the camera, ran his fingers though his perfectly coifed hair and then pretended to mess with some big piece of equipment strapped to his chest. It made an assortment of loud and annoying beeping sounds. "She sure is," he said.

The medium's head stopped bobbling and he was having a one-sided conversation, saying things like, *I'm sorry, it's not your fault*, and *you need to move into the light*. I booed at the TV and said things like *bull crap*.

I guzzled the rest of my Diet Coke and went to get a refill. Gracie sniffed my part of the couch for dropped cookie crumbs. When she found nothing, she jumped off the couch and followed me into the kitchen. I grabbed the Diet Coke from the fridge and poured it into my glass, still watching the medium on the show, when the TV went to snow and static. A few seconds later it came back on and both the host and medium looked spooked.

The host turned away from the camera and asked someone off screen, "Are we back on?" He nodded, faced the camera and then explained that something had happened to their electrical circuits, something he believed was caused by the ghost bride.

The medium shook his head. "No, it wasn't her." He rubbed his ear and then nodded several times. "Yes. Yes, I will."

The host spoke to someone off screen again. "You're getting this, right?"

The medium paced in circles around the screen, his head nodding continuously. "She has a message for someone," he said, and then stopped pacing and stared into the camera. It felt like he was looking right at me. She says, "Ah Madone, trying to use the Ouija Board was stupid. Wake up, for crying out loud, because your Ma's got stuff to tell you."

I held the Diet Coke bottle in midair and screamed. "Josh!"

He ran into the kitchen, panting. "What's wrong?"

I pointed to the TV and said, "Uh, the...the..." Nothing coherent came out of my mouth and my son eyeballed me like I had snot dripping from my nose.

"Yeah, Mama. It's a TV." He turned to go back to his not-yet-a-man cave.

I shook my head and stomped my foot. "No, Josh, I know that. I mean, I want you to watch the show."

"I'm in the middle of a game. Can I watch it later?"

"No. I want you to watch it now," I pushed him into the family room.

"But I'm in the middle of a game."

"It's just two minutes."

"But they're gonna kill my guy, and I was winning."

I clenched my teen in frustration. "It's two minutes, Josh. Come on."

"Gee Mama, chill." Josh shook his head.

"I'm chilled. Now watch this with me, please. I wanna know what you think."

*   *   *

"Cool. Grandma's on TV."

"So you think it's her, too?"

"I mean, she said, *Ah Madone* and everything. No one else says that."

"Can you tape the show for me?"

"Nope."

"Josh, please stop giving me such a hard time and help me, okay?"

"Uh, Mom? I can't tape the show because it's already over."

"Oh." I rubbed my arms. "Are you sure?"

He grabbed the remote and hit a bunch of the buttons. "There. I recorded the episode when it's on again tomorrow night. You know, Turner's mom isn't drinking Diet Coke anymore and he says she's really nice now. Even got him a new phone for no reason."

"Thank you," I said, ignoring his psychoanalysis of my Diet Coke issues. I opened my arms to him and we hugged. "Thank you for helping me."

"You're welcome."

He shook his head, too.

I shooed him away with my hand. "Go play your game. Love you."

He smiled. "Love you too, Mama."

*   *   *

I called Jake and left him a cryptic message about the show. Cryptic messages usually got a quick return call. "Hey. Ma was on TV. Hope your day was good. Love you, mean it, bye."

I sent Mel a text. "Ma contacted me."

"What?" She wrote back.

"On TV."

"Hole-eee crap! How?"

"She interrupted the ghost hunter show with the guy who has the huge biceps."

"Oooh. He's hot."

"He's gross. You can have him."

"Duly noted. So what happened?"

I called her and gave her the details and told her Josh had the DVR set to record it the next night.

"Told you the Ouija Board was a dumb idea."

"That's what you got outta this?"

"Absolutely. So what happens now?" She asked.

"Beats me. I guess I'll keep doing what I'm doing. Seems to be helping."

"What exactly is it you're doing?"

"Uh, winging it?"

"Good Lord."

"What?" I asked.

"Gotta go. Nick is actually talking to me. Look outside, I think pigs are flying."

"Good luck."

"I don't need it. He does."

"True."

"Let me know if anything else happens," she said and hung up.

*   *   *

I cleaned the kitchen while I waited for Jake to call. The counters sparkled and my oven was streak-free, at least in the dim light. An hour later Jake still hadn't called and I'd waited long enough. I turned off the lights and decided to read in bed. I told Josh to shut off the game and reminded him to brush his teeth—we didn't pay five thousand bucks for braces for his teeth to rot and fall out, and told him to hit the sack. He didn't argue.

"Night, Mama."

"Night, Little Man, love you."

"Love you too."

I snuggled under the covers as Gracie jumped up on the bed, turned in circles and landed right in the middle of Jake's pillow. I thought about Ma's message and laughed. "You're right, Ma," I said. "The Ouija Board was pretty stupid, wasn't it? But seriously, watching Mel run out of the room in a tizzy was hilarious. And I'm trying, Ma. I'm really, really trying."

I powered on my iPad to read for a bit before I went to sleep. I'd just purchased Martha Reynolds's second book, *Chocolate Fondue*, the second in her *Chocolate* series. The first book's title, *Chocolate for Breakfast*, caught my eye, so I bought it. It was a great story about a woman who gave a baby up for adoption. When I saw the story continued, I couldn't help but wonder what happened next, so I bought both the second and the third book, *Bittersweet Chocolate*. I read the first two pages and my eyes began to close, so I shut off the iPad and closed my eyes. Seconds later, Ma's image flashed in my mind's eye.

"Angela."

I sat up, wide-eyed. "Ma?" I couldn't see her, but the room felt different. The air felt cooler and I heard a slight buzzing, like a strong electrical current humming in my ears. My heart raced and I felt my underarms sweating. Gracie jumped off the bed. She stood in the middle of the bedroom, tail wagging and ears up. "Who's here, Gracie?"

She popped her front legs up and crouched down. Her tail wagged ferociously and she barked.

"Grandma?"

I flipped on my bedside light. Josh stood just inside my door, his face beaming, cheeks glowing. "Mama, I can see Grandma."

I jumped out of bed. "Where, Josh? Where is she?" I scanned the room but saw nothing. My shoulders sank and I felt my heart break a little.

He pointed to Gracie. "She's right there. Can't you see her?"

"No. What's she doing? Can she see you?"

He held his finger up. "Hold on. She's talking to me."

My eyes bulged and I bit my lip. He nodded and listened to a voice I so desperately wanted to hear. I was so excited he could hear and see her, I almost wet myself. I ran to the bathroom. "Don't let her leave," I said. "I gotta pee."

He laughed. "Grandma says you're a pain in her big Italian ass and she's glad someone can finally see her. She says she's tired of talking to a brick wall." I came out of the bathroom and he pointed to me. "I think you're the brick wall."

I laughed too. "Tell your Grandmother that works both ways."

"She can hear you." He paused. "And she's not gonna leave because she's got something important to tell you." He listened and said, "It's about Emily. She's in truuuuub-bull. Grandma says it's not good."

My pulse quickened "What's not good?"

"She says she's at a party right now and she's gonna get her cherry popped." He scratched his head. "What's her cherry?"

I rushed to my closet to put on clothes. "I'll explain later. What party, Josh? And where?"

"An ill repute one," he said. "What's ill repute mean?"

My daughter was at a brothel losing her virginity? Good God. Did those things even exist anymore? I pulled a pair of sweats from my closet shelf. "I'll explain later. Ask Grandma to tell you where it is. Get a pen and paper from my nightstand and write it down, please. I'm getting dressed." I shut the closet door. When I came out of the closet he handed me the address. "Josh, this is Hayden's house. Ma, what's going on?"

Josh listened to Ma, and I paced my room. I rubbed my right thumb with my left hand over and over. "This is ridiculous, using my son as an interpreter because my gift is broken. I want to help people, I do. I'll show you that—whoever you are. Just please, give me my freaking gift back already."

"Ah Madone, stop yellin', you'll wake the dead," Ma laughed. "Too bad you can't hear that 'cause I know you'd think it was funny."

I froze. "Ma?"

"Angela?"

"Ma, I can hear you." I pivoted around, convinced I'd see my mother floating just above the floor, dressed in the blue nightgown she died in, but she was already gone. "Ma? Where'd you go?"

"Whadda ya mean, where'd I go? I'm right here."

I scanned the room but couldn't see her anywhere. "I can't see you."

Josh pointed to the entrance to my bathroom. "She's right there."

Ma laughed. "Well now, ain't this gonna be fun for me?"

Josh giggled.

"Shit." I grabbed my shoes. "Can't deal with this now. Ma, we need to get to Emily."

"Oh, yah. That child is getting into something bad. I can feel it. You gotta save her from getting knocked up."

"Ma, she's at Hayden's house. It's not a house of ill repute."

"All I know is that girl is getting herself in trouble so *muoviti*."

I finished putting on my shoes. "I'm moving, Ma. I'm moving."

Josh tapped me on the shoulder. "Can I come?"

"No, honey. I'm sorry, but I need you to stay here, okay?"

His head dropped. "Man, I never get to have any fun."

I hugged him. "Keep your phone with you. I'll let know what's going on."

"Or I can pop in and give you an update," Ma said.

"Yeah, do that Grandma. I missed you."

"I never left ya, my little *bambino*."

I wiped the tears from my eyes. "Let's go."

*　*　*

I pulled out of the garage and started talking. "Have you been throwing rocks at me?"

My mother didn't respond.

"Ma?"

"Boo."

I slammed on the brakes. "Mother! Don't do that when I'm driving! I could hit another car or something!" I leaned my head back on the headrest. "Cheese and rice. You scared the crap out of me."

Ma laughed. "I wouldn't have done it if there were cars around. Geesh."

"Well thank God, but please, don't do that again. I'm over forty now. I don't want to have a heart attack. And seriously, why have you been throwing rocks at me? I called Roxanne and she told me the dream so why'd you keep doing it?"

"Rocks? Oh, yah. At the Walmart you mean? Yah, that was me. What was I supposed to do? I couldn't get your attention any other way. Lord knows I'd tried."

"Ma, rocks have been everywhere. It was getting annoying."

"Huh? Whadda ya talking about?"

"The rocks, Ma. In the woods at the park? In the basement? All over the damn house, actually."

"That wasn't me, Ang. I just used the rock at the Walmart is all."

"The other rocks? Those weren't you?"

"Nope. I tried all sorts of tricks to get you to notice me but you're blind as a bat."

"For your information," I said, "I've had several ghosts vying for my attention. How was I supposed to know which was you?"

"Because I'm your ma, that's how."

"So what'd you do? How'd you try to get my attention?" I turned left onto the main road into Hayden's subdivision. "And tell me fast because we're almost to Hayden's house."

"The time your bedside light went out. It made that big pop sound. That was me."

"What about the light in the bathroom? Was that you?" I asked.

"Nope."

"Be a little more original then."

"I dropped my picture from the wall in the hallway once," she said.

I shook my head. "Never saw it."

"Yah, Josh picked it up and put it back. He said hi, too. At least he knew it was me."

I held my hand up in the air. "Well, I guess he's smarter than me."

"I heard brains skip a generation," she said.

"Nice."

"That one time the back door kept opening? That was me. And I gotta tell ya, it was funny to watch you get beetroot red every time you got up to close it."

"You thought annoying me was the appropriate way to send me a sign?"

"Well, yah. It worked when I was alive so I figured it'd work with me dead, too."

There was a lot of truth to that. "Did you blow up my microwave?"

"Nope. That was your father."

I felt a slight fluttering in my stomach. "It was dad? That's what Josh said, too."

"Yah, I told him not to do it on account of you hate shopping so much and that microwave was new but he's all about electrical stuff right now. It's pretty common for the newbies, ya know, the new spirits."

I swallowed a lump in my throat.

"Oh." Her tone went up an octave. "And that time you and Jake were getting ready to have a little hanky panky? Ya know, do the wild thing? When Gracie ran in circles, chasing her tail? Yup, that was me." She snorted.

I bit my bottom lip to stop from smiling. "Good Lord. I'll never have sex again."

"Ah Madone, Angela. I didn't stick around. I got limits, ya know. But I gotta tell ya, that Jake of yours? He's got a big one, that's for sure."

I glance at the passenger's seat, my mouth wide open and said, "Please stop. Please."

"Well you asked what signs, so I'm telling ya. Don't blame me if you don't like the answers."

"Oh, for the love of Mike."

"What? Who's Mike?"

"It's an expression, Ma."

"Well it ain't a good one. What if you're Mike and someone says it to you? That'd be confusing."

I laughed. "Welcome back, Ma. I've missed you."

"Like I said, I never left."

We pulled onto Hayden's street and counted ten cars parked on the road and driveway. I pulled up next to the driveway and shut off the engine. The main floor of Hayden's house was lit up and girls' shadows shone through the window, filling the front room. I stayed in the car with my invisible mother, whom I assumed was still hovering next to me. "Well, you're right. Something's going on," I said.

"Uh huh, and you're not gonna like it. All those doodads and creams."

I wrinkled my nose. "What doodads and creams?"

"The sex stuff. Ya know, that stuff they sell in those adult only shops on the interstate. They're all over that house. Some floozy brought 'em over and is showing the girls how to use 'em. She's telling them all how it's gonna make sex better, make 'em feel good. We gotta get Emily outta there before I go in there and start throwin' that crap through the windows."

"No throwing anything through the windows, Ma. Promise me, okay?" She didn't respond. "Ma? You still here?"

"Ah Madone, yes. Now let's go, we gotta hurry."

I didn't need to be a rocket scientist to figure out what was going on in Hayden's house. "It's a sex toy party, Ma, that's all."

"I don't know about that. All I know is she's got creams and doodads and some electric stuff. Says it'll make 'em feel good, but Emily could shock herself or something. I don't know, but I bet gettin' shocked in your twat would hurt like a son-of-a-gun."

I dropped my head onto the steering wheel and sighed. "Ma, nobody calls it a twat anymore and besides, they use batteries, and I don't think you can get shocked from batteries."

"Batteries can still give you a shock, Ang. Remember that time your brother Pauly made you lick the battery? Sent you flying, the shock. Ah Madone, that was funny." She snorted again. "And how do you know those things use batteries anyway? You got one?"

Whoops.

"Mel has stuff, Ma. And I'm pretty sure it's just a sex toy party. I'm not thrilled she's here, but she's not going to lose her virginity tonight, and I'm certainly not going to barge in there and embarrass her. She'd never live that down."

"You're right, you can't go in there. Girls are horrible. I remember how you were."

"What's that mean?"

"You were a *cagna*, ya know."

"I was not a bitch, Ma."

"Were too."

She was half right. There were times I was a *cagna*, just not all of the time. "Okay, so I was sometimes, but not all of the time."

"You say tomato, I say tomahto," she said.

"You're funny."

She ignored that. "Be right back. I'm gonna go take a peek and make sure she's not boinkin' that boy in the closet or something."

That boy?

"Ma, please don't break or move anything."

She didn't respond.

"Ma?"

Still nothing.

"I know you hear me, Ma. Keep everything intact, please."

"Well I'll be damned," Ma said.

I jumped in my seat. "Please don't startle me like that, and what? What'd you see?"

"I've never seen anything like that in my life," she said.

"Is she with a boy? What boy?" Emily didn't have a boyfriend, or at least not one I knew about.

"Nah, she's not with a boy. It's the stuff. They're gonna go to hell in a hand-basket using that stuff, that's for sure."

"I'm sure it's just a few gadgets and body lotions," I said.

"Oh yah? Well I've never seen body lotion shaped like a pecker, and with a finger growin' outta it. I don't know what that's for, but I'm telling ya, it can't be good. They called it a rabbit, but it doesn't look soft and fluffy to me."

Oh boy, they had a *rabbit*. I knew what it was but only because I saw pictures. Honest. "Did Emily have one?"

"No. She said no when that floozy told her to try it out in the bathroom. Thank God for that. It's probably full of germs and she'd end up with that crotch disease like Al Capone."

My temples throbbed. "Emily isn't going to get syphilis, Ma."

"Ya never know. You need to get that girl a chastity belt."

*   *   *

Josh was waiting for us when we got home. "Is Emily okay? Grandma, you were supposed to keep me posted."

"Ah, Josh, your sister, she's fine. Don't you don't worry your little head about her, ya hear? I'm sorry I didn't come back, but your Ma and me, we got to talking, and I forgot. We've got a lot of catchin' up to do, now, too, ya know."

"I know. Look, I got my braces off." Josh smiled big at someone I so desperately wanted to see.

"And you look mighty good, too, more handsome without those braces. You're becoming such a big boy. You got good genes, from my side."

His eyes lit up. "Thanks, Grandma. I got a lot to tell you, too. Will you come back soon?"

"I'm always around. Just call for me, okay my *bellissimo ragazzo*? My beautiful boy?"

"Okay."

I put my hands on Josh's shoulders and gave him a kiss on his head. I realized that one day he'd be taller than me and I wouldn't be able to do that. My emotions were heightened and feeling the sadness about my baby growing up, I hugged him tight. "It's bed time now, Little Man."

"What about Emily?"

"She's fine. Grandma misunderstood what was going on."

"So she's not in trouble?"

"I didn't say that."

"Awesome. Love you, Mama. Love you too, Grandma."

I shook my head. "That boy loves to see his sister in trouble." I walked into the family room. "Ma, you here?"

"Like mother like son," Ma said.

"What?" I shook my head. "That's not how the saying goes, Ma and besides, it's not true anyway."

"You did the same thing to Pauly. He was such a good boy and you were constantly getting him in trouble. *Demone bambina*, you were."

"Me, the demon child?" I shook my head. "He locked me in the neighbor's shed. He pushed me down the stairs and told me I was going to die in a plane crash." I threw my hands up. "While I was on a plane for the first time! He was the demon child, Ma, not me."

"Boys will be boys."

"He locked me in a shed, Ma. In a shed. I only got out because the neighbor heard me crying."

"Well, you always were a little loud."

I threw myself onto the couch and sighed. "I give up. Welcome back, Ma."

"You gotta learn to forgive and forget, Angela. Holdin' all that bitterness inside, it's not good. Like Linda said, you should meditate."

"Oh, geez. I wanna see you try it. It's not easy."

"Hum. Hum," she sang, completely off key. "Us celestial beings, we meditate all the time."

"I can't see you, Ma, and it's *um*, not hum."

"Well, it's different in the afterlife."

"Uh huh. If you can meditate, then I'm the Virgin Mary."

She laughed. "That's a load of bull hockey if I've ever heard one. You got your father's genes, ya know."

I sniffed and wiped my nose. "I can't believe he's gone." A lumped formed in my throat. "Forget it," I said. "I can't talk about him, not yet."

"I heard you, ya know."

I crossed my arms and ran my hands up and down my shoulders. "What do you mean?"

"After he died. I heard you. I was here. Even though you couldn't see me anymore, I never left."

My chin trembled and my heart ached. "I can't do this now, Ma. I just can't."

"You gotta talk about him, ya know. Get it out. It helps."

The temperature in the room rose and my cheeks got hot. "Ma, please, just drop it."

"You want I should go see one of your brothers? They don't yell at me."

"That's because they can't see you."

"Yah, well, neither can you."

"You know what I mean." I rubbed my eyes. "I'm sorry, Ma. I've waited months to be able to talk to you and what do I do? I bitch. I'm a horrible daughter." I cried more and sniffled the snot back into my nose.

"What are you cryin' for? That's what we do. We kvetch at each other. It's the way we show our love. Ah Madone, stop cryin' already. Your face gets all swollen and puffy and it ain't pretty."

I wiped my eyes again and laughed. "I missed you, Ma."

"I never left you, Ang. Never."

CHAPTER FIVE

"MAMA, WAKE UP." Josh shook me awake.

I rubbed my eyes with my fists. "Hey, Little Man. What time is it?"

"Eight fifteen."

I sat up. "Oh, geez. I fell asleep on the couch."

"Uh, yeah. That's where you are now," he said. "Where's Grandma?"

I scanned the room, and then remembered I couldn't see her anyway. "I don't know. Can't see her, remember?"

He walked around the room, came back to the couch and crouched down on the floor next to it. "She's not here. What if she doesn't come back?"

I pulled him onto the couch and wrapped my arms around him. "She will, Little Man. I don't think she ever really left us. I think we just couldn't see or hear her is all."

"Stuff because of Grandpa, right?"

I nodded. "Probably, but I think now that we're feeling better things will go back to how they were before."

"Why can't you see her?"

"Beats me, but I can hear her, so that's good."

"What about Grandpa? Do you think I'll see him?"

"I don't know."

"I miss him."

I squeezed him tighter. "Me, too."

"Mama?"

"Yeah?"

"I can't breathe."

"Oh, sorry." I released my death grip.

"And can you make pancakes?"

"Why? Your hands broken?"

He held his hands up, fingers pointing in different directions. "I think so."

"Okay, fine, but you're cleaning up."

"It's Emily's turn."

I stood. "She's not even here, Josh."

He shrugged, and we walked into the kitchen.

Josh got out the pancake supplies while I checked my phone. Mel had sent four text messages.

"Nick trimmed the rose bushes in the back yesterday and woke up today with poison ivy. Think it was Fran?" She wrote.

"Probably," I wrote back. I decided to tell her about hearing Ma after breakfast.

I made pancakes in the shape of Mickey Mouse and one in the shape of a penis. Inappropriate? Probably, but it made my son laugh and sometimes that was more important than acting appropriately. Neither of us could bring ourselves to eat the penis pancake though, so Gracie got a special breakfast treat. I laughed because Josh cringed as the dog scarfed it down.

Wide-eyed, he said, "Wow. She's got a big mouth."

I held back a giggle. "Go ahead and get dressed. I'll clean up."

"You sure, Mama?"

"I can change my mind if you'd like."

He jumped out of the chair and bolted up the stairs. I gathered the dishes and turned on the water. It immediately shut off and I heard Ma laugh. "You're funny, Ma. Can you turn it back on, please?"

It turned back on. "Thank you."

I rinsed the dishes and shut off the water and it came back on again. "Having fun?"

The garbage disposal switched on. "Seriously?"

It shut off.

"Thank you." I didn't let her little game annoy me. Happy to have her back, I decided I'd let her have her fun, at least for as long as I could stand it. I piddled around in the kitchen a little longer and then texted Jake before I headed upstairs to take a shower.

"I CAN HEAR MA!" I used the all-caps feature on my phone for effect. I was a little miffed he hadn't called me back last night, especially since I sent a cryptic message to get his attention. He'd probably stayed up late entertaining clients, and his phone died, but it still annoyed me. Since he didn't respond, I texted Mel the same message.

"OMG! COMING OVER NOW!"

"Give me a half hour. Getting in the shower."

"Hurry, I don't want to see you naked."

"Most would kill for a peek," I responded.

"Ew."

I finished my shower and called Jake again. This time he answered, so I told him about Ma.

He laughed about Ma messing with me in the kitchen. "That's Fran, all right."

"Yup. And I didn't even get mad. You'd have been proud."

"More like shocked."

"Thanks for your support."

"Anytime."

I passed on telling him about Emily and the sex toy party, knowing it would set a negative tone for his day. As for talking to Emily about it, I couldn't let her know I knew, so I had to think of a way to discuss sex—and the fact that she couldn't have any until she was at least thirty. I figured I'd say something like, "You better not be having sex or I'll ship you off to a convent. That's it. You're grounded for life. Go to your room."

Yup, that would work.

* * *

When I got downstairs, Mel was already at the kitchen table talking to Josh. She hadn't brought coffee or cupcakes. I held my hands up. "What the heck? Where's my red velvet?"

She looked me up and down. "Looks like it's attached to your boot-tay."

I pointed at her and said, "Watch it, Melissa," and then giggled under my breath.

"Oooh, she called you by your full name," Josh said. "You're in trouble now."

I winked at him. "He's right."

Mel laughed and waved a hand at my son. "That's alright, Josh. I can handle your mother."

"In your dreams," I said.

"Thankfully you're not in my dreams, especially when they're about Ryan Reynolds."

Josh got up. "Awkward," he said as he scooted out of the kitchen.

We both laughed. "Easiest way to get rid of a kid," Mel said. "Just mention sex and they're running like a Kenyan in a marathon."

"Interesting comparison."

"I just read an article about Kenyan runners and how they're genetically predisposed to being good at it."

"I made a penis shaped pancake for breakfast."

She nodded. "Nice."

I shrugged. "We couldn't eat it so we gave it to Gracie."

"Probably best."

"Coffee?"

"Thought you'd never ask."

I put on a pot of dark roast and sat down at the table with Mel. She put her hands on the table and leaned toward me. "So tell me what happened and don't leave anything out."

I told her how Josh saw and heard Ma but how I couldn't and that it ticked me off and then I could hear her and we went to Hayden's because Emily was there for a sex party. "And they had the Rabbit," I said, and shook my head.

"Oh my."

I nodded.

"Did she buy one?" she asked.

"She better not have or I'm sending her to a convent."

Mel laughed. "They don't accept women who aren't Catholic, you know."

"I'll lie and tell them she was baptized Catholic but I didn't force her to go to church."

"Yeah, that'll work."

"You never know."

"Seriously though, I'm so happy for you." She grabbed my hands and shook them. "You can hear Fran!"

I smiled. "I know, it's amazing, isn't it?"

"Hey," Mel said. "Do you think she's the one who gave Nick the flat tire? And the poison ivy?"

"You betcha," Ma said.

I jumped. "Jesus, Ma." I slapped my hand against my chest. "You scared the crap outta me."

Mel shot up out of her seat. "Fran's here? 'Hi Fran.'" She waved. "I'm so glad you're back."

"Ah Madone, tell her I'm a celestial being. I never left. We don't screw things up, it's you who did that."

I shook my head. "Oh, geez."

"What'd she say?"

"She told me to tell you she never left, that I screwed up and that celestial beings don't."

She sat back down. "God, I love your mother."

"Harumph. At least someone appreciates me," Ma said.

"I appreciate you, Ma, and you're not helping, Mel." I got up and poured us both coffee.

"What'd I do?" Mel asked.

"Yeah, what'd she do? All's she said is she loves me. Nothing wrong with that, is there?"

I wanted a shot of rum in my coffee, but it wasn't even noon, so I grabbed a bag of Oreos instead and sat back down at the table.

"I sure do miss coffee," Ma said. "I just want to smell it. Just one more time."

"Ma, we've had this conversation before. A few times, actually."

"So? It's important for me to express my feelings. You wanna deny me that?"

Maybe that rum wasn't such a bad idea.

"What's she saying?" Mel asked. "I hate that I can't hear her."

I raised my eyebrows at my friend. "Now you know how I've been feeling." I handed her an Oreo. "Ma, we need to talk to you about Nick." I dipped an Oreo into my coffee.

"That's gross," Mel said.

"Nuh uh," I said with a mouth full of coffee-drenched Oreo. It was heavenly. I dunked another one and then dangled it in Mel's face. "Want some? I'll even dunk it more for you, if you'd like."

She stuck her finger in her mouth. "Blech."

"That's fine. I'll enjoy the food-gasm without you."

"Did your mom leave?"

I dunked the Oreo again and stuffed it in my mouth. I said, "Ma, you still here," but with a full mouth of Oreo it sounded more like *maf-youf-stiff-herf*.

She didn't respond.

"Ma?"

Mel's coffee cup moved across the table, sending Mel out of her seat, about three feet into the air. "Holy crap!"

I think I peed a little, watching her jump. I guffawed, spitting Oreo onto the table. "Gosh, it's really funny when it happens to you."

She gave me the stink eye. "No, it's not." She straightened her shirt and sat back down. "Good God, that would drive me crazy."

I nodded. "Ma, stop screwin' with Mel. She's gonna wet herself."

Ma howled. "Ah Madone, that's so much fun."

"I think I did wet myself," Mel said.

"I think I did, too," I said.

All three of us laughed. "Okay, can we focus here?" I wanted to talk about Nick.

"I'm practicing moving stuff. Getting pretty good at it, too. I'm gonna scare the bejesus outta that cheating son-of-a-gun, Nick, you just wait."

I made an O shape with my mouth.

"What'd she say? Is she talking?"

"Oh yeah, and you're gonna love what she's saying."

"Tell her I've been keeping my eye on him and she's right. He is cheatin' on her with that new assistant of his, that little *sciattona*. The poison ivy and the flat tire? Yup. Those were me. Pretty darn clever too, if I do say so myself."

Oh boy. I knew Mel *thought* Nick was cheating but Ma's confirmation took things to a whole new level. Ma rarely called anyone a *sciattona* —Italian for slut, so I knew it was bad.

"Well, what're ya waiting for, Angela? Tell her."

"Hold on, Ma. Lemme think this through."

"What? What'd she say?" Mel asked.

I dunked another Oreo and swirled it around in my coffee. Yeah, I was stalling but I wasn't sure how to tell her. Plus, I was scared. Mel could get pretty angry when pushed too far and I didn't want to be on the receiving end of that.

She snapped her fingers in my face. "What did she say?" She scowled at me, so I did what anyone would do. I panicked, and blurted it out. "She said you were right. Nick is cheating." I gasped and covered my mouth with my hand. "Oh my gosh, I'm sorry. I didn't mean to say it like that."

She was silent for a moment, but then she took a deep breath and nodded. "I told you. I know a cheating rat bastard when I see one."

She was calm in the way the wind gets before a tornado and I knew eventually she'd lose it. I just hoped I could be there to help her when it happened. I filled her in on the poison ivy and the flat tire hoping it would make her feel better.

"God, I love your mother. Thank you, Fran." She took an Oreo and dunked it in her coffee.

I frowned. "Copy cat."

She shoved the entire mushy mess into her mouth, smiled and then said, "Good Lord, this *is* orgasmic."

"You okay?" I asked, knowing full well she wasn't.

Her nostrils flared. "My husband is having an affair."

"I know. I'm sorry."

"I am not okay."

"Ah Madone, are we gonna get this cheater or what? I got a good plan. You wanna hear it or what?"

"Yeah, Ma. We wanna hear it." I turned back to Mel who was dunking her second Oreo. "Ma's got a plan. You up for it?"

"Abso-freakin-lutely. Especially if it includes more poison ivy, like on his balls."

I cringed. "Yikes."

"My husband is cheating on me. The least he deserves is itchy balls."
What could I say to that?

I played messenger between Ma and Mel. We discussed catching him in the act but I put the kibosh on that crazy notion immediately. None of us needed to be in that position, especially Mel. Instead we decided to find whatever proof we could to give Mel a legal advantage. Actually, it was whatever proof Ma could find, though Mel and I committed to more amateurish private investigating. I had a feeling I would regret that.

Mel, who had eaten eleven dunked Oreos in record time, smiled bigger than I'd seen her smile in months. "I can't wait for this to be done," she said. "I'm so ready to move on with my life."

I figured Mel said that more to convince herself than because it was true. "Are you sure you're ready for this?" I had a funky feeling in my gut that this wasn't going to be as satisfying as Mel thought. "It might be harder than you think."

"I'm ready. Not everyone has a relationship like you and Jake. Nick and I have never been that solid."

I hadn't realized Mel compared her relationship to mine. "Jake and I aren't the perfect couple. We have our struggles, too."

"Maybe, but at least Jake doesn't drop trou for anyone but you."

She had a point there.

"Just thinking about Nick makes me want to hurl," she said.

"Yah, I was like that with your father, too," Ma said.

Excuse me?

"Ma, Dad didn't cheat on you."

"No, but he sure made me wanna hurl at times."

I shook my head. "Ma, please, that's my father you're talking about."

"All's I'm sayin' is with his travel, I was alone a lot and that don't make a marriage easy. Maybe I shoulda got me one of those sex toys like at that party. We mighta not got divorced if I did." She was silent for a second and then said, "Nah, it probably woulda happened anyway."

I shook my head again.

Mel giggled. "She's giving you a hard time, isn't she?"

I nodded. "She said my father made her want to hurl at times, too, because she was alone a lot, and that she should have had a sex toy."

She laughed. "Tell her she can borrow mine."

"Good Lord."

"Ah Madone, I wish," Ma said.

"Seriously, mother."

"What'd I do?"

I rubbed my temples. "I'm getting a migraine."

Mel laughed. "Remember a few days ago when all you wanted was to talk to your mother? How's that working for ya?"

"Ma always said, be careful what you wish for 'cause karma has a way of biting you in the butt."

"Ass. I said ass. We're all adults here, you can say ass, ya know."

I just shook my head. Sometimes being silent was best.

Mel got up to leave. "I gotta go. You'll let me know if Fran does anything, right?"

I nodded.

"I'm gonna pop on over to that little floozy's house right now and see if Nick is there," Ma said.

I held up a finger to tell my mom to wait a second, and walked Mel out to her car. "I'm worried about you."

"I'll be fine." She hugged me. "I'm so glad you can hear Fran again and not just because of the Nick stuff. I know how much you missed her."

I hugged her. My heart broke for her. "Remind me of that when I'm ready to lose my mind."

"I can hear you, ya know," Ma said.

Mel got in the car. "Good luck with Fran. I think you're gonna need it."

I walked back inside and cleaned up the coffee and Oreos. If Ma was still with me, she didn't make a sound.

* * *

Emily burst in about an hour after I'd cleaned up the kitchen. "I'm gonna be late," she said as she zipped by me.

"Hold up there a sec, Speedy Gonzales. I need to talk to you."

She stopped at the foot of the stairs. "Mom, I'm running late."

"For what?"

"I'm like, meeting friends at the lake. I was supposed to be there like, an hour ago."

"I don't remember you talking to me about going to the lake."

Cue the hissy fit.

"Mom, it's, like, my only day off this week. Everyone's going today so, like, I can go. I told dad about it, like, last week."

Parental manipulation struck again. The rule was to come to me, not their dad, when they needed approval. He was distracted during work hours—which were usually twelve a day, and they knew they could get a yes because he wasn't really paying attention. They also knew if they got busted, whatever they'd planned was off. "So, what's the rule about that?"

Emily clenched her fists and shook them. "Mom, I already made plans. I can't just, like, change them. Everybody's already there."

"Well, I sure can. Give me your phone and I'll text everyone for you."

She hopped on her toes. "Dad said I could go. Please, Mom."

Josh walked out of the den, saw Emily's red face, and then stepped back into the den and closed the door. Smart kid.

"Have you been in the basement recently?" I asked.

Her chin sunk to her chest and she exhaled. "I haven't had a chance to clean it, Mom but I, like, promise I will when I get home tonight. Okay?"

"You need to clean it now, Emily."

"I promised everyone I'd be there, Mom. Come on. Can I please clean it, like, when I get home? Please?" She turned and headed up the stairs.

I walked over to the bottom of the staircase and said, "Let me make this perfectly clear. You are not going anywhere today except to the basement to clean it. End of discussion."

"But Mom—"

I cut her off. "Toss me your keys, Emily."

She didn't move.

"Now, please."

She took her keys out of her purse and dropped them on the stair below her and ran into her room. "I never get to do anything," she said as she slammed her door.

I grabbed the keys from the step and stood there. My jaw hurt from clenching my teeth. A second later I felt the steam leaving my ears and raced up the stairs to her room. She'd already locked her door, so I grabbed the master key for bedroom doors from above my bedroom doorframe, unlocked the door and walked in.

"This is my room, Mother. You can't just, like, walk in."

Jake and I didn't raise her to be entitled and that attitude made my blood boil. "Your father and I own this house, therefore this room is ours. We're being gracious by allowing you to use it, but trust me, you keep up this attitude, you'll lose it."

She threw her pillow on the floor. "What's your problem? I like, didn't do anything and you're yelling at me." Her bottom lip trembled and she started to cry.

"Are you serious? You really don't think you did anything? There's pizza in the basement with mold on it, Emily. Mold. We probably have ants and rats now, thanks to you."

"Way to be dramatic, Mom." She wiped her nose on her pillow.

I took a deep breath and let it out slowly. "Emily, you're barely ever home. I'm pretty sure you'll survive if you miss one day with your friends." I sat on her bed next to her and pushed her hair off her face. "And seriously, you left the basement a wreck. I need you to go clean it."

She leaned back on her pillows, the ones she didn't throw on the floor. "Can I please go and do it, like, when I get back?"

I shook my head. "Now, please."

"Talk to her about that sex party," Ma said.

My body stiffened at the sound of my mother's voice. I wasn't sure I'd ever get used to hearing and not seeing her, but I didn't dwell on it for fear I'd lose her again.

"Tell her them toys will shock her woman parts and she won't ever give you a grandbaby," Ma said.

I thought I saw a shadow near Emily's door but if I did, it was only for a second.

"Go on Ang, tell her."

I ignored her.

Emily wouldn't let it go. "Please, Mom?"

"It's that boy, I'm tellin' ya," Ma said.

I realized Ma was right. Emily had a boyfriend and hadn't told me about him. I held her hand and asked. "What's his name?"

She flinched and pulled her hand away. "What? Who?"

"The boy you're supposed to meet at the lake, Emily. What's his name?" Her eyes dropped to the bed and she picked a hair off her comforter. *Busted.*

She lifted her eyes to me, but kept her head down. "Chandler."

"That boy's gonna pop her cherry. You're not gonna let her go, are ya?" Ma asked.

I so did not need to hear that.

"I really like him, Mom. Please, can I go?"

"Are you two dating? Why haven't you told me about him?" Emily and I weren't extremely close—who's actually close to their teenage daughter? But I thought she'd at least tell me when she'd started dating someone she was serious about.

Tears pooled and dropped onto her cheeks. She wiped them away. "I didn't think you'd understand."

"Honey," I said, and snuggled up next to her. Surprisingly, she didn't flinch. "I was a teenager once too, you know. You'd be surprised at how much I understand."

She pulled away, eyes a little brighter than a few seconds before. "So I can, like, go?"

Even though the teenager in me was empathetic to her situation, I knew this boy was likely one of many, and I needed to set a precedent for acceptable behavior. The adult in me knew she was harboring some pretty serious feelings for the boy and I preferred to chain her to her bed and get a chastity belt. That Angela won. "If he really likes you, Emily, he'll understand why you can't make it today."

She pulled her knees into her chest and cried, rubbing her nose on her work pants. "He's like, not going to like me now, that's for sure. No one likes someone who's treated like a child."

I knew we'd hit a place of no return and that nothing I said from then on would matter, so I dropped it. I stood and walked to the bedroom door. "I'm not getting into this any further. Get the basement cleaned and remember this the next time you have friends over. Hopefully you won't do it again."

She grabbed her phone and started texting. I knew if I let her keep it, she'd spend the day texting and the basement wouldn't get done so I took it from her. "Mom, like, I need to tell him I'm not coming."

"I'm sure he'll figure it out."

"But Mom, he's waiting for me."

"I'm sure he'll get distracted by the other kids there, too, Emily."

She cried harder, and shook her head.

"No one else is going, are they?"

She shook her again head and rubbed her eyes. They would be red and puffy tomorrow and she'd probably be upset about that, too.

"Well, I guess you should have considered that when you asked your dad instead of me for permission to go." I slipped the phone into my pocket. "You can have your phone back once the basement is done, and you know what I mean by done, right?"

She got up, pushed by me, and stomped down to the basement.

"This ain't good," Ma said. "You got any rubbers?"

I bowed my head and muttered, "Good Lord."

* * *

Emily scoured the basement, her face set in a permanent scowl the entire time. Her cleaning skills astounded me and I was amazed that something I'd taught her actually sunk in. Who knew? When she'd finished, I held out her phone and she plucked it from my hands. Her fingers pounded the touch screen in rapid motion with a desperation that bordered on pathetic. I realized at that moment my daughter was *that girl*. The one whose insecurity was so overwhelming she needed the acceptance of a boy to give her self-worth. I was sad for her but knew it wasn't the right time to approach the issue.

Her fingers continued to pound on the phone screen and I assumed she was texting Chandler, who'd sent several texts demanding to know where she was. He was livid she'd blown him off. I knew, because I read them. His texts were disturbing, but I'd kept my cool, and didn't text him and tell him to go screw himself like I'd wanted. "Good Lord, Emily. It's just a phone, it's not made of steel."

"He's like, super mad at me, Mom," she said.

Ma was right. Emily was going to do something I'd regret, and I had no idea how to stop it. My shoulders stiffened, and my jaw ached. "Just blame it on me. If he's got a problem with that, have him give me a call."

She rolled her eyes and I walked away.

I snuck up to my room, hid up in my closet and called for my mother. "Ma, you here?"

The air chilled and a shirt dropped from the shelf.

"Oh geez. No games, please. It's about Em. I think you're right. She's gonna get her cherry popped." I winced hearing those words from my mouth.

Another shirt dropped.

"Mother." I opened my mouth wide, hoping to relax my jaw.

"I'm here. Geesh, I was playing with Paul's cat. I pop up in front of him and it scares the bejesus outta him. He meows and hisses and then takes off running. Cracks me up every time."

I grabbed the shirts and shoved them onto the shelf. "It'd be great if you stopped dropping my clothes on the floor. Gracie's dog hair is everywhere."

"Huh?"

I pointed to the messy pile of shirts on the shelf. "The shirts. They didn't just jump from the rod themselves, you know."

"I didn't drop any shirts and I'm gettin' a little tired of you accusing me of stuff I didn't do."

I stared at the messy pile, and then picked through the hanging clothes for the empty hangers and hung everything back up. "I think you were right about Em," I said.

"Of course I'm right. I've been watching that girl for months. She's ready to be deflowered, all right."

Deflowered? I guess that was a better term than *cherry popped*, but it still made my heart race. "I've got to talk to her."

"You've told her about the birds and the bees, right? About the honey and the buzzing and all that?"

I sat on the closet floor and rubbed my forehead. "No one uses that analogy anymore. It's a little outdated."

"Doesn't matter anyway. I told you about the birds and the bees, and you still got your cherry popped too young."

My jaw tensed. "I'm not discussing my cherry-popping with you."

Another shirt fell from the rod.

"See?" I pointed to the shirt on the floor. "You did that, didn't you?" I picked up the shirt and hung it back up.

She giggled. "Well, if you're gonna blame me, I figured I might as well have a little fun."

"Did you check on Nick or just play with Paul's cat?"

"I did what I said I'd do, geesh. Then I played with the cat."

I raised an eyebrow. "And?"

"Meh, the cheater was sittin' in his office working."

I nodded. "Well, that's good, I guess."

"Don't you worry though, Frances Richter the ghost detective is on the case. The next time he's with that floozy, I'll be there."

Frances Richter, ghost detective? Ma was getting a little too into this. "Please don't do anything I wouldn't want you to do."

"Ah Madone, you spoil all my fun."

I laughed. "I kind of need you to keep an eye on Emily too, if you don't mind."

"Oh yeah, spy on her. Been there. Done that." She snickered.

When Ma returned from the dead, Emily got involved with some friends doing drugs, so I'd asked my mother to keep an eye on her. Ma called it spying, but I called it keeping a watchful eye over a young, impressionable child. "Yeah, Ma. Spy on Emily." I piddled with the hanging clothes. "Just don't make it too obvious, okay?"

"So moody. Your brother's cat's got a better attitude than you."

"Sorry. Blame it on Emily. She's wearing me out."

"Been there, done that, too."

I nodded. I'd probably been about as dramatic as Emily at times. "Lemme know if you bust the cheater."

"You betcha."

I imagined her shimmering away like she did when I could see her. I examined the clothes hanging on the rod. If Ma was telling the truth, and she hadn't touched them, that meant someone else was doing it. "Whoever you are, you're not earning any brownie points."

Another shirt fell. I shook my head, opened the closet door, and walked out.

* * *

Emily spent the rest of the day hiding in her room. Josh escaped to Turner's house while Emily cleaned the basement. Family bolted when she had meltdowns. Sometimes I envied Jake and his traveling. My escape was a quick run in the park, a workout at the gym, or coffee with Mel. It helped me de-stress, but inevitably the drama was still mine to handle. I knew one day Emily and I would be friends, but from what I'd heard, that wouldn't happen until she was at least thirty, and I wasn't sure we'd both make it that long.

I spent the evening meandering around the house doing a lot of nothing. I sat on the floor in front of the microwave and willed my father to take responsibility, but he didn't. At ten p.m. Gracie came down, nudged me, and then went back upstairs. I took the hint, followed her.

I'd just buried myself under the covers when I felt the temperature in the room change and the hairs on my arms rise. Gracie, snuggled on Jake's pillow, barely raised her head, so I figured it was Ma.

"Boo," she said.

"Eep. You scared me. Not."

"Bubble burster."

"Learned from the master, Ma." I sat up and switched on the light. It seemed strange to talk to her in the dark, even though I couldn't see her.

"I got it," she said.

The edge of my bed dipped. "Did you just sit on my bed?"

"Yah, why?"

"I can see the dip."

"Dip? What dip? Is it big?"

The dip went away. "No, it's not big."

"Then why'd you have to mention it?"

"Because I noticed it and I'm trying to adjust to how my gift works now. Watch for signs of you, since I can't see you."

"Oh, yah. I thought you were calling me fat. Which would have been rude since I lost all that weight from having the big C and all."

Lung cancer stole my mother's voluptuousness before it took her life. When she died she weighed less than one hundred and twenty pounds. Her ghost looked more like she did before cancer, a size fourteen hourglass with a whole lot of *va-voom*. She didn't know and I didn't have the heart to tell her. "You're not fat, Ma. You never were."

"Nope, us Italian women? We're curvy. Like you, all hips and no torso."

I ignored that. "So, what'd you get? Does it have something to do with Nick?"

"You betcha."

* * *

"You're gonna love this one."

When Ma told me what happened, I grabbed my phone and called Mel.

"Have I told you how much I love your mother?" Mel asked.

"Not even once."

"That's funny, I thought I'd mentioned it."

My lips curled upward and I snickered. "It's safe to say Nick's probably gonna have a black eye."

Mel choked.

"You okay?"

Through a cough, she said, "Yeah."

"You sure?"

She coughed again. "Yeah, I just choked on my Oreo."

"Oreo?" I knew what she was doing. "You're dunking it in coffee, aren't you?"

"I plead the fifth."

"Copy cat."

"Tell me about the black eye."

"Ma went on a Nick hunt."

"Obviously. Where was he? He said he had to work late again but we know that's BS."

That was the part I'd hope to skip. "Her apartment."

"Oh." Her voice cracked.

"I'm sorry."

"I'm fine. Just tell me what happened."

"I was hoping they'd get to the good stuff but they didn't," Ma said.

I didn't pass that on to Mel. "She said the girl's name is Carrie, and that he told her you two had another fight."

"I knew it. Carrie's his new assistant. I called earlier and found out."

"Did you two fight recently?"

"Pfft. We'd have to actually speak to each other to fight."

"Tell her what he said about her," Ma said.

I covered the phone. "Shush. Gimme a minute, will ya?"

"What'd you say?" Mel asked.

"I was talking to my mother. She said he said you've become volatile." I waited for the Asian explosion.

It came, big time. Expletives shot from her mouth like ammunition from an automatic weapon. "I'll show that son of a bitch volatile."

Oh boy.

"I'm sorry."

She calmed down a bit. "It's not your fault. I just don't even recognize him anymore. I don't understand who he's become."

"I don't either," I said.

"He's become a shuck, that's what he's become," Ma said.

"A what?" I asked.

"A shuck, ya know, a cheat, a liar."

"I've never heard that before."

"Back in my day it's what we called men like Nick."

"What'd she say?" Mel asked.

I told her.

"A shuck. I like that," she said. She rattled off questions. "When was this? Is he still there? Where does she live? Is it the place where you got skunked?"

"Tell me when you're done so I can finish."

"I'm listening," she said.

"Yes, it's the place of the unfortunate skunk incident."

"I knew it."

"She tripped him."

"Huh?"

"Ma. She tripped him. That's why she thinks he's gonna have a black eye."

Mel busted out laughing. "I love your mother."

"I know."

"How'd she do it?"

"That's the million dollar question."

"Huh?"

"She said she just thought about it and suddenly he took a header right into the glass table. Chipped the glass."

"Too bad he didn't castrate himself."

"Probably the angle wasn't right."

Ma said, "I could probably do that, once I'm a little more advanced in my spirit super powers."

"Oh geez."

"What?" Mel asked.

"Ma says give her time and she can probably do that."

"Seriously?"

"Mel."

"Gotta go. The shuck just got home."

"Okay, I'll fill you in on the rest later."

"Nick's officially the shuck," I told my mother.

"If the shoe fits."

"Poor Mel. I don't know what I'd do if Jake cheated on me."

"Luckily that's not a problem 'cause you'd get all angry-Italian-wife on him and beat his ass."

I raised an eyebrow. "How do you know it's not a problem?"

"Maybe I checked on him a time or two. Ya know, just in case."

"You spied on my husband?"

"I like to think of it as keeping tabs on a family member."

"That's spying, Ma."

"You say tomato, I say tomahto. Besides, you want me to spy on your kid, so what's the big deal?"

I rolled my eyes.

"You didn't seem to mind when I told you about him and the granny hooker, remember?"

To convince Jake that my dead mother was back, Ma told me about an old woman prostitute who'd hit on him while he was on a business trip. When I told him, he became an instant believer. "That's different."

"How?" She asked.

"You did that so I could prove to him you were back from the dead."

"Ah, I get it. It's not spying if it helps you."

Yikes. She'd got me there. "That's not what I mean. Please Ma, don't spy on my husband."

"Fine, but if I happen to accidentally notice something I think you should know..."

"Okay, then I guess you can tell me."

"That's what I figured."

CHAPTER SIX

"ANGELA? ARE YOU ASLEEP?" Ma asked.

I threw the covers off and sat up. "What? Who?"

Ma laughed. "That's never gonna get old, I tell ya."

"Cheese and rice, Ma. You know I hate when you do that."

"Yah, and that's what makes it fun. Like when you were a kid and I'd come in and scream, *wake up and pee the world's on fire*."

I yawned. "That wasn't funny either, Ma."

"To me it was. I always sorta hoped you'd pee, but I didn't wanna have to clean it up."

I flipped on the light. "Why are you here? Is everything okay?"

"I found something in Emily's room. You gotta go get it. You can use it when you talk to her about the birds and the bees and that sex party."

I rubbed my eyes and looked at the clock. It was four a.m. I didn't recall falling asleep. I clicked the light off and snuggled under the covers again. "It's four o'clock in the morning. I'm not gonna go in there and risk waking her up."

"Ah, you won't. She's not there. Snuck out a few hours ago."

I jumped out of bed. "What? Why didn't you tell me?"

"'Cause you were sleeping and I was keepin' my eye on her like you asked."

I pulled off my pajamas and grabbed my clothes from the day before. "You should have told me. Where is she?"

"She's at the Waffle House with that boy."

At least she was in a public place. "You still should have told me."

"Why? So you'd go get her? How'd you plan to tell her you found her?"

I took my cell phone from my nightstand and waved it in the air. "See this? It's magic. I can bust her without letting on that I know where she is."

"Oh, yah. Forgot about that. Never could figure out those things anyway. How'd they get a phone to work without plugging it into the wall?"

I suppressed a giggle and went to check Emily's room.

"What? You don't believe me?"

Truth was, I didn't know why I checked. "Yes, I believe you, I just felt the need to check."

I called Emily's cell but she didn't pick up so I sent a text: "Fifteen minutes." I paced in my room, my heels pounding into the carpet. I threw my hands up. "Who the hell does she think she is, sneaking out in the middle of the night?"

"Your daughter."

I glared in the direction of Ma's voice. "I never snuck out."

"Sure you did."

I did many things but sneaking out wasn't one of them. "No, Ma. I didn't."

"Remember that one time you sat on the roof with that boy? What was his name again? Ya know, before your dad and me split."

"I sat on the roof. That's not sneaking out."

"You left the inside of the house and went outside. That's sneakin' out."

"I stayed on our property so that doesn't count."

"You mean you snuck out and stayed on our property."

"Oh geez."

"You say tomato-"

I cut her off. "I say tomahto. I know."

"Before she gets home, you gotta go get that stuff behind her make up mirror. It looks like a tube of Chapstick. Hurry. She's almost home."

I shook my head. "Whatever it is, I don't wanna know."

"Ah Madone. You're a parent and sometimes you gotta do the hard stuff whether you wanna or not. Now go on."

I grunted and relented because she was right. Behind Emily's make up mirror I found a tube called *Breast's Buddy, A Tingle Tube of Delight*. My stomach did a little flip.

"She's gonna end up knocked up if you don't do something. I'm tellin' ya."

I popped the top and smelled the waxy stick. It smelled like fake watermelon. I probably shouldn't have, but in the name of motherhood,

I licked it, too. It tasted waxy but nothing like watermelon. "This is gross. And she's not going to get pregnant from a waxy boob stick." The words *boob stick* made me cringe.

"Not from the stick she ain't, but what she does after she uses that stick is a whole nother ball of wax." She laughed at her play on words.

I rubbed the vein in my forehead. "I'll buy her condoms. Put her on birth control. Lock up her vagina with a steel chain and triple key locks." Okay, that was a bit extreme, but I didn't rule it out.

"Oh, now that'll be fun, taking her to the twat doc."

I hated that word. "Mother."

I heard the front door open and snuck out of Em's room, the boob tube hidden in my fist, and waited at the top of the stairs. Emily, head down, creeped up the dark stairwell and smacked right into me.

"Good luck," Ma said. "I'm outta here."

Scaredy cat, I thought.

I hit the home button on my phone, illuminating the hallway. "We'll talk in the morning." She walked into her room and closed the door without a word.

I went back to my room and Googled *Breast's Buddy A Tingly Tube of Delight* and then I texted Mel. "Emily bought some boob cream at that party."

She must have been awake because she texted right back. "Must have been a *Pleasure Party.*"

I googled *Pleasure Party.* It was a home based party company focused on *toys to make sexual acts more pleasurable, whether alone or with a partner.* Acid rose in my esophagus. I swallowed it down. "How'd you know?"

"Seriously?"

"Forget I asked," I wrote.

"Did she buy Breast's Buddy?"

"Yup."

"Jar or stick?"

"The stick."

"Which flavor?"

"Watermelon."

"What's it taste like?"

"Seriously?"

"Come on. You know you tried it."

"Waxy watermelon."

Mel texted the description from the company website. *The sensitizing ingredients of the Breast's Buddy Tingly Tube make for a tantalizing tingle on the go or when you're in the heat of the moment with that special someone. This enticing, erotic balm is ideal for a nibble by your partner or for a quick rub on the lips. Enjoy it alone or to get your partner to linger longer and pleasure you more, just apply to the nipples and feel the tingly sensation to make your nipples pop.*

"I feel a migraine coming on," I wrote back.

"At least she's frugal. The cream was three bucks more," she wrote.

"There's a plus. Why are you up?"

"I wasn't. Forgot to turn off my ringer."

"Oh, sorry."

"No prob. Did you read my text?"

"Didn't see it. Hold on." I typed.

I went back and read Mel's text from several hours before.

When Nick came home he told Mel he'd fallen at work and hit the side of a chair. "Nice cover," I wrote.

"I know. Shuck thinks I believed him."

"I don't know who he is anymore."

"I do," she wrote. "Nick the prick. Or shuck the f---". She didn't finish the word.

I giggled. "Fitting."

"Wait. How did you find out about the boob cream?

"Guess."

"Have I told you how much I love your mom?"

"Maybe once or twice. Emily snuck out tonight to meet Chandler."

"Holy crap."

"Yup, and Ma told me. TWO HOURS LATER."

"Oh boy. Where was she?"

"Waffle House, but she's in bed now. Thinking of putting a padlock on her door."

"Good idea. Did you ground her for life?"

"Not yet. Told her we'd talk in the morning."

"It's already morning."

"You're right. I should wake her sneaky butt up."

"Yeah 'cause dealing with a cranky teenage daughter at four a.m. is fun."

"Good point."

"Going back to sleep," she wrote.

"Me, too. Night."

"Night."

* * *

An hour later I was still awake, so I tiptoed downstairs and put on a pot of coffee. I powered on my laptop and checked email and Facebook while the coffee brewed.

The coffeemaker finally beeped and I grabbed my second favorite coffee cup from the cabinet. It was from a family trip to Disney and had a photo of me, Jake, and the kids—younger versions, smiling, printed onto the sides. As I poured the coffee into it, the cup skated across the counter, spilling coffee along the way. "Not cool, Ma."

The cup glided back to me. I grabbed the handle so she couldn't move it again, and poured coffee into it. I pointed to the spilled coffee. "You need to clean that up." The cup plunged off the counter and smashed onto the floor. "Seriously? My second favorite cup? Nice, Ma. Real nice." I grabbed the broken pieces and tossed them in the garbage, and then used a wet paper towel to wipe up the rest of the mess, including the previously spilled coffee. I grabbed another cup from the cabinet and held it in the air as I poured the coffee. "Na na na-na na," I sang. "I win."

"How come she can see you, but not me?" A male voice said.

The hairs on my arms rose. "Who's here?"

"My name is Bill, ma'am." The accent was southern, and though the voice didn't seem threatening, my heart raced.

I straightened my shoulders and cleared my throat. "Well, Bill, it's not polite to come into someone's house uninvited."

"They said you could help me," he said.

Word of mouth spread fast in the afterlife. A ghost named Heidi once told me that my gift was common knowledge to ghosts and that more would find me. That would have been fine if I could hear and see them but I couldn't. "Well there's a better way to ask for help than scaring the bejesus out of me."

He didn't reply.

"Bill?"

"Yes, ma'am."

"Do you understand?"

"Yes, ma'am. I'm sorry. I don't mean any harm." Bill spoke like a native Georgian, slow and with a long drawl.

I closed my eyes and focused my attention on the air in the room. I'd been trying to determine what it felt like when Ma came around so I could tell when she was here, but I hadn't quite pinned it down. I didn't feel anything funny, nor did the energy seem different than before. "Is my mother here?"

"Yes, ma'am."

I nodded. "Did you break my cup, Bill?"

"No, ma'am."

"Well crap," Ma said. "You didn't have to rat me out like that."

"I'm confused," he said. "She saw you break the cup but then she asked me if you were here, and if I broke it."

"I can hear her, but I can't see her," I said. "She's been messing with me lately so I kind of thought she broke the cup, but I wanted to be sure." I didn't want to wake up my daughter, so I walked to the door to the garage and said, "Come with me. Both of you."

Ma grumbled, but Bill was silent. Bill was a smart spirit.

I yanked a University of Georgia camping chair off the wall, pulled it open and sat in it. "Are you two here?"

"Yes, ma'am," Bill said.

I raised an eyebrow. "Ma?"

"Yah, yah. I'm here. Let the tongue lashing begin."

Bill spoke before I could. "I'm truly sorry to bother you, ma'am."

Ma'am. Ugh.

I cut Bill some slack. He'd fallen victim to my mother's shenanigans so I felt sorry for him. "What can I do you for, Bill?"

"I'm dead."

I nodded. "Pretty much."

"My wife and son don't know yet, ma'am. You see, my body was just found a little while ago. I need to get them a message and they told me you could help me."

Them again.

"Wait," I connected the dots. "You were murdered?" Murder would involve police and then my secret would be out, and I'd be labeled that crazy lady who thinks she talks to the dead. We'd have to change our names and move—dear God—Emily would never let me hear the end of it. My stomach ached.

"No, ma'am, I wasn't murdered. Two days ago I drowned in the big lake. Fell out of my boat trying to reel in a fish. Biggest catch in years, too. Knocked my head on the side of the boat, passed out, and drowned. Never felt a thing, either. When the authorities found me, the fish was still on the hook. The police said it was a grand catch, too."

I giggled about the fish, but the rest of it, painless or not, was depressing.

"My wife and me? We were separated. She wanted a divorce but I wanted to come home. I didn't think she'd let me though, so I didn't try."

I didn't know where this was going. "I'm not sure I'm following you, Bill."

"Ever since I died, I've been with my family. My wife, she cries on the phone to her friends and mama. Says she misses me, but doesn't think I want to come back. Says she's afraid to ask for fear I'll say no. I want her to know I would have, that I still loved her. And my boy, I think he sees me. He told her I was there, but she didn't believe him. Just cried more. I want him to know that was me he saw, and that everything's going to be okay. It's going to be okay, isn't it?"

Not jaded by fear or social stigmas, children often saw the dead. I guessed Bill's son was young, and I was sad for him and his family. I tried to reassure him. "I'm sure everything will be okay Bill, but the truth is, I haven't done this is a long time and I'm pretty rusty. Is there anything you can tell me that will help your wife believe me?"

The prospect of riding that horse wasn't appealing, but I knew it would be worth it once I got back up and moving.

"Jessica—that's my wife, she's a believer, ma'am. She watches them ghost hunter shows all the time. I know she'll believe you."

"I'm still going to need something, Bill, just in case."

"Yes, ma'am. I understand."

I told the ghost I'd help, but not until later that day. I suspected Bill wasn't a one-shot thing and I was getting my gift back, and I wanted to manage it better than before. Plus, I needed to deal with Emily—she came first.

"Thank you, ma'am."

"Don't thank me yet—and Bill?"

"Yes, ma'am?"

"Don't call me ma'am. My name is Angela. If you call me ma'am again, I'm not going to help you."

"Yes, ma-," he stopped himself. "I'm leaving now."

I smirked. "Thank you."

"And Ma," I said. "We'll deal with the cup later."

* * *

"So you're back to helping my kind again, huh?" Ma's voiced boomed over the water in the shower.

I yanked my towel from the rod and covered myself, soaking the towel in the process. "A little privacy, please?"

"Ah Madone."

I stood motionless, not sure if she'd left. "Ma? You still here?"

"If you don't want me to see you in your birthday suit, quit talking to me for cryin' out loud."

"I just wanted to make sure you were gone, Ma, that's all."

"I was, but now I'm not."

"Then leave, please."

"Geesh. Make up your mind."

"And you owe me a new cup."

"I can't hear you because I'm gone."

"Oh geez." I hung the wet towel over the shower and rinsed off.

After I dried off, I called Jake and got his voicemail. "Call me when you wake up."

He called right back. "That was fast," I said.

"I'm on the toilet, playing Angry Birds."

"Thanks for sharing."

"You're welcome."

"So guess what?"

"You're reading that bestselling raunchy novel? The one you called mommy porn?"

"Uh, no."

"You bought sexy lingerie?"

"What's the point? It just comes right off."

"That *is* the point."

"Oh right, but no, no sexy lingerie."

"We'll go shopping for something this weekend," he said.

"Oh geez. Fine."

"And I'll come in the dressing room with you."

"Uh, no. The mirrors are horrible. I won't even try stuff on in stores because of them."

"You're no fun."

"You'll be retracting that statement later. So guess what?"

"Oh great. What did Fran do now?"

I laughed because I'd have gone there if I were him, too.

"Aside from breaking my second favorite cup, nothing. It's not about her."

"Then I got nothin'."

"I saw another ghost, or heard one, at least."

"Define heard. Like, heard noises that could be another ghost or heard another ghost speak?"

"Heard another ghost speak. A man, named Bill. Hit his head at the big lake while fishing and died."

"Obviously he's dead if he's a ghost, honey."

"Oh, yeah."

"I'm not sure what to say. Is this a good thing or a bad thing?"

"Actually, I'm kind of excited."

"Then that's great news!"

I laughed. "What would you have said if I said I wasn't excited?"

"Uh, that sucks?"

"Figured."

"So fill me in."

I did. He wasn't thrilled about Bill being in the house but was happy that I was happy.

"I gotta go, got a meeting in five minutes," he said. "Love you."

"Love you, too."

I finished getting dressed and read a text from Mel. "Nick's eye is a lovely shade of blackish purple. Have I told you how much I love your mom?"

"Oh geez," I responded.

"Said he's got an early meeting this morning but he's probably going to Carrie's. Might do another drive-by. Wanna come?"

How do you tell a person they're not thinking straight without making them angry? I stopped texting and called her. "I don't think driving by will accomplish anything but upsetting you more."

"I'm not upset."

I put my phone on speaker while I applied my makeup. "Of course you're not," I said, even though I imagined little red horns growing from her head.

"I'm pissed."

"And that's better than angry, how?"

"Are you coming with me or not?"

"I can't. I'm sorry. I've got an appointment."

"It's okay."

"Be careful, please," I said.

"I will. I promise."

My spidey senses told me this would be the first promise Mel broke.

* * *

I ate breakfast and contemplated my talk with Emily. I dug into the bowels of my brain for an approach that would keep her defenses intact, but my bowels were empty. Emily was the queen of angst and drama, and never missed an opportunity to let that be known. The conversation wouldn't be pretty. I sipped hot coffee from my not-second-favorite-coffee cup as she barreled into the kitchen, ready for a war.

"Can we like, get this over with now?"

My best defense against her anger was to remain calm, but as an Italian and the mother of a teenage daughter that wasn't easy. "Absolutely." I sipped my coffee and attempted to be casual and nonchalant. "You're grounded for two weeks. No car, no cell phone, no computer, or iPad. There. It's over with now." I took another sip of coffee.

Her face reddened and tears pooled in her eyes. "That's not fair."

"Life ain't fair, kiddo. Best you learn that now." I got up, rinsed my cup, and loaded it into the dishwasher.

"I just went to Waffle House. At least I wasn't, like, out drinking or doing drugs."

"Sneaking out is unacceptable, Emily, regardless of where you sneak out to."

"Fine, Mom. I snuck out. Ground me, but don't, like, take my stuff away. I only did one thing so I should, like, only have one punishment."

I gave her my one-eyebrow up look. "And you became a parenting expert when?"

She rolled her eyes. "It was just Waffle House."

"With Chandler, I presume?"

"Does that matter?" She snipped.

My daughter was lucky I had self-control. I pointed at her. "And that's another week added for being a smart-aleck."

"Can I at least have my phone?"

"Nope. Not until you have an attitude adjustment." I held out my hand, palm up. "Keys, please."

"What? Why do you want my keys? I'm grounded, remember? I can't go anywhere."

"Rumor has it you're prone to sneaking out and I'm not taking any chances."

She got up and stomped out of the room while muttering, "I have to get my purse."

"Bring the phone too, please."

She clomped up the stairs like a horse. I followed, trying hard not to giggle at the drama of it all. She threw the keys on the kitchen table, but set her phone down with care. I grabbed the keys and stuffed them in my pocket.

"I guess I'll have to quit my job since I can't get to work."

Oh, puh-lease.

"The cafe isn't more than five miles, round trip. You can drive to and from work and I'll check the mileage. Every night I want the keys on my nightstand."

She shook her head. "Whatever."

I ignored that. "You never answered my question. Were you with Chandler?"

"Yes," she mumbled. Her shoulders dropped. She knew she'd screwed up. "He was mad that I, like, blew him off for the lake. He said if I didn't meet him he'd, like, break up with me."

Chandler needed a serious ass kicking. "He threatened you so you'd do what he wanted?"

"It wasn't, like, a threat, Mom. He was upset. He didn't, like, mean it that way."

My daughter was naive, and Chandler was a jerk. "He most certainly did mean it that way, and the next time he threatens you like that, call his bluff. Stand up for yourself, and he'll back down. Never let someone threaten you like that, Emily."

"I don't want him to break up with me."

"If he breaks up with you because you don't take orders from him, then he doesn't respect you, and if he doesn't respect you, he'll treat you like crap. Is that what you want?"

"You don't understand, Mom. Things are different than, like, when you were my age."

Ah, yes. *That line.* Emily pulled that out every time she didn't have a worthy comeback, so I retorted with my standard reply. "Things may be different kiddo, but people still want the same things."

"But you don't know what Chandler wants. He loves me. I'm like family to him and he was really mad that I, like, chose you guys over him."

What?

"Chose us over him for what?"

"The lake, Mom. He was mad because I, like, chose to stay home and do what you said and not go to the lake. He said it hurt him and that he, like, loves me more than you, so I should do what he wants."

I had a choice to make and had to do it fast. I could say what I knew to be true, that this guy was an absolute idiot and she better run like hell from him, which would do nothing but push her even closer to him or I could be sarcastic and pretend it wasn't a big deal. I chose sarcasm. "Wow. That's pretty serious. When's the wedding?"

She rolled her eyes. "We're not like, talking about that kind of stuff yet, Mom."

Yet. "Good to know because your dad and I haven't started saving for it yet, either."

Emily was serious about this kid, and all I could think of was the damage he could do to her heart, not to mention her already fledging self-esteem. It was time for drastic measures. "Guess we should get you to the gynecologist, huh?"

Her mouth dropped and her eyes widened. I choked back a laugh.

"Mom, I'm not, like, having sex with Chandler."

"Not yet," I said. "But better safe than sorry."

"I'm not having sex," she repeated.

"You've already said that, but I still think you need to be prepared."

"Fine, mom. Whatever."

"I don't think you're having sex, but like I said, better safe than sorry."

Ma spoke and I didn't even flinch. "Tell her about the bees."

"Em, I'm not gonna tell you the story of the birds and the bees but-"

"Seriously, Mom? I'm seventeen. I don't need the sex talk."

Phew. Dodged that bullet.

"I just don't want you to rush into anything."

"I'm not having sex," she repeated.

"I'm still making the appointment."

"Is it a guy or a girl?"

"She's a female."

"Fine. I'll go." She stomped to the bathroom and closed the door.

As if she'd had a choice.

The conversation exhausted me and all I wanted to do was crawl back into bed, but first I had to change the computer and iPad passwords and take a picture of the car mileage, and then head out to Bill's wife's house.

"Maybe you should take it outta her room," Ma said, referencing Emily's computer.

"Can't believe you broke my second favorite cup." I whispered.

"Ah for cryin' out loud Angela, it was just a coffee cup. It ain't expensive china. By the way, where's my china? Did you sell it or something?"

"I thought you were all-knowing now. Shouldn't you know where your china is?"

"Huh. Probably I should."

I laughed. "It's in the basement storage closet."

"Oh gee, thanks. Hide my stuff in the basement."

I was a still miffed about the cup. "Why'd you have to break the cup? I got that at Disney with the kids. It had a photo of us on it, and I don't have a copy of that picture."

"It was an accident. I just meant to push it a little, but I guess my mind's stronger than I thought, and it went flying right off the counter."

I nodded. "It sure did."

"Well, I felt bad for the guy. When I popped in and he was standing there, talkin' to you, and you were ignoring him, I decided to help him out."

"Wait, he was talking to me and I couldn't hear him?"

Ma yelled. "You oughta get your ears checked. Can you hear me? Hello? Angela? Can you hear me?"

I shook my head. "I can hear you. But that doesn't make sense. Why could I hear him when you broke the cup but not before?"

"I dunno, I wasn't there the whole time. Maybe he was talkin' soft or something?"

"So lemme see if I got this right. You showed up and he was talking to me and I didn't respond. Then you broke my second favorite cup and he talked and I could hear him?"

"Yup."

I snapped my fingers. "I got it. It's you."

"Whadda ya mean, it's me?"

"You're the link. I couldn't hear him because you weren't there, but when you showed up, I could. I can't hear other ghosts without you here, Ma. You're my connection to the dead."

"Huh. Ya think?"

I nodded. "What else could it be?"

"You think I'm the connection?"

"That's what I'm sayin'."

"That sounds important."

I nodded. "I'm pretty sure it is."

"I'm gonna have to ask about that. They haven't taught that in celestial being school."

Oh geez.

"I'm going to see Bill's wife's today and I think you better come with me. If I'm right and you're not there, I'm gonna look like a nut case in front of her."

She coughed. "Well, it wouldn't be the first time."

"Feelin' the love, Ma."

My phone dinged with a text from Mel.

"Went by the 'ho's but he wasn't there. Car's at the office though. Thinking of going in to see if he's there. Need a reason. STAT."

"Oh boy."

"She's at his office, isn't she?" Ma asked.

"It's really creepy how you do that."

"I know. If I coulda done it when I was alive, your life woulda ended up different."

Just thinking about that sent a shiver up my spine. "Let's not go there, please."

"You're no fun."

"Mel's making a mistake doing this. What should we do?"

"Tell her to chill out and hold on a minute. I'll pop in there and check."

"Have I told you how much I love you?"

"Nope. And it's nice to finally hear it. Be back in a jiffy."

"Love you, Ma!"

I texted Mel and told her Ma was going to pop into Nick's office.

"Have I told you how much I love your mother?" She wrote back.

"Funny, I just stole that line from you."

Ma was back in a jiffy, like she'd said. "Tell her to go home, he's at his desk and he ain't goin' nowhere for a while."

I didn't like the sound of that. "I'm not even gonna ask."

"Probably smart. Just tell her so she doesn't run in balls to the wall, for cryin' out loud. She's in her car shaking like a leaf, that girl. And tell her to switch to decaf coffee before she has a heart attack."

I dialed Mel's number. "He's in the office. Ma says go home and stand back from the caffeine."

"What's he doing?"

"My guess is he's working. Go home, Mel. Don't make this worse than it already is."

"Fine." Her voice shook. "Tell Fran thanks." She hung up before I could say goodbye.

"She says thanks. I think she's mad at me."

"Probably. You were kinda rough."

"I didn't mean to be. I just don't want her to make things worse."

"Can't think of anything worse than your husband cheatin' on you."

She had a point. "I need to try to be more sensitive, don't I?"

"Sensitivity was never your strong point. You're more like your dad in that you say what you want without thinking about the other person's feelings. Me? I have more tact about things like that."

I snorted. "Uh, you don't seriously mean that, do you?" Ma was the queen of verbal diarrhea.

"'Course I do."

"All righty then. Let's move on. I'm probably gonna regret this, but tell me what you did to Nick."

"Aw, Madone. Nothing big. Just blew his papers off of his desk, is all. So he's gotta do a little reorganizing. No big deal."

Relief swept over me. Nick was almost as anal retentive as me so he was probably frustrated and confused about the sudden burst of wind. Ma really knew how to hit where it hurt. "Awesome. That'll keep him occupied both physically and mentally."

"That was the plan."

I texted Mel to let her know and added, "Yes, I know how much you love my mother," to the end.

"I gotta go to Bill's now. You're coming, right?"

"Wouldn't miss it."

I went downstairs and found Emily exactly as I'd left her—sitting on the couch, rendered a TV zombie. "Heading out to run an errand. I'll be home in a bit, okay?"

No response.

"Grunt if you heard me."

"Ugh."

"That works."

CHAPTER SEVEN

"MA, CAN YOU DO ME A FAVOR?" We were driving to Bill's wife's house.

"I'll think about it."

I ignored that. "Can you leave for a few minutes so I can see if I can hear Bill without you?"

"Oh, yah. Good idea. I'll just pop in on Emily real quick and make sure she's not boinkin' that boy while you're out."

Good Lord. "This will only take a second."

"I travel fast, so it's okay."

"I know." I waited a few seconds to make sure she was gone and then said to, "Okay here's the thing, Bill. I think I need my mother to hear other ghosts but I'm not sure, so I need you to talk to me and I'll let you know if I hear you. But I need you to talk to me right away, okay? On the count of three. One. Two. Three."

Silence.

"Okay, Bill?"

More silence. I hand-palmed my forehead. "Oh, duh. If I do need Ma then you've probably answered and I didn't hear. I'm not the sharpest nail in the box, am I? Okay, so say something right now just to make sure."

I turned down the radio and pushed my hair behind my ears, thinking maybe that would help me hear him. "Okay, one more time. So, how's the weather in your neck of the woods, Bill?"

Nothing.

"Well, guess I do still need my mother, huh? Ma, you can come back now."

Silence.

"Ma?"

"Boo."

"That doesn't work anymore. How's that make you feel, huh?" I wiggled my head. "I win."

"You don't have to be obnoxious about it," she said.

I gloated more because it was fun to get one up on my mother since it happened so rarely. "You didn't see it coming did you? That's because you didn't raise no fool, Ma."

"Says who?"

"I'm not talking about Paul or John."

"Me neither."

"Do you two always talk to each other like this?" Bill asked.

In unison we said, "Like what?"

Bill laughed.

It was good to have my mother back.

* * *

I parked down the street from Bill's house and gripped the steering wheel to stop my hands from shaking. I willed the butterflies in my stomach to fly away, but they didn't.

"Why're you shaking? This is old hat for you," Ma said.

I checked my reflection in the rearview mirror and patted down my hair. "What if she doesn't believe me?"

"She'll believe you, ma'am," Bill said.

I rubbed my temples with the balls of my hands. "Thank you Bill, and please don't call me ma'am."

"Oh, sorry, ma'am. I forgot."

Ma laughed.

"Oh," Bill said.

We all laughed. I laid my head on the steering wheel. "I hate feeling like this."

My car door opened and Ma said, "Come on Ang, don't be a wimp. I got stuff to do, ya know."

"I'm coming," I said, and got out of the car. "Don't leave me, Ma."

"And miss the good stuff? No way."

"Ya'll are a stitch," Bill said.

"Stick around, Bill. You might change your mind about that," I said.

"Pfft. People loved me. Not sure about her, though," Ma said.

"There is that," I agreed.

I rang the doorbell and Bill's son answered. He was practically a baby. His mother came to the door, "May I help you?"

I shuffled my feet. "Um, yes, my name is Angela and I um...I heard about your husband, Bill. I'm sorry for your loss."

"Bill? How? I just found out myself a few hours ago."

"I um, heard from—may I come in?" I half smiled. "This is going to sound strange but I have a message from your husband."

Her mouth twisted. "Excuse me?"

"Jessica, right? I'm sorry. I know this sounds crazy. Honestly, it's still pretty crazy to me and I'm still a little rough around the edges here, but I promise you I'm not a nut case. Not when it comes to this anyway. I'm a medium."

She didn't say anything, just moved to the side and held the door open. The boy hid behind his mother's legs. "William, go on into the den and watch TV while Mommy talks with this nice lady, okay?" She shooed him away with her hand and he ran toward the back of the house. She walked into the living room and sat down. "Please, have a seat."

I sat. "I'm truly sorry for your loss."

"We were getting divorced," she said, her face solid as stone.

"I know, he told me." I sat up straighter, and pushed my shoulders back. I didn't feel confident but I could act the part. "I guess I didn't really explain myself well. I can communicate with the dead."

"Yes, you said you're a medium."

"No. Yes. Well, sort of, I guess." I tripped over my words, which I'm sure did nothing to win her trust. I breathed in and out deeply. "My mother died and then came back and something happened—she flipped a switch I guess, and now I can talk to the dead."

"That's amazing."

It was easier than I expected and I relaxed. "I know! But then my dad died, and I wasn't able to see spirits anymore, not even my mother."

She frowned. "What about now?"

"I don't see them now, but I can hear them. Well, my mother and your husband at least. I just started hearing my mother again and then this morning I heard your husband. I don't know about others yet."

"Wow."

"Exactly. Your husband is a nice man. Or, was, I mean."

Awkward.

"Bill is—was a wonderful man."

"He said that right after he died he came here and heard you on the phone. He knows you still love him and he wants you to know he still loves you, too."

She fidgeted and searched the room. "Is he here?"

"Bill?"

"Yes, ma'am. I'm here."

I nodded.

"Can he hear me?"

"Tell her I can."

Ma spoke too, "Hellooo? And me."

I shook my head. "He can hear you. I have to tell you though, there's another little hiccup to my gift."

She raised an eyebrow.

"It's not a big deal, really. It's just that I can only hear other ghosts if my mother is around, so she's here too and she can hear you. I'm sorry."

Ma said, "Why's that make you sorry?"

"Ma, please."

"Pfft," she said.

Bill laughed.

"Your husband thinks me and my mother are funny."

She took a tissue from the box on the table and blew her nose. It sounded like a horn. "He had a great sense of humor."

"Tell her I wanted to come back, please. I need her to know that."

"Jessica, Bill wants you to know he wanted to come back, but he wasn't sure you wanted him to."

That one got her and the floodgates opened. I sat next to her and put my arm around her. "He says he loves you very much."

"I love him too." She blew her nose again.

"Please tell her it's okay. Tell her we both know now, and tell her I want her to be happy," he said.

I told her.

"I don't know if I can do this without him." She cried again.

"Yes, she can," Ma said. "You tell her she'll be just fine and she'll be married again, too."

"She will?" Bill asked. "How do you know?"

"Bill, I'm an advanced spirit. I got connections. One day you'll be advanced too. After we're done here I'll tell you which classes to take and teach you a few tricks of the trade."

"That would be nice, ma'am."

"Oh, geez," I said.

"What's happening?" Jessica asked.

"My mother says that you will be fine, and that you'll be happy again."

Her mouth dropped. "Really? How does she know?"

"That's what Bill asked, too. Apparently there are different levels of spirits in the afterworld and the higher up one is, the more information they can get."

Jessica smiled. "I didn't know it worked that way."

I shrugged. "It's news to me, too."

"Yeah, she'll be just fine and dandy. She's gonna have another baby boy, too," Ma said.

"She says you're going to be just fine, Jessica." I left out the part about another boy.

Her head dropped. "It doesn't feel that way now."

"I know. But it will get easier, I promise. It just takes time."

At that moment her son walked in the room. "Hi Daddy," he said, and then turned to me and said, "Hi ma'am." He did a half circle and then pointed at nothing. "You're really old," he said.

I laughed because I knew he was talking to my mother.

"It'll happen to you one day, too kid," Ma said.

"Hey big guy," Bill said.

Jessica cried again. "Honey, do you see Daddy?"

"Yes Mommy, he's standing right next to you, silly."

"That boy's got the gift," Ma said.

"Whose Grandma is that?" The boy asked.

"That's my mother Miss Fran, and my name is Angela."

"Oh, hi." He turned back toward my mother's voice and pointed at her again. "Why's she in her jammies?"

"Because they're comfy," Ma said.

"Mine are comfy too." He looked down at his pajamas. "These are old though. I just got a pair of Iron Man jammies. Wanna see 'em?"

Ma said, "Heck yeah, I wanna see 'em!"

William held out his hand, and I saw his hand clasp around something invisible. My heart raced. Even in death my mother had a way with kids.

"Awesome. They're in my room," he said.

"I'll be right back," Ma said.

"But Ma, I can't hear Bill when you're not here."

"Gimme a minute. This is important. It's Iron Man jammies."

I stood. "Let's go. If we follow them, we can still talk to your husband."

William talked to my mother like he'd known her forever. "My Daddy is dead," he said. "Mommy says I can't see him again but he's here now. I don't understand."

"Ah, little William, it's all kinda confusing isn't it?" Ma asked.

"Yeah. Mommy says when you're dead you go to see God but God's not at my house so how come my Daddy is here? Does that mean he's not dead?"

"Actually, God is here. He's everywhere, ya know. We just can't see him. He's sneaky like that. It's how he makes sure we're okay, too, being around and not being seen. And sometimes God lets us come back from his house and tell the people we love that we love them one more time so we can all feel better, like your dad is doing now. When my Pa died he came back and kissed me on the cheek. That's how I knew he was safe."

My grandpa died when I was in my twenties, but I couldn't remember my mother crying or even appearing upset. I was probably just too self-centered to notice.

"Did you cry?" William asked.

"When my Pa died? I sure did. I cried like a baby, and my nose got all snotty, too."

I pretended to wipe my nose to cover my smile.

"I didn't cry," he said. "Mommy cried and she said I'm stronger than her but I can't pick up the dog food bag and she can, so I think she's wrong about that, too."

"Nah, she ain't wrong. She means a different kind of strong. It's confusing but there's other kinds of strong that don't involve big muscles. I bet you got big muscles, dontcha?"

"Uh huh. Wanna see?"

"Sure do," Ma said.

William held his arms up and grunted, showing Ma his muscles. It was adorable.

"Yah, those are some big ones, William. You'll be lifting that bag of food in no time. Your mom is crying now 'cause her heart is sad. She misses your dad, so she's gonna cry a lot. She'll be better soon, but for now, she's gonna need a lotta hugs and kisses from you, you got that?"

"I got that," he said and hugged someone I wished I could see.

I was jealous that William could see and touch my mother. I wanted that so much I could I could almost taste it. I didn't know how, but I was going to find a way to get the rest of my gift back.

William walked into his room and he showed Ma his Iron Man pajamas. Jessica and I stood outside the door and watched.

Bill said, "She's right about God, son. He's here. Just like they say at church. He's all around us, and he's going to help you and your mom but she's going to need you too, just like Miss Fran said. She's going to need lots of love and hugs and kisses from you, okay?"

"Okay, Daddy."

"It's time for me to go now William, and I don't know if you'll see me again but I want you to remember something, all right?"

William nodded. I swallowed a growing lump in my throat.

"I'll always be close by, even if you can't see me, okay? I love you, son."

"I love you too, Daddy. Bye-bye." He wrapped his arms around his father and though we couldn't see Bill, Jessica and I knew he was hugging his son. We wiped the tears in our eyes.

"Angela, can you tell Jessica I love her?" Bill asked.

I nodded and turned to Jessica. "He's got to go now, but he said he loves you."

She said she loved him, too. I told her that Bill had promised to keep an eye on William and Ma said he was gone. Jessica and I cried, and William crawled up on his mother's lap, hugged her tightly, and showered her with kisses, just like Ma and Bill said he should do.

Jessica thanked me several times, and I gave her my phone number just in case she had any questions or just needed to talk. When I got back to my car, my floodgates opened. I was emotionally drained but it wasn't a bad thing. I'd helped three people. It felt good.

"You here, Ma?"

"Yup," she said.

"That was freaking amazing."

"You made me proud, Angela, real proud."

"Thanks, Ma. That's nice to know."

On the drive home I called Mel and told her about Bill.

"Wow, that's amazing," she said. "So you think your mom's the link?"

"She has to be. There's just no other explanation."

"It makes sense. It's like you're getting your gift back in bits and pieces. Maybe it's a series of tests by the universe. Each time you pass, you get another nugget back."

"It sure would be nice to have it all back at once."

"Understandable. But be careful what you wish for."

"You know what? It would be fine with me if I got it back completely. I actually want it back. What just happened was emotionally exhausting but invigorating, too."

"Who are you and what have you done with my best friend?"

"I know, right? It's weird."

"I'm happy for you, and I'm sure you'll have your gift back completely in no time."

We chatted a bit more about nothing important and conveniently avoided the monkey on Mel's back. Sometimes it was better to avoid something than continue to beat it into the ground.

* * *

Jake and I sat outside by the fire pit, a beer in his hand while I sipped on a glass of Riesling. I filled him in on the Emily drama, sparing no details about the sex toy party, her sneaking out and what the manipulation attempts by her jerk of a boyfriend.

He sipped his beer and rested his feet up on the fire pit. "Wow, you had a busy few days, huh?"

"That's it? That's all you're gonna say? Our daughter is going to have sex with a loser and you have no comment?"

"She's not gonna have sex. She probably went to that party because she didn't want her friends to think she's a prude. I'm sure that's why she bought that stuff."

My husband needed to get a clue. "Denial isn't just a river in Africa."

"Funny."

"Did you not hear me tell you how this boy is manipulating her? He's definitely going to use manipulation to boink her?"

"I just don't think we have to panic yet. Emily isn't stupid. She won't let him treat her bad, and please, choose a better verb. *Boinking* should never be used in the same sentence as *our daughter*."

"Okay." I licked my lips. "How about banging?"

He shook his head.

"Screwing?"

"Ang."

"Bumping nasties?"

"Really?" He said, his face red.

I took a sip of my wine. "Play hide the sausage?"

He shot me a nasty look and guzzled his beer.

"You're not panicked about this kid pounding your daughter's punanni pavement?"

He raised an eyebrow. "Pounding her punanni pavement? Have you been Googling again?"

"I got that from Mel." I poured more Riesling into my wine glass.

"Pounding her punanni pavement," he said again.

I scratched my upper lip to hide my smile but Jake busted out laughing and I couldn't hold back.

"That one's new to me," he said.

"Mel's got a descriptive vocabulary."

"Obviously."

"It's not as funny when it's about our daughter, though," I said.

"Nope." He shook his head. "Not so much."

"I don't have a good feeling about this boy. And Emily likes him so much, I'm afraid she'll do something stupid. She's already said she's afraid he's going to break up with her."

Jake picked up his phone and swiped his fingers over the screen. "She'll be fine."

"You don't know that, but hey, don't worry. Whatever's gonna happen will happen when you're gone—because you're always gone, so you won't have to deal with it." I regretted saying that as soon as I finished. I got my verbal diarrhea issue from my mother.

He looked up from his phone. "Real nice."

"Well, it's true. While you go off and have dinner out and stay by yourself in a fancy hotel room with a bunch of pillows and a fluffy comforter, I'm at home dealing with my kid's cherry being popped by some kid whose mother clearly had a crush on Chandler Bing." If I'd had on a sock, I would have stuffed it in my mouth. Instead I chugged my wine.

Jake ran his hand through his hair and then leaned toward me, something he did with people when he was pissed. "Fine. I'll switch to a desk job and be home every night. It'll be less money so you'll have to get a full time job and we'll have to downsize, but then you won't be a single parent. Sound good?"

Truth be told, that wasn't what I wanted. We'd agreed years ago that our life would be the way it's been, and it wasn't fair of me to throw it in Jake's face like that. He felt guilty when I vented my frustration about our life, and then I felt guilty for making him feel that way. "No." I shook my head. "I don't want you to switch jobs. I'm sorry. But my mother's intuition tells me this is a bigger deal than you think. Emily's never been this intense about a boy before. And contrary to what our children think, I was a teenager once— real live teenage girl, so I'm pretty sure I'm the expert here." I took another gulp of wine and sank back in the plastic chair. "Oh, that tastes good."

He nodded. "Can't argue with that. And I know most of the parenting falls on you. When we talked about having kids, I had no idea it would be like this. I'm sorry, honey." He chugged the last of his beer and grabbed another one from the cooler, popped it open, and swallowed half of it down.

I got up, swayed a little more than I expected, and sat on his lap. I snuggled my face into his neck, smelled his familiar, comforting scent. It smelled like home to me and if I could have, I wanted to stay nuzzled into him forever. "I'm the one who should be sorry, not you."

He kissed me with a forgiving passion that felt good and my stomach fluttered. After practically an eternity together—some days seemed even longer—he could still give me butterflies. I wanted to take it upstairs.

"So what do you think we should do?" he asked.

"More stuff like this," I said, and nibbled his earlobe.

A low groan escaped his mouth. "Yes, this will definitely save Emily's punanni."

I bit his ear a little harder.

"Ouch," he said, pulling away. "That hurt."

I smirked. "Mood-killer." I got up and sulked back to my chair. I topped off my Riesling and took a swig then leaned back in the chair. I sank into the nylon material and seemed to wrap itself around my body. I was instantly sleepy. "Oh," I said and sat up, energized. "How about we lock her in her room until she's forty?"

He laughed. "That works. Except we'd have to put bars on the windows and that'll be pricy."

"Silly Jake." I let the chair envelop me again. "Love can't be stopped by metal bars."

"But it can be by a Smith and Wesson."

"Then you'll be the one staring out between metal bars and that would suck." I hiccupped. "Oh, 'scuse me. I think I'm a little tipsy."

He tilted his head and smiled. "Maybe just a little."

"Your window is closing," I said, batting my eyelashes. "Maybe we should go upstairs and bump nasties before it shuts?" I hiccupped again. "Oh wow. That one hurt."

"I thought you'd never ask," he said.

We stood and gathered the empty beer cans and then Emily walked outside. "Hey Dad," she said, sulking and ignoring me.

"Hey honey. I hear you've had some fun lately," Jake said.

Cocky and confident from the Riesling, I rolled my eyes and dove in for the attack. "Yup, she sure did." I pointed at my daughter. "Oh, since you're gonna be banging your boyfriend soon, you're definitely going on the pill." I held up my wine glass and guzzled the last of my Riesling. It wasn't one of my finer parenting moments.

"Mom," Emily said, embarrassed.

"What? We already talked about you going to the twat doc anyway, so what's the big deal?"

Jake spit his beer and it splashed onto the fire pit. "Can we talk about this later, honey?"

"Why? I think now's the perfect time. Oh and Emily, we'll pay for the doctor appointments but since you're the one who's gonna be using it, you get to pay for the prescription." A loud burp roared out of me, and I laughed. "'Scuse me."

"Fine. Whatever. I'm going to bed," Emily said, and got up and went inside.

I shrugged my shoulders. "That went well."

"Yup," Jake said, and took a big swig of beer. "That window close yet?"

I winked. "Hell no. Let's go."

He beat me to the door.

CHAPTER EIGHT

THE NEXT MORNING I WOKE UP HUNG OVER. "Ugh," I said, and then I rolled over and snuggled up next to Jake. "How much wine did I drink?"

"The whole bottle."

"My head's throbbing."

"So's mine, but not the one on my neck."

"Lovely."

He flipped over and kissed me. "I missed you while I was gone."

"I missed you, too."

"I was hoping for two-fer last night but after round one you were flat on your back and snoring."

"I don't snore."

"Uh, yeah, you do," he said, laughing.

"Nuh uh."

He grabbed his phone, swiped his fingers a few times, and then the phone grunted like a pig.

I cringed. "That's not me. It doesn't even sound anything like me."

He flipped the phone in my direction, and laughed. "See your face? Oh, and here comes my favorite part."

Just as my mouth opened, the phone snorted. Busted. Jake laughed so hard no sound came out. His head just bobbed up and down. I would have been mad but I'd videoed him snoring in the past. "Touché, but it's 'cause of the wine. It messes with my sinuses. What's your excuse?"

He laughed harder.

I pressed my temples with the palms of my hands. "Stop laughing. It's hurting my brain."

"Hair of the dog, babe."

I shook my head. "Never. Drinking. Again."

"It'll make you feel better."

"Stop. The thought of that makes me want to yack. I need grease. Oh! I need hash browns from McDonald's." I fluttered my eyelashes at him.

He nodded. "An Egg McMuffin does sound kind of good, actually."

I turned on my side and pulled the covers over my head. "You go and I'll keep the bed warm. I'll love you forever if you'll feed Gracie before you go."

He got out of bed. "I feel like you're pregnant again, and I'm rushing out to get you ice cream."

I scooted further under the covers. "Good Lord, Jake. Don't jinx me like that."

"With our luck we'd have another girl."

"I'd be institutionalized."

He laughed and walked into the bathroom. A few minutes later he'd fed the dog and left to get breakfast.

I scooted out from under my blankets, grabbed my phone off of the nightstand, and texted Mel. "Wine is evil."

"Wine is my friend."

"It's not mine."

"Have a little too much last night?"

"The whole bottle," I texted.

"Ouch."

"Yup."

"Nick came home pissed off last night."

"I know, you love my mom," I wrote.

"I do."

"What're you doing today?"

"Purging," she replied back.

"Please explain."

"Decluttering. Was up half of the night doing the kitchen and kids' bathrooms. Doing their bedrooms now."

"Your house isn't cluttered."

"It feels like it. It's making me claustrophobic."

"That's not physical clutter doing that."

"I know, but it's the only clutter I can get rid of right now, so I gotta work with what I've got," she wrote.

I got that. "Need help?"

"No, thanks. The kids are helping whether they want to or not."

"Good idea."

"Are you still in bed?"

"Yup. Jake went to McDonald's."

"The grease craving. I know that well."

"Jake said I should drink more wine but a Diet Coke sounds better."

"Hair of the dog. Best hangover cure ever," she replied back.

"Good grief. I'm not twenty. I can't even think about wine without wanting to throw up."

"I can. Probably it's because I'm still young."

"You're only a year younger than me," I wrote.

"The key word in that sentence being younger."

"Beyotch."

"Take a shower. You'll feel better. Gotta declutter."

"Later."

I considered the shower but nixed the idea because my bed was too comfy to leave. I heard Josh get up and called him into my room. "Hey Little Man. Sleep good?"

"Yup," he said, and lay down next to me. He grimaced. "Ew, your breath stinks." He fanned the air and pushed away from me.

I mimicked him. "Yours doesn't smell like roses either, dude."

"I haven't brushed my teeth yet."

"Neither have I."

"Well, you should because your breath is horrible," he said.

I rolled over and pushed myself out of bed. "Fine. If I have to, you have to, too."

"I will after I eat."

"Josh."

"Then I gotta brush them again and that's a waste of toothpaste."

"Okay," I said, and got back into bed. "Then I won't either. Dad's getting me McDonald's and will be home soon anyway." I breathed in his face again and he cringed.

"He's getting us McDonald's?" he asked, backing away from me.

"No, he's getting *me* McDonald's. You were sleeping."

"But I want something, too."

I handed him my cell phone. "Call him."

He called and asked for a sausage McMuffin and two hash browns and an orange juice.

Emily came into the room. I caught myself tense, and then quickly chastised myself for it. She was smiling. "You're in a good mood today," I said, knowing I was treading on thin ice.

She shrugged. "I guess I slept good."

I nodded. If she was in a good mood, I certainly didn't want to push it.

"Dad's getting breakfast," Josh said, handing her the phone.

She gave Jake her order. We all snuggled under the covers and chatted while waiting for Jake to return. It was one of those rare moments when everything seemed like a Norman Rockwell painting. Gracie, propped on her chair by the window, expelled a big breath.

"You wanna come up here, Gracie girl?" Josh asked.

"All she hears is blah, blah, blah, Gracie, you know," Emily said.

"So," he replied. "She's still smarter than you."

They sliced up my Norman Rockwell painting with a butcher knife. "How about we all pretend to get along for a change?" I asked. "It'll be something new and different."

They grunted.

"Should I make you hug?"

"Please don't, Mama. I don't wanna shower yet," Josh said.

"You're funny, loser," Emily said.

"Come on guys. Five minutes. Can I have five minutes of no bickering, please? Pretend it's Mother's Day or my birthday or something."

"We bicker then too, Mama," Josh said.

He had a point. I sighed and hid my head under the covers.

I heard the garage door open and peeked out of the top of the covers. Jake yelled, "Breakfast is served," and the kids took off running.

Gracie raised her head and her ears stood at attention.

"Crap," I said to her, "I wanted breakfast in bed."

She got up and went downstairs too.

"Traitor."

"Boo." Ma said.

I didn't budge.

"I gotta tell you something. Wow, you look like crap."

"Thanks, Ma. I'm hung over. Too much wine last night. Jake's got breakfast downstairs. Can we chat later?"

"Okay, but I gotta talk to you soon," Ma said. "It's important."

If I was smart, I would have stayed and listened to what she had to say.

*   *   *

Breakfast made me partially human, so I went upstairs and showered, hoping that would seal the deal. While I dressed, Mel sent a text, and Ma showed up as I read it.

"I didn't do it," she said. "Okay, I did it, but I didn't mean to do it."

I finished reading the text. "Nick was in an accident last night. Please tell me you're not talking about that."

"That's what I said. I did it, but I didn't mean to do it."

"Why didn't you tell me last night?"

"You were busy, you know...playin' hide the salami. I didn't think it was the right time."

I shook my head, and closed and locked my bedroom door. "Tell me what happened."

"All's I did was change his radio station. How was I to know he got distracted so easily?"

I sat on my bed, and put on my socks. "Tell me everything, Ma."

"Like I said, I was playing with his radio, you know—"

I cut her off. "I thought you said all you did was change the station?"

"Yah, well, that and I might a turned it up a little."

"Uh huh." I nodded. "Go on."

"So I found a Randy Travis song—you know how much I like Randy Travis—and maybe I turned it up a little more 'cause I was dancing a little. Line dancing, like I used to at that country music bar I used to go to back in the day. You remember? The one with the peanut shells on the floor? Ah Madone, I loved that place."

"I remember, Ma. You used to make me go with you. I hated that place."

"That's where I met Buddy, ya know."

After my parents divorced, my mother met Buddy. They fell in love and were engaged, but in a tragic turn of events and before they'd had a chance to marry, he died from a heart attack. Ma never dated anyone seriously after that. "Buddy was a great man, Ma."

"He still is," she said. "As a matter of fact we just went—"

I waved my hands. "Can we talk about Buddy later? I wanna know about the accident."

"Oh yah, I got distracted. Like I was saying, I was dancing to Randy Travis—*Diggin' Up Bones*—so he goes to turn it down, and I guess maybe the knob wouldn't move. He's trying to force it and all, and he went off the road, and hit the gas station sign over across from that Starbucks you always go to. You know, the BP?"

Good Lord. "Why didn't the knob move, Ma?" I knew what she was going to say, but wanted to make her say it.

"It was Randy Travis. You gotta play Randy Travis loud. And Nick? He's fine. Just a bump on his head 'cause he wasn't wearing his seatbelt. And it's the law, ya know, so that's not my fault. If he'd had it on, his head wouldn't have hit the steering wheel. Can't blame that one on me."

"Ma, you can't go around causing accidents. Nick could have been seriously hurt, and regardless of how angry Mel is right now, I know she doesn't want anything to happen to him."

"I wouldn't bet on that."

"He's the father of her children, Ma."

"I'm just sayin'."

"You have to be more careful, Ma. Please."

I texted Mel. "Talking to my mother about it. Get back to you soon."

"Have to drop the cheating rat bastard at the car rental place near Starbucks. Meet me there in an hour?" she asked.

"Okay," I wrote back.

I walked to the bathroom to throw on some make up, shaking my head the entire way.

"Ah Madone. It was an accident," Ma said, and then laughed. "You know what I mean. It was an accident yah, but it was an accident that the accident happened. I'll be more careful next time."

"Promise?" I asked.

"I promise," she said.

* * *

Jake and the kids were hanging out watching some tree house show when I came downstairs. I was happy to see them all together and not arguing. The kids definitely needed that bonding time with their dad, so I just said a quick goodbye and left. I wasn't even sure they heard me.

At Starbucks I ordered two mocha frappes and sat outside, waiting for Mel.

"Boo," Ma said.

"So not workin' anymore."

"Drats."

"You here to apologize to Mel?"

"Apologize for what? I didn't do nothing."

I rolled my eyes. Obviously my daughter got that annoying little habit from me.

"Ah Madone. He's fine. Just a little bump on his head is all."

"You could have seriously injured the father of her children, Ma. You need to at least acknowledge that."

"Uh, Ang?"

"I'm serious."

"Uh, Ang, there's another ghost here, and he's uh...he's naked, and juggling. And he's staring at you."

"Oh yay." I clapped my hands and squealed. "That's the British guy. I love him."

"Well hello my lady." The naked, juggling man said in his British accent.

"How are you?" I asked.

"Gobsmacked, I am. I've been talking to you for months, but it would seem you didn't notice my presence."

"Gobsmacked?" I asked. I didn't understand.

"Ah yes, my apologies. I'm *surprised* you can hear me. I've been here many times and sat with you and that lovely Asian woman, but have been ignored."

I took a sip of my frappe. "Yeah, sorry about that, but I didn't see or hear you. In fact, I can't see you now but—"

Ma interrupted. "And that's too bad, too. He's a looker, I tell ya."

I shook my head. "I've had a little trouble with my gift lately, but it's working again, sort of."

A woman walked out of Starbucks, and looked at me funny, so I grabbed my phone off the table and pretended to talk. "Just took you off speaker because people think I'm talking to myself."

Embarrassed, the woman walked to her car.

"Geesh," I whined. "Totally forgot how stupid I look. I need to remember to use my ear buds."

"I like this man, he's my kind a spirit," Ma said.

"And you're quite dishy, yourself," the ghost said.

"Dishy?" Ma asked. "What's that?"

"It means lovely, my lady. You're quite lovely. I certainly admire a woman of your beauty."

I sensed a potential love connection, and pictured my mother running naked through the Starbucks parking lot, her big boobs bouncing as the man juggled his balls—not his *balls* but his balls. I shuddered at the thought. "Let's not go there."

Ma busted out laughing.

"Might you like to attend my next performance?" the ghost asked.

I pressed my palm to my forehead and pushed, hoping to make the pain stop.

"Ah, thanks for asking, but I can't. My daughter needs me right now, so I gotta stay."

"Right. Very well. I hope to see you again soon. And I'm glad you are able to talk to me again, young lady."

"Me, too," I said.

"Very well," he said. "Until we meet again."

"Now that's an attractive man," Ma said. "All of him."

I cringed. "Is he gone?"

"Yup. Left like a bat outta hell, bouncing all the way, too."

"Good Lord."

"Hey, he ain't wearing any clothes so he must be okay with showing his stuff. What's the harm in looking?"

"I just threw up a little in my mouth."

"You sick?" Ma asked. "You always were prone to stomach issues. It's the acid. You got the reflux. You should see a doctor."

Mel walked up. "Saved by the Mel," I said. "Thank you. How's Nick?"

She sat down, and took off her sunglasses to rub her eyes. They were swollen and puffy again. "He's fine, just a bump on his head. Matches his eye perfectly."

"You've been crying," I said, grabbing her hand. "Are you okay?"

She shook her head, then put her glasses back on. "I'm fine, really. Is Fran here?"

I released her hand and sat up straight. "Yup, and she is going to apologize to you for what happened too, aren't you Ma?"

"She doesn't need to apologize, Nick's fine." She frowned. "I guess that's a good thing."

I nodded. "It may not feel like it, but it is, at least for the kids."

She agreed. "So what happened?"

I played a verbal tennis match, carrying my mother's part of the conversation between her and Mel. We decided it was time to make a plan, and be more organized in getting what Mel wanted for the divorce. It was obvious we weren't detectives because other than following him, all we could think to do was have my mother spy on him and report back.

"I think it's time we tell Jake what's going on," I said.

"Yeah, I think so," Mel agreed. "He texted the other day and asked why we hadn't gotten together in a while."

"Jake texted you? You must be special. I can barely get him to text me back, let alone text me first."

She laughed. "No not me, Nick. I read his texts."

"Ah. So what did Nick say?"

She shrugged. "Last I saw he hadn't responded."

"What a tool. They're supposed to be friends."

"Yup."

"Tool," Ma said. "I like that word. I'm gonna use that."

I ignored her.

Mel placed her elbows on the table and rested her head in her hands. Her hair, normally smoothed straight and shiny, looked frizzy and dull. She'd lost weight and the dark circles under her eyes were showing behind her sunglasses. "Have you been eating?"

"Some," she said and took a sip of her frappe. "I don't have much of an appetite lately."

"I can imagine, but you need to eat." The grease sat like lead in my stomach but for Mel, I could toss a bagel in there, too. "How about a bagel? We could go to that New York bagel place that just opened."

"No thanks. The thought of food makes me nauseous. I'm going to run by Nick's office. He got a white Taurus from the rental car place, and I want to see if he went to work or to the ho's."

"Okay, I'm going with you. We'll take my car. Sooner or later he's going to see you out there." I texted Jake and said that I'd be home later.

"I'm comin', too," Ma said.

"Ma's coming, too."

"Great. Maybe she can give him another bump on the head."

"Don't give her any ideas."

They both laughed, and I pressed my palm to my forehead again, hoping to stop my headache from getting worse.

*   *   *

Mel pointed at a white Taurus. "That's his rental."

"So he's here. That's good."

"It's a little late for anything he does to be considered good," she said.

"I know, I just meant it's good that he's here, and we don't have to go to Carrie's house."

"Don't count on that," Ma said.

I rubbed the back of my neck. I knew I'd regret asking, but I did anyway. "Why not?"

"'Cause he ain't at work."

"What's she saying?" Mel asked.

"Ma says he's not here."

She straightened her shoulders. "I'm going up there."

"What? Why? He's gone."

"To find out where they went."

"Don't you think that's a little odd, going to his office? You never go there."

She shook her head. "I'm checking on him. He just got in a car accident and refused to stay home and rest. I want to make sure he's okay. He could have blood on the brain or something and not know it. Plus, he's my husband, and I can visit him at work any time I damn well please." She opened the car door and left.

"Ma, can you go with her, please?"

"You betcha."

I leaned my head back on the headrest and prayed that Mel wouldn't do something she'd regret. She was reaching her tipping point and it was going to get ugly.

Five minutes later she still hadn't returned. I busied myself reading status updates on Facebook to pass the time. What took so long? She went in and asked for Nick. They said he wasn't there, so she asked for Carrie. They said she was gone, too, so she asked where they went. They said to her house to have sex, so she became that crazy Asian woman who destroyed the office, but got out before anyone stopped her. Based on my time estimate, she should have been back two minutes ago.

"Well that was close," Ma said.

I let out a breath I didn't know I'd been holding in. "What took so long? I've been going crazy out here."

Just then Mel opened her door. "She's twelve!" She screamed. "She looks like a freaking twelve year-old." She sat in the passenger's seat and slammed the door with a bang. "Nick wasn't there, and Carrie was in the bathroom, throwing up. I know because I was in there pulling myself together before I went into the office, and heard her yacking. I figured it was her because when she came out of the stall and saw me her eyes got all bulgy, and she rushed out without checking her make up."

"She puked and didn't check her make up?"

Mel nodded. "Didn't even look in the mirror and see if she had puke on her face. Nick has a family picture on his desk, so I'm sure she recognized me." Her hands were shaking, and she made a growling sound, but her mouth stayed closed.

That wasn't a good sign.

"So did you go into the office or what?"

She nodded. "I went to the reception desk and asked to see Nick. She said he was out at a meeting with his boss, which is probably why his car is here. Then I asked to see Carrie, so she called her up." She let out a quick snort. "She could barely hold it together when she saw me—that ho."

"Girl was shakin' like a leaf on a tree if you ask me," Ma said.

"So what did you say to her?" I asked.

I told her I was checking on *my husband* because *my husband* had been in an accident and *his family*, you know, *his kids and his wife*, *me*...were worried about him."

"Oh boy."

"Yah, that's what I said, too," Ma said.

"And then what happened?"

"She mumbled something about leaving him a note, and then skirted away with her slutty tail between her legs."

I grimaced.

"She is so screwin' my husband, and now she knows I know it, too." Mel said.

"Wow...just, wow."

"And guess what?" She smacked my arm. "You're gonna love this."

Ma agreed. "Oh yah, this is good."

I tilted my head. "Okay?"

"The ho is Asian."

"You're shitting me."

"If I'm lyin', I'm dyin'," she said.

"He's a tool," Ma said.

I tried not to snicker.

"Again, wow...just, wow."

"Let's go," Mel said. "I gotta get outta here."

I turned the key in the ignition. "Where to? Back to your car?"

She shook her head. "No, I wanna eat."

I closed my eyes and nodded. "Good. How about a sandwich or something from the bread and soup place?"

"No, I want an Obnoxious One," she said.

An Obnoxious One is a cupcake from a local cupcake specialty shop by the mall. They make the most incredible, albeit expensive, cupcakes ever. They're creamy and moist and the size of a five-pound bowling ball. The Obnoxious One was the best cupcake-gasm this side of the Mason-Dixon Line, if not in the whole country. It was the big guns, and I knew Mel was suffering through some serious emotional turmoil to want that.

I pulled out of the parking lot and headed to the shop. "I'm getting Key Lime Pie and Red Velvet," I said.

"I'm getting two. It'll be a double cupcake-gasm."

Oh boy.

"Ah Madone, what I would give for a cupcake, and an orgasm. If only I knew when I was alive, what I know now," Ma said.

I shook my head. Sometimes my mother dropped bombs full of information I just didn't need.

"You're shaking your head," Mel said.

"If Fran were your mother, you would too."

"Hey! I can hear you, ya know." Ma yelped.

I waved my hand. "I know, Ma. I know."

Mel didn't even ask what my mother said, she just laughed.

We sat in the car and ate our cupcakes, sipped on Diet Cokes—I know, ironic, and tried to come up with ways to catch Nick. Ma was helpful, but hadn't yet been able to get the kind of hard evidence Mel wanted. "We need to watch more crime dramas," Mel said.

"Probably would help," I said, the cupcake in my mouth muffling my words.

"I'm all for a few little harmless incidents here and there, but I need something that unequivocally proves he's having an affair." She shifted her head toward the backseat. "Not that I don't appreciate what you're doing, Fran, because I do."

"Tell her I know, will ya? And tell her I'm working on it," Ma said.

I took a bite of my Red Velvet cupcake. "Masaysyougottabepatient." Cupcake spit out of my mouth and landed on Mel.

"Seriously?" She wiped her shirt. "Stop talking with your mouth full. Who taught you manners?"

"Hey!" Ma screamed. "That's rude. You tell her I taught you all kinds of manners. It ain't my fault you don't remember them. You tell her it ain't polite to talk about how I raised you when she can't hear me defend myself."

I held my finger up, and chewed the bite of orgasmic delight. "Ma said you're a bitch."

Mel spit pieces of the Obnoxious One onto my lap. I'd be lying if I said I didn't think about eating them.

"That's not what I meant!" Mel said. She eyed the back seat again. "I'm so sorry."

I laughed. "Ma's gonna haunt the crap outta you for that one." No one ever tells an Italian woman she didn't raise her kids right. I picked off a piece of cupcake and stuffed it into my mouth. "Good luck," I said, but kept the cupcake from flying out that time.

"Don't give her such a hard time. For cryin' out loud, her husband's gone and knocked up another woman, and you gotta give her a hard time like that?"

I dropped the rest of my cupcake into my lap.

"Oh, crap. I didn't mean to say that. Pretend you didn't hear it. So, how 'bout that Michael Jordan? I bet he's still got it after all these years, huh?"

Ma dropped the nuclear bomb of Mel's lifetime, and I wasn't sure what to do. I eyed my cupcake, sitting icing side down on my lap. Mel nudged me. "Dude. Don't just leave it there like that."

My eyes darted to Mel's face, and I quickly looked away. My stomach did a flip flop and I was no longer hungry. I grabbed the cupcake and put it back in its plastic container. "I can't eat this," I said. "I feel sick all of a sudden."

Mel nodded. "Me, too." She put her cupcake back too. "But that's pretty much how I feel all of the time lately."

She had no idea how much worse it would get.

"Anyway, back to catching the cheating rat bastard. Anymore ideas?" she asked.

Catching cheating husbands wasn't my area of expertise, and I really wasn't sure I wanted to be too involved without Jake knowing. "We really need to talk to Jake. He helped our friend Neil when he went through his divorce, so I'm sure he'll know what to do."

I called Jake and told him Mel and I had some stuff to talk to him about and would be there shortly. We drove back to Starbucks so Mel could get her car, and she followed me home.

If Ma was in the car then, she didn't say anything, and I wasn't about to bring up the bomb she'd dropped earlier. I needed to let that one sink in first.

CHAPTER NINE

THE KITCHEN SMELLED OF FRESHLY BREWED COFFEE, and Jake was standing near the pot, smiling. "You made coffee? For us?" I asked.

Ma whined. "Ah Madone, the torture. I just want one cup. One stinkin' cup."

"Ma's mad."

"Why?" Jake asked.

"Can't have coffee. Can't smell coffee. Can't live as a ghost—I mean a celestial being—apparently, without coffee. Must really suck to be a ghost."

"Well, that's rude," Ma said.

"It must," Jake said. "Popping in and out of everywhere whenever you want, not having any bills to pay, no responsibilities. Yeah, it must suck. Seeing anyone you want naked."

I shook my head. Jake was a professional at redirecting conversations to sex.

"I got responsibilities," Ma said. "I gotta take care a all a you. And with the trouble you got all of the time, that's a big responsibility."

"And we greatly appreciate it," I said, ignoring her comment about our constant trouble. Just then Mel walked in through the garage door. I grabbed a cup from the cabinet and handed it to Jake. "Here, pour yourself some. You're gonna need it."

He raised his eyebrows at me. "Great." He poured himself a cup, and then grabbed cups for Mel and me, too. He even poured Ma a cup, and sat it at the fourth seat at the kitchen table. "For you, Fran. Even if you can't have it, you can at least look at it."

"Aw, he's such a nice son in-law. How come you never pour me cups of coffee like that?"

Mel sat at the table and said, "Jake, have you talked to Nick lately?"

"Yeah, actually, just this morning. Said we needed to get together, but he said he's been busy, and a lot of things have been happening. He told me about the accident, but said it wasn't anything serious."

"Too bad, too." Mel said.

Jake rubbed his chin and shot me a look.

"Nick's having an affair," I said.

"Nick? Having an affair?" He leaned back in his chair, and shook his head. "No way, not Nick. He swore he'd never do that again."

My mouth dropped, and I was about to say something, but Mel yelled, "That bastard. I knew it."

I shot my husband my look of death. He glanced at me, and then dropped his head and stared into his coffee cup. We had a *no secrets* policy, and he'd just been busted.

"Mel," Jake said. "He said you knew—that you'd talked it out and made a decision to stay together. He said he made a mistake, and he wouldn't let it happen again." He shook his head. "And I thought he meant it."

"Well he lied to us both then, because he's banging his little Asian assistant, probably as we speak," Mel said.

"How do you know?" he asked.

Mel filled Jake in on what she knew, and then I told him what Ma saw. He wasn't happy.

"I'm not sure having Fran pulling little ghostly pranks is a good idea." He drank some of his coffee.

I stiffened. "She's not pulling ghostly pranks, she's helping Mel." I guzzled my lukewarm coffee, got up and poured myself another cup, and sat back down. I chilled out a bit and continued. "I told Mel about how you helped Neil. Do you think you could tell her about it?"

Mel took a notepad and pen from her purse. "I know Georgia is a no-fault state, but I want to make sure I do everything I can to not get screwed in court," she said.

He nodded. "Are you sure that's what you want to do? Divorce him?"

"I deserve better, Jake," she said.

He nodded. "Okay, but be prepared. Neil's divorce got ugly, and that could happen to you too."

She nodded. "It probably will, because I'll make it that way."

Jake spit out a list of things Mel needed to get: bank statements, emails, phone bills, itemized call logs, photos of his phone with text messages to name a few. He told Mel he would help her in any way he could, and I knew he'd decided his relationship with Nick was done.

An hour later I walked Mel out to her car and promised her we'd get what she needed. "You'll probably have Nick's testicles hanging from your rearview mirror, too." I said.

She smiled a half smile. "Thanks."

"Ma, you here?"

"Yuppers," she said.

I walked back inside, and glared at my husband. "I'm going to talk to my mother for a minute, and then I wanna know why you didn't tell me what you knew about Mel and Nick."

He nodded but kept quiet. Probably smart of him, too.

I walked outside to the deck. "Are you here?"

"Boo."

"Tell me you made that up before, please." I said, throwing myself onto a deck chair.

"Made what up?" she asked.

I closed my eyes and leaned my head back. "What you said in the car earlier, about Carrie being pregnant. Please tell me you made it up."

"Okay, so I made it up."

I sat up. "Seriously?"

"No, but that's what you wanted me to say, so I said it."

I rubbed the back of my neck. "Ma, no jokes now, please. This is serious."

"Yah, I know. I'm sorry."

"How do you know? I mean, you can't see into her uterus or anything, can you?"

"Of course I can't see into her uterus, but I'm gonna check on that 'cause that'd be one super celestial power to have, don't ya think?"

I sighed.

"I saw her take the test, and I snuck a peek at the stick. The rabbit died, Ang. That girl's having Nick's baby."

"Criminy." I stood and paced the deck.

"Are you sure it's Nick's?"

"If you're asking if I saw it happen, no I didn't, but my ghostly juju says it's his and I haven't been wrong yet. Kinda like when I was alive, too. I was never wrong."

I ignored that. "Does Nick know? Were you there when she told him? What'd he say?" I rubbed my forehead. "Good God, don't tell me he said he's gonna marry her. That'll kill Mel."

"Don't get your undies all up in a bunch. I don't think she's told him yet. I haven't heard them talking about it, and she's actin' all kinds of nervous around him. She's gonna have to soon though. It's been over a month already, and that girl's tiny, she's gonna be showing in no time."

I stopped pacing. "Wait. You've known this for over a month?" I didn't need to be a rocket scientist to understand. "So you knew this before I could hear you, and you're just telling me now?"

"I was waitin' for the right time, is all."

"When did you think that would be? Her baby shower?" I shook my head. "I've gotta tell Mel."

"I wouldn't do that if I were you. She's about ready to blow a gasket now. You telling her that is just gonna make it worse."

"She's gonna blow a gasket regardless of when she hears it. Wouldn't you?"

"Yah, I'd blow a gasket all right. With one of them big rifles Jake's got up in your closet, aim it right at Nick, that's what I'd do. Ain't no way I'd let him get away with stickin' it in some other woman and knockin' her up. Nope. No way."

Ma was right, Mel was going to blow a gasket and I didn't want that to happen, at least not before she had what she needed for court. Scared about her reaction, I decided to sit on it for the time being. Eventually I'd tell her, but I wanted to wait until the time was right.

"Do not speak a word of this around anyone, okay?" The only other person that would hear my mother was Josh, but I figured better safe than sorry.

"Who me? My lips are zipped." She made a zzzzzz sound.

"Thank you. Now I need to talk to Jake about keeping secrets from me."

"Uh," Ma said.

I waved her off. "Yeah, pot callin' the kettle black, I know."

I walked into the kitchen, and Jake's mouth curved into a half smile. "You're angry."

Ma snorted. "You betcha she is," she said.

"Ma, could you give us a minute, please?"

"Ah Madone. Fine. I'm leavin'. You don't want your mother around to support you, to be here for you, fine. I'll leave. Use me when you need me, then toss me aside. Your brothers, they'd never do that. That's why they're my favorites."

I laughed. "Bye Ma, don't let the door hit you on your way out."

"I don't open doors, ya know. I go through them."

I laughed. "Good point." I sat at the table across from Jake, propped my elbows on it, and plopped my head in my hands. Eyebrows raised, I said, "You were saying?"

He smiled. "I was saying sorry."

"Oh, really?" I smirked. "And for what exactly are you sorry?"

He leaned back in his chair. "So this is how it's gonna be, huh?" He exaggerated slumping his shoulders, and sighed a long, fake sigh. "For being a rotten husband."

That one surprised me. "You're not a rotten husband. At least not compared to Nick."

"You'd be hard pressed to find a husband more rotten than him right now," he said.

"Actually, I could name some politicians." I smiled again. "But go on, I won't interrupt you again." I made a cross sign over my heart. "Promise."

"I figured you knew and were sworn to secrecy, too."

I straightened my back. "When have I ever kept a secret from you?"

"You're right." He nodded, more to himself than to me. "What was I thinking? Everyone knows you can't keep a secret to save your life."

What the?

"I can keep secrets."

He shook his head. "Not really."

My voice rose and my body stiffened. "Tell me one time I haven't."

"When we got Emily her car."

I shook my head. "That's different. That's not a real secret, so it doesn't count."

"I didn't know there were different kinds of secrets."

I nodded. "Try again."

"When I lost my job at Por-Tel."

I scrunched my eyebrows. "I didn't tell anyone."

"You told Mel."

"Well, of course I told Mel. She's my best friend. No one keeps secrets from their best friend."

"Do you see a pattern here, Ang?"

I shook my head. "This isn't about me anyway. This is about you keeping things from me."

"It wasn't my secret to tell."

"But it was about my best friend, so you should have told me." I knew that was weak, but it was all I could think to say.

"If Mel wanted you to know, she would have told you."

"But she didn't. Not until recently anyway."

"Why aren't you mad at her too, then?"

"Because you're my husband, you should tell me stuff."

"But she's your best friend and no one keeps secrets from their best friend."

Score one point for Jake.

I stuck my bottom lip out. "I hate when you do that."

"Really? I don't."

"You're rude," I said, smiling.

"But you love me."

"Only because you're good looking and handy."

"And great in bed."

"So you say. I'm waiting to find out."

"I can show you right now, if you'd like."

"No, I'm mad at you. You have to suck up first."

"Make up sex is incredible," he said.

"You have to make up first to have make up sex, Jake."

"I said I was sorry. Twice, actually."

"I hear foreplay for make up sex is all you can eat crab legs at the resort on the lake." I batted my eyelashes.

"What about the kids?"

"Pfft." I waved my hand. "They're expensive, and noisy. They can stay home and fend for themselves."

"I like how you think."

"If you play your cards right, you'll like how I act later, too."

He got up. "Gimme a few hours to get some stuff done, and then I'll shower and we'll go. Sound good?"

"Oh, yeah. Clean Jake. I like him much better than dirty Jake."

"I prefer dirty Angela."

"That's not what I meant, you dork."

"Dammit."

He went down to his office. I stayed at the kitchen table, feeling like a hypocrite. I knew I was keeping a very important secret from Mel, and I felt like a heel for doing it, but I convinced myself I was stopping her from doing something she'd later regret. I figured I was following Jake's example—ask for forgiveness, not permission.

* * *

We went to eat all you can eat crab legs at the resort on the big lake. It was casual—the kind of place where people came in wearing flip-flops and bathing suits under shorts, but I wore Jake's favorite skirt and tank top. I figured I'd tease him a little before I shoved obscene amounts of crab in my mouth. He'd always said watching me sucking a crab leg turned him on. I didn't get that, but I figured whatever floated his boat was good with me.

We decided not to mention Mel or Emily or my mother and just focus on us for a change. Until Ma popped in, that is.

"Ang."

I hung my head. "Ma's here," I groaned.

Jake's eyes narrowed. "She wasn't invited."

"Tell him to zip it. You got a visitor," Ma said.

"I'm on a date with my husband. Can't this wait?" I turned to Jake. "She's not alone."

He wiped his mouth on his napkin, and then tossed it onto the table. "And here we go again."

"I'm sorry. I'll make it quick, I promise." I cracked another crab leg and dipped the meat in butter. "I'm listening."

"This here's Harold and he ain't happy. Seems his wife is having some financial issues, but he says he's got money hidden, and he's been trying to tell her where it is, but, like you, she don't got no clue what's going on. And now she's gonna sell the house and he doesn't want her to, what with that money hidden and all. He needs you to tell her where the money's at."

"What's going on?" Jake asked.

"Ma says this man wants me to tell his wife where he's hidden some money so she doesn't lose the house," I said. "Said she's moving, but he doesn't want her to." I cracked open a crab leg and pulled out the longest, most perfect piece of leg ever.

"How much money did he hide?" Jake asked.

I shrugged. "How much money are we talking about?" I sucked the leftover parts of the crab leg out of the shell.

"Two million."

I choked, and took a sip of my water. "Two million?"

Jake dropped his fork full of coleslaw. "Two million?"

I nodded, and took another sip of water. "Two million. Holy shit."

"Two million," Ma said. "Well I'll be damned. I could a used someone hiding two million buckaroos for me back when your dad and I split."

"When is she moving?" I asked.

"Day after tomorrow," Harold replied.

"Okay, Harold. We'll meet tomorrow first thing. Ma, can you make sure he's with you, and meet me at Starbucks at nine?"

"You betcha," she said.

"You're making plans to meet a ghost at Starbucks?" Jake asked.

It did sound pretty strange. "She's moving the day after tomorrow, and it's two million dollars."

"I'm going with you," he said. "This, I gotta see."

* * *

On the ride home, I gently rubbed Jake's leg. "That was amazing make up sex foreplay," I said. I touched my belly. "Good Lord, I'm bloated."

He rolled his eyes. "So I guess make up sex is outta the question then?"

I stuck my belly out as far as I could. "No way, baby. This thing is all yours."

He laughed. "I'm good with that."

Unfortunately when we got home the opportunity for intimacy disappeared. Emily was gone.

Josh was sitting on the couch, watching TV. "Josh, is Emily home?" Jake asked.

"Nope. Haven't seen her all day."

I shook my head. "She went out straight from work." I ran my hand through my hair. "Dammit. I knew this was gonna happen."

I grabbed my cell and checked my calendar for her work times. "She got off at six."

"Son-of-a-bitch," Jake said, gritting teeth. He sent her a text to get home immediately.

"We need one of those swear jars," Josh said, switching channels on the TV. "We could go on a vacation with the money you two would have to put in it."

"Pray you don't have a daughter, buddy," Jake said.

"Oh no way. I'm not having girls."

"You don't have a whole lotta control over that."

"Uh, yeah, I do. My health teacher says the man determines the sex of the baby, so I'm having boys."

"Good luck with that," I said.

"He's learning sex ed in health class?" Jake mouthed.

"Apparently so," I whispered.

Emily hadn't answered Jake's text, but he had an app on his phone that allowed him to locate hers, so he used it. "She's at Central Park. Let's go."

"This isn't going to be good," I said.

"Josh, we'll be back after we get your sister," Jake said.

He nodded. "Good luck."

In Jake's car, I said, "You know she's with Chandler."

"I know."

"I told you this was serious."

"Yes, you did."

"My mother was supposed to be keeping an eye on her. Where's Ma?"

"I don't really know, honey. I can't see her."

"Yeah, well neither can I." I leaned my head against the back of the seat. "Could use a little help here, Ma."

"Boo," she said.

"Ma, why didn't you tell me Emily wasn't home?" I glanced at Jake. "Ma's here."

He nodded.

"Whadda ya mean she's not home? She sneak out again?" Ma asked.

I shook my head. "Josh said she didn't come home after work."

"Oh boy," Ma said.

"I thought you were gonna keep an eye on her," I said. "What happened?"

"I didn't know," Ma said. "I'm sorry. I was with Harold and then I went to bingo and I got a little distracted. It happens."

"What? You went to play bingo?" I shook my head. "I don't understand what you're saying."

"Bingo, you know, the game?"

I nodded. "I know what Bingo is. I don't—what do you mean you played it?"

"I went to the assisted living. You know, the one I lived in 'til I got the big C. I go there sometimes, and I play Bingo."

"Honey," Jake said, but I ignored him.

"Oh. Well, since I can't actually *play*, play, I just sorta helped Suzanne play."

"How on earth did you do that?"

"I might a made the Bingo machine pick her numbers so we could win."

"You fixed the game?"

"Angela, seriously. We're almost there."

I'd totally forgotten about Emily. "Oh, crap."

"If that kid is there, I'm gonna beat his ass," Jake said.

"Oh boy," Ma said.

We pulled into the Central Park parking lot. Except for two small lights at the park's entrance, the entire park was dark. We spotted Emily's Scion parked at the back of the lot, next to an older model Honda something-or-other. Their fronts faced out, toward us. Jake cut the lights, and let off the gas, but the lot was on a slight hill, so we coasted toward them. I rolled down my window and listened. "I can't hear anything." Just then something dark moved inside Emily's car. "Did you see that?"

Jake nodded. "They're in the back seat."

I dropped an F-bomb.

"I'll handle this," Jake said, and moved to get out of the car.

"Don't let him do it, Ang," Ma said. "He ain't gonna be happy."

"Honey wait. Lemme do this, okay?"

He shook his head. "I'm gonna have a 'come to Jake meeting' with this kid," he said.

"Fine, but let me go to the car. You just wait behind me, okay? Let them get out first. Neither of us needs to see what might be happening in there."

We stayed as quiet as possible getting out of the car. I put my hand out to stop Jake a few feet away from their cars, and whispered, "Let me do this part, just in case, okay?"

He shook his head, and went to respond, but stopped when all four doors to Emily's car opened at once. The headlights on our car went on. I muttered a thank you to my mother for those nifty little tricks.

Both Emily and Chandler's heads popped up in the back seat, and then ducked back down a second later. I heard Emily say, "Shit, it's my parents."

Jake shot for the car, but stopped himself. "Out of the car now, both of you," he said.

"Okay, Dad. Just a second," she said, her voice shaking.

Chandler was the first to get out, and did so buttoning his jeans. *Buttoning his jeans.* The kid had balls, that's for sure. Jake was up in the boy's face in less than a second. "Chandler, right?" His eyes gave the kid a once over, and he shook his head and grunted.

"She can do a hell of a lot better than you."

Go Jake.

Chandler stepped back and stumbled over his words. "Uh, yeah...I'm... I'm Chandler."

Jake pointed to the side of the car formerly known as Emily's. "Wait over there, and don't move."

"Uh, I gotta...I gotta go," Chandler said. Dropping his shoulders, he turned toward his car, but Jake stepped in front of him, and blocked his path.

"Over there," he said, pointing to Emily's car again. "Now."

Chandler did what he was told.

Emily got out of the car, and walked over to us, her body stiff, her jaw set. She stood defiant and smug, but didn't say a word.

And that's when I lost it. I laid out a verbal lashing full of things I promised myself I'd never say to my kids. I even used my mother's favorite saying, *I'll knock you into next week.* I was up close in Emily's face, and I was loud. She flinched, but kept her mouth shut.

Jake put his arm on my shoulder. "Hold on, honey," he said and then shifted to Chandler, who was still standing at the side of the car, busying himself on his phone. Jake walked over to the boy, took his phone and put it in his pocket. "I'm going to make sure there's nothing on this that can cause my daughter harm, and then I'll think about letting you have it back."

Emily and I watched as Chandler muttered, "Yes, sir."

Jake motioned for Chandler to come with him, and walked back over to us. He looked at both of the kids and said, "This is the last time either of you will see each other again, you hear me?"

Neither of them spoke.

"Do you understand?" Jake asked, a tone in his voice I rarely heard.

Chandler nodded, but Emily stayed still and silent.

Jake's eyes shifted from Chandler to Emily. "I'm not playing around here." He pointed to the boy, and then made eye contact with him again. "If I find out you've been anywhere near my daughter, I'll come find you. We'll go for a little drive. There are a lot of places in this town to bury a body, kid, and no one will ever find you."

Chandler's mouth went slack, and his eyes widened. He nodded his understanding.

Ma said, "Ooop."

I kept quiet because I knew Jake wasn't kidding. Emily must have known too, because tears dripped down her cheeks, but she didn't touch them, and she still didn't speak.

Jake looked through Chandler's phone and hit the buttons. We all stood there, watching. He handed Chandler back his phone. "Don't forget what I said," he told him. "Now get out of here before I decide to take that drive now."

Ma guffawed.

Chandler stuffed his phone in his pocket and high-tailed it to his car. He was gone in less than a minute. He didn't even glance at Emily the whole time.

Jake set his eyes on our daughter. When he spoke, his tone was sarcastic. "Congratulations, Emily. I've never known how it felt to be disappointed in my child." He nodded. "But thanks to you, now I do."

Her head dropped to her chest, and her shoulders shook. I looked at Jake, and saw the sadness in his eyes. "Why don't you go home, and I'll drive back with Emily?" I asked.

He nodded, and then shifted around and walked to his car.

I stood and watched him drive away, my arm around my daughter, whose tears were coming out in buckets now.

I walked over to the driver's side back door to close it. I shouldn't have, but I couldn't help myself—I looked on the seat and saw Emily's thong panties, and a used condom lying there. It was then that I understood how Jake felt. I shook it off, and walked to the other side of the car, and closed that door, too. "Come on, Em," I said. "Let's get you home."

She lifted her head, saw my face, and cried harder. "I'm sorry, Mama. I'm so sorry." She ran to me and we hugged.

"It's okay, Emily." But it really wasn't. Things had changed, and they'd never be the same, and I wasn't sure I was ready for that. "I'm going to make the appointment with the doctor."

"Okay."

I let go, faced her, and wiped the tears from her cheeks with my thumbs. "Was that your first time?"

She nodded, and rubbed her nose with her hand.

"Well, you're certainly never going to forget it."

"Yeah."

"Listen, I have a lot of things I want to say to you, but I think it's best that we sit on this for the night. We're all dealing with some pretty strong emotions right now, and I think it's best we pull back so we don't say anything we'll regret."

"Am I grounded?"

I leaned my forehead into hers. "Oh, honey, you're so grounded you're lookin' up at dirt."

"Great," she said.

We got in the car, and I pointed to the thong and condom. "That needs to go away when we get home."

She looked behind her, and nodded.

*   *   *

When we got home, Emily went straight up to bed. Jake and Josh were in the den, playing on the X-box with the doors closed, and I watched as Emily paused in front of the den, only to turn and walk upstairs.

I walked into the den. "I'm going to hang out outside," I said. "Wanna have a chat with my mom. You going to bed soon, honey?"

Jake nodded. "Yeah, we'll be done here in a bit," he said.

"You okay?" I asked.

He nodded, but didn't take his eyes off of the game.

"Okay. I'll be up soon, too," I said and closed the door.

I walked out the front door and sat on the step. "You here, Ma?"

"Yah, I'm here," she said.

I leaned back and moved my neck in circles. My shoulders ached, and my jaw hurt. "She was having sex."

"Yah, I know."

"She's just a child."

"Yah, she is. She don't know how stupid she is actin'."

"I don't wanna deal with this. I really just want to pretend it never happened."

"I know, but you gotta. Now's the time you gotta show her that you love her. It's when she needs it most. You know she's thinking about you and Jake being mad at her. She's ashamed. She's embarrassed. You gotta make her understand that you're mad at her, but that doesn't stop you from loving her."

"You're such a better mother than me, Ma. I know that's what you'd have done, but I'd rather crawl under a rock." I cracked my neck again.

"Hell no, I wouldn't a done that. I'd a chased your ass around the dining room table with a butcher's knife, like your grandmother did me."

I laughed. "I'm pretty sure I don't have a butcher's knife."

"Probably a good thing, too."

"What a night," Jake said after we'd gone to bed.

I snuggled up next to him. "Remember that time we went out for all you can eat crab legs? When was that?"

He rubbed my back. "Feels like a month ago, doesn't it?"

"Tonight was intense," I said, and lifted my head off his chest. "What you said to Chandler, though? That was hot."

"I wasn't kidding."

"Oh, I know that. That's what made it hot." I kissed him.

He kissed me back, but it lacked passion. "I'm thinking tonight's not a good night for make up sex."

I lay on my back. "Seriously?"

"Our daughter had sex in the back seat of a Scion."

"At least it wasn't a pickup truck. We do live in Georgia, you know," I said.

"Yeah."

"You okay, honey?"

"No, not really."

"Me neither."

He turned and faced me. "What if we never have sex again?"

"We will, eventually."

"I don't know if I can do it without picturing Emily."

"Oh, yuck."

"You're welcome. I didn't want to have to carry that burden on my own."

"Since we're sharing, her thong panties and a used condom were on the backseat."

"You're gonna have to throw away all your thongs now."

"Uh huh." I kissed him on the cheek. "This too shall pass."

"Like a smelly fart, I hope."

"Lovely. Night babe."

"Night."

CHAPTER TEN

I COULDN'T SLEEP. Emily had sex. There was a used condom in the car. If I ever did sleep again, I was sure I'd have nightmares about that. No parent should ever have to see a condom used during sex with their daughter. It was just wrong on every level.

I was pretty sure Jake wasn't sleeping either, but just in case I carefully got out of bed, grabbed my phone and went down to the den.

Mel had already texted. "Where are you? I haven't talked to you since you left for crab legs. And now I want crab legs, and I'm thinking about being a lesbian. I read an article about it online. It's pretty common with divorced women. They've done studies on it. So I need your opinion. And crab legs."

"You're not going to become a lesbian. It would be weird," I texted back.

"FINALLY," she texted back. "Jake finally get off you?"

"So didn't happen tonight."

"You okay?" she wrote.

"Long night. Tell you about it later. How are you?"

"Eh. Same. But I'm serious about the lesbian thing."

"I don't think you can just wake up and decide one day you're a lesbian. I think you're just born that way."

"Not true. The study showed that seventy percent of women who'd never had a sexual encounter with a woman before they got divorced ended up in some kind of intimate situation or relationship with a woman afterwards."

"They've been hurt and they're angry, but I think you'll get through this without switching teams, Mel."

"If I do, I'll be a lipstick lesbian."

"A what?" I wrote.

"A lipstick lesbian. Google it."

"Don't have to. You're not going to become a lesbian. Besides, it would be strange."

"Why? It's not like I'd hit on you or anything."

"Obviously. We're best friends."

"That and you're not my type. Too stuffy and controlling."

"Good to know."

"You and Jake get in a fight tonight or something?"

"Nope. Emily stuff."

"Coffee tomorrow to discuss?" she wrote.

"Sure. Same time?"

"Yup."

"Oh," I texted. "I can't. I'm taking a ghost to his house to show his wife where he hid TWO MILLION DOLLARS."

"Excusawhat?"

"TWO MILLION DOLLARS!"

"I'm coming with you."

"That's what Jake said. We'll meet you at Starbucks. Ma is bringing the ghost there, too."

"That's not something I'd ever thought I'd read in a text."

"Never thought I'd write it either."

"Going to bed. Try to get some sleep."

"Okay, you too." I wrote. "And stay straight."

I yawned, and made my way back to bed. I snuggled up next to Jake, and when his hands wandered, I realized he was half asleep, and not thinking about Emily, so I didn't stop him. Our lovemaking was comfortable, and I knew our love was solid, and we'd weather this storm together just like all of the ones before, and the ones that would come later, too.

* * *

The next morning Jake and I woke up wrapped in each other's arms. Though we'd snuggled often, we never slept that way because his body temperature was usually somewhere near boiling, and my not-yet-peri-menopausal-but-probably-pretty-darn-close-body couldn't tolerate temperatures above freezing. I lived in my own personal summer four seasons a year.

He snuggled closer. "Phew."

"Phew?"

"We did it. We had sex."

"I knew we would."

"I didn't. I really was afraid I'd picture Emily. That'd be enough to drive any man to the brink of celibacy."

"Well then, thank God for me you're not just any man."

"You're one hell of a lucky woman, Angela Panther."

I rubbed his chest, "Yes I am, and it appears you're gonna be one hell of a lucky man again, too."

"Praise God." He pulled the covers over our heads.

After our little morning escapade, and a joint shower, I told Jake that Mel was meeting us at Starbucks to go to Harold's, too.

"I think I should stay here with Emily," he said.

"Okay, but you're not gonna give her a hard time, are you?"

He shook his head. "I'm not even sure I can talk to her just yet."

I told him what Ma told me. "She needs to know you still love her, even if you're mad at her."

"I know, and she needs some kind of consequence," Jake said.

Truth be told, neither of us had a clue about how to deal with Emily. Parenting was a shot in the dark. One minute things were moving right along, no worries or issues and then suddenly you're smacked in the face with a fast pitched ball of drama, clueless about how to deal with it. Eventually you'd figure out how to patch up the injury, and move on, but they kept throwing those fast ones, especially the girls. It was never-ending.

"I think at the least, considering she was having sex in the car we gave her, the car should go away for now," I said.

"What about for work?" He asked.

"I'll drive her, but she's going to have to tell her boss her availability has temporarily changed because I'm not picking her up after they close."

He softened. "She's gonna lose her job."

"Stuff happens when you screw up. Not my problem," I said.

"Maybe it's consequence enough for her to be embarrassed from being busted by her parents while having sex and being forced to end her relationship with that jag-off."

I shook my head. "I don't think the embarrassment was big enough to impact her and my guess is she'll be all about the drama and make it a Romeo and Juliet type of thing."

"Great," he said.

"I gotta go," I said. "I'll be home right after I'm finished, okay?" I kissed him goodbye. Our lips lingered a little longer than usual. Post-sex days were always the best.

*   *   *

Mel was waiting at Starbucks when I arrived.

"There are some really cute women in this town," she said, glancing at a woman through the Starbucks window.

I sat and shook my head. "Good grief. How long am I gonna have to deal with this? A week? Two weeks? Or is it gonna be like the time you gave up shaving your legs? You made me feel the hair on them for a month. It nearly ended our friendship."

She stuck her tongue out at me. "You're such a fuddy-dud."

"Uh huh. And where's my coffee? You always buy me coffee."

She sipped hers. "I gotta save my cash for my soon-to-be new girlfriend. I'm guessing she'll be a shopper since you're not."

I shook my head.

"Kidding," she said. "I got you a frappe. Jenn's making it now, Miss No Sense of Humor."

"You're awesome," I said, and blew her a kiss, and walked into Starbucks.

"I told you you're not my type!"

Jenn and I caught up for a minute, and she gave me a sample of a new frappe to take to Mel. "I told her I'd make one for her," she said. "Tell her to let me know if she likes it."

"I will. See you later."

She waved, and went back to making drinks.

I gave Mel the sample. "Jenn wants to know what you think."

She took a sip and grimaced. "Ew, that's horrible."

"Really?" I took a sip, and grimaced, too. "Ew. You're right." I pushed the drink aside and sipped my mocha frappe.

"So when's the millionaire ghost supposed to be here?" Mel asked.

"Wow, that's what I called him earlier. Scary."

"Great minds," she said.

"Boo," Harold said.

I dropped the frappe in my hand. "Aw come on, Ma. That's cheating."

"What?" Mel asked, looking around.

"Harold just said *boo*," I said, shaking my head.

The three of them laughed.

"Gawd, I love your mother," Mel said.

"What's this about Mel bein' a lesbian? To each his own, I say—but me, I like a pecker. It gets the job done," Ma said.

I rubbed my forehead. It didn't matter how old I was, hearing my mother talk about sex was gross.

"What'd she say? Mel asked.

"I can't repeat that."

"Ooookay."

"Okay," I said, and rubbed my hands together. "Is everyone ready?"

"We are," Ma said. " We'll just float around twiddlin' our thumbs, waiting on you to finish your dessert there."

"They're ready. Let's drink and drive," I said.

"Great," Mel said. "Let's go find some money. Lord knows I could use some."

"Uh, ma'am," Harold said. "Your friend here isn't going to try to take any of the money, is she?"

I busted out laughing. "No Harold, my friend won't take any of your money." I gave Mel a dirty look. "I promise."

"Oh, well then, I'll tell you where to go."

We got in my car and Harold gave me directions to the Laurel Valley subdivision. It was a wealthy golf club community with obnoxiously large, beautiful homes decorated to the nines. Every year they did a Christmas home decor tour and Mel and I went.

I pulled into the neighborhood and Harold gave me the entry code to pass through the gate.

"It's the first street on the left," he said. "Number 4755."

I parked on the street just up from Harold's house.

"She lives there?" Mel asked.

Harold answered, not realizing Mel couldn't hear him. "Yes, we bought the house five years ago, but since I've died, she's not been able to keep up the payments. I never got around to telling her where I'd hidden the money, and I don't want her to lose the house. With that she can pay it off, and have plenty left over to live off, especially if she invests it wisely."

I repeated what he said.

"How did he die?" She asked.

"Oh, yes, well," he said. "It was a terrible accident. I was playing golf. I was on the lower nine, and was hit in the heart with a golf ball. Damned thing hit in just the right spot, at just the right time. I was dead before I hit the ground."

"Oh my God," I said. "You're that man. It was all over the news. I'm so sorry. Horrible way to die."

"What man?" Mel asked.

I filled her in.

She held her hand to her heart. "Oh no. I remember him. His wife tried to sue the country club and lost. The news said she spent her life savings on attorneys, and had nothing left," Mel said.

"Yes, that's true. That's why it's so important she knows where to find the money," he said. "I'd like that sign to disappear."

He was talking about the short sale sign stuck in the front yard. They'd popped up all over town, but especially in the bigger, over-priced subdivisions. We were hit hard when the market crashed, and many people still hadn't recovered. "Your house is beautiful," I said.

"Yes, thank you. It was our dream home. The children love it."

"Oh, I forgot about that. He has kids, Mel."

"Yeah, I remember. Two boys. Grade school age, I think."

"She's right. Brendan and Kyle. Twins. They're in fourth grade now."

"I'm so sorry," I said.

"It's the way things go. I talk to Kyle often. He knows it's me. I come to him in his dreams. He's told Maya—my wife, but she thinks it's just his subconscious wanting to see me."

"I can understand. Unless you've been there, it's impossible to believe we can communicate with our loved ones who've passed," I said.

"I know. I used to dream about my father," Harold said. "But I never knew it was actually him until he told me."

"He told you?"

"Yes, when he came to get me."

"Our family comes to get us when we kick the bucket," Ma said. "Your grandma and your Auntie Rita came for me. Didn't I tell you that?" Ma asked.

If she did, I didn't remember. I shrugged and asked Harold, "Do you think Maya will believe me?"

"I think so. Once you get her to look behind the bookcase, she will. She'll have to then."

"Do you think that will be a problem?"

"It might. She doesn't know it can move so you'll have to convince her."

Great. That wasn't what I wanted to hear. I told Mel that Maya didn't know the bookcase moved and I had to figure out a way to convince her.

"Meh, no problem. You'll make it happen."

"Where is the bookcase?" I asked.

Harold gave me the basic layout of the great room. "Okay then," I said. "Let's get this party started." I got out of the car and Mel followed.

"Too bad there ain't no finder's fee for ya, Ang," Ma said. "You could use it for a little nip and tuck, ya know?"

My mother had the best timing. She knew how to throw out those zingers right when I wasn't able to fight back. Very deliberate and extremely effective, too. "Yeah, it's too bad, Ma."

I rang the doorbell, and Mel bounced on her toes.

"Stop that. She's gonna think we're here to scam her."

She rolled her eyes. "Like she's not gonna think that when you tell her why we're here?"

I nodded. "True."

Maya answered the door, her posture rigid and her eyes narrowed. "May I help you?"

Why were my hands sweaty? I rubbed them on my shorts to try and dry them off, but it didn't help. I cleared my throat. "Uh, yes. My name is uh, Angela Panther, and this is my friend, Mel. I uh...I was hoping you could, uh—we could talk to you about your house."

She scowled. "No thank you, I'm not interested." She stepped back and pushed the door to shut it, but Mel stuck her foot in it before she could.

"Ms.—I don't know your last name—Ms. Harold's wife, you're gonna wanna talk to my friend here, okay? Your husband Harold contacted her, and told her something that could stop you from moving or losing your house." She glanced up at the detailed stone and woodwork above the front door. "And this looks like an amazing house, so if it was me, I wouldn't want to leave it."

Maya leaned her head into the crack of the door left opened with Mel's foot. Her face was red. "My husband is dead, so it's impossible for him to have spoken with your friend." She pulled her face away from the crack, and pushed hard enough on the door that it forced Mel to pull her foot out as she slammed it shut.

Mel said, "That's one scary woman right there."

I glared at my friend. "That went well." We walked back to the car.

We sat in the car and focused on the house. Ma ranted at Mel, and then ranted at me for not repeating it. She threw Josh's discarded lacrosse balls in the back seat up front.

"What the hell?" Mel screamed. She shook her head—probably realized it was Ma trying to ping her with one. She tossed a ball between her hands. "I screwed up. I'm sorry."

I made the inch sign with my fingers. "Maybe just a little."

"I know. I'm sorry." She pinched the top of her nose with her fingers. "I haven't been myself lately."

"Ya think?" I shifted toward her. "What was your first clue? Telling me you're gonna start batting for the other team? Or how about practicing your peeping tom skills at Carrie's?" I shook my head and ran my fingers through my hair. "You've got to get it together, Mel."

Her face tightened. "My fifteen year marriage is ending. Forgive me if I'm struggling because of it." Her eyes glassed over from tears.

I was the crappiest best friend ever. I dropped my chin to my chest. "I'm sorry. I'm a horrible friend." I raised my eyes as she wiped the tears dripping down her face.

"No, you're not," she said. "The lesbian thing was pretty nuts. And you're right, sneaking around Carrie's apartment complex in the dark was pretty stupid." Her mouth curled into a smile, and she laughed. "But man it was funny watching you practically suffocate that skunk." She let out a belly laugh.

I snorted. "I'm glad I can add a touch of humor to the insanity." I put my hand on her knee. "I'm sorry. I can't imagine what you're going through, and it's not fair of me to be critical. You wouldn't do that to me."

She clasped my hand in hers. "It's okay. You're not being critical. You're being honest, and I appreciate that. I need you to tell me when I'm going off the deep end. It may upset me, but I'll get over it."

"Ah Madone, can we quit with the Hallmark commercial, and figure out how to help Harold here? I got stuff to do," Ma said.

I raised my eyebrows at Mel. "Ma said we gotta get the ball rolling here for Harold."

Mel's eyes widened. "Oh, crap. Totally forgot about him." She spoke toward the back seat. "Sorry, Harold."

He accepted her apology.

I glanced at the house again. "I don't know what to do except knock on the door, and try again." I shifted my head toward Mel, and smiled. "Think you can keep your lips zipped this time?"

She pulled her fingers across her lips in a zipping motion, and nodded.

"I'm gonna knock on the door, and if she answers, I'm just going to blurt out as fast as I can that I talk to the dead and have a message from her husband," I said. "Harold, maybe you can tell me something to say to her so she'll believe me?"

"Let me think about this for a moment," he said. "Ah, yes, I do know of something you could mention. Perhaps she'll believe you if you tell her you know that she was originally pregnant with triplets, but one did not grow properly, and died in utero. It was attached to our son Brendan when he was born. The doctor had to surgically remove the fetus from his shoulder. We never told anyone about it for fear of what it would do to our sons—knowing they'd had another sibling that didn't make it."

"Wow. It' a like a story from *Reader's Digest*."

"What?" Mel asked.

"I'm not telling you," I said, smiling. "I don't want you running up to the door, and screaming it to the poor woman."

She stuck her tongue out at me. "Touché."

"She gets that from me," Ma said.

I ignored my mother, and got out of the car. "Promise you won't say anything?" I asked Mel.

"Pinky promise," she replied.

We stood in front of the door, but none of us touched the knocker or doorbell. I bounced on the tips of my toes, and stretched my shoulders back. "Okay, here goes," I said and tapped the knocker on the door three times. I rubbed my hands together. They were sweaty again.

The door opened a crack, and a chain pulled tight across it. "Do I need to call the police?" Maya asked.

I quickly stuck my foot in the door—just in case—and blurted out, "I know your husband is dead, but I have a message from him."

I tensed my leg, waiting for the door to push on it, but it didn't.

"He's been dead two years. If you had a message from him why would you wait until now to tell me?"

I squared my shoulders. "Because he just told me yesterday."

I felt the door push on my foot, and I kept my foot pressed into the ground.

"Ah Madone," Ma said. "Someone's gonna lose a foot in that door."

"He said you'd believe me if I told you I knew about the triplet attached to Brendan's shoulder."

The pressure from the door relaxed, and Maya's face appeared in the crack. Her head was slightly tilted. "No one knows about that but Harold and me."

I nodded. "I know. That's why he told me to tell you. May I please come in? It's important."

Her face softened, and she looked down. My eyes followed, and when I saw my foot, I pulled it out. The door shut, and I heard her remove the chain. She opened the door again and moved to the side. She shook her head. "I don't know why I'm doing this, but come in."

I released a deep breath, and walked in. Mel followed.

The house was stunning. The foyer grandeur was over the top, and bordered on tacky. Centered in the middle of the entrance was a spiral staircase with marble flooring, framed by two huge vases that held fake floral arrangements, and a naked woman statue on a grandiose foyer table.

"Wow," Mel said. "This is incredible."

Maya flipped her hand in the air. "Harold liked it. I prefer things more simple."

"It really is beautiful," I said. "I'm sure it made your husband happy to have it how he liked it."

"Yes." She led us into the great room.

"Wow," I said. It was decorated like a French villa. Colored in creams and reds with gold accessories, and a soft cream, half-circle couch. There were four bookcases separated by an ornate stacked stone and wood fireplace. I knew the money was hidden behind one of them, but I wasn't sure which.

"Harold again?" Mel asked, hesitantly.

Maya nodded.

"Holy moly," Ma said. "I think I've died and gone to heaven. As Josh says, *it's da bomb* ain't it? Though mauve and gray would a been a better choice. That's what I had in my place, ya know. The red makes it look kinda like a whorehouse, you ask me. I wonder if they got an ice maker? I always wanted an ice maker."

"Yes, we have three, one in each refrigerator," Harold said.

"Oh, I forgot you were here," Ma said and snorted. "Sorry about the whorehouse comment."

"Similar comments have been made," he said.

I covered my mouth, and giggled.

"I figured. And hey, whadda ya need three fridges for?" Ma asked. "Your wife cook a lot?"

"No, but our maid did."

"You got a maid? I always wanted a maid, but all I got was Angela here, and she never had any interest in cooking."

I ignored my mother, and focused on Maya.

"I know this is hard to believe, but Harold came to me last night. He doesn't want you to lose the house."

She raised an eyebrow. "He came to you last night? How is that possible?"

"Honestly," I said. "It's a long story, and I don't want to bore you with the details, but he gave me some information, and it's huge. You won't have to move."

She pulled her face back, making her chin multiply, and shook her head. "I don't understand."

"He says there's two million dollars hidden between a bookcase and the wall." I twisted toward the bookcases. "I'm guessing it's behind one of those."

She pivoted toward the bookcases, and then swung her head back toward me. Her face was red. "That's impossible. Those bookcases are built into the wall. Besides, Harold wouldn't hide two million dollars behind a bookcase." She stood. "Now, please, you need to leave. I have too much to do to be wasting my time with you."

"Harold, I could use some help here," I mumbled.

"You see that photo on the first bookcase?" He asked. "It's a picture of us in Mexico the day we found out she was pregnant. We had to pay a hotel worker to drive into town and get a pregnancy test because she was too afraid to leave the resort. Tell her you know she still has the test stick in her jewelry box, and that I wanted her to throw it away because it seems too unsanitary to me."

I walked over to the photo and picked it up. "Harold just told me this was taken in Mexico, the day you found out you were pregnant." I held the picture toward her. "He said he had to pay a hotel worker to go into town, and get a pregnancy test for you because you were too afraid to go."

She walked to me, and snatched the photo from my hand. "All of our friends know that story."

"Do they know you've still got the test stick in your jewelry box?" I asked. "Harold said he tried to get you to throw it away because he thinks it's unsanitary, but you wouldn't."

She swayed, catching her balance on a bookcase shelf. "I wouldn't let him tell anyone that," she said. "It *is* unsanitary to keep the stick, but I couldn't make myself throw it away. I just couldn't."

I nodded. "I kept both of my test sticks, too."

Maya stared at the bookcase. "Two million dollars?"

"That's what he said."

She ran her hand along the edge of a shelf. "Is this the one?"

"Harold?"

"Yes, that's the one," he said.

I nodded to Maya.

Her eyes scanned the great room. "Is he here?"

"Yes."

"Oh." She shuffled her feet. "What does he want me to do?"

Harold told me how to move the bookcase.

"He wants you to move the bookcase."

She faced the bookcase, and tilted her head. "But I don't know how."

I stepped to her side, and showed her the electrical cover on the back wall of the second shelf. "Flip that up. There's a latch behind it. Release the latch, and it unlocks the bookcase. Then you just have to pull the bookcase forward, and it should open."

She just stood there, her eyes glued to the bookcase.

"Would you like me to do it for you?" I asked.

She nodded. "I don't think I can."

I flipped up the electrical outlet cover. Harold was telling the truth. Behind the cover was a latch, I released it, and heard it snap.

"The bookcase is heavy," Harold said. "You'll need two people to pull it out."

I turned to Mel. "Harold says it's heavy. Wanna help?"

She touched her hand to her chest. "Me? Oh, yeah, sure." She jogged to the bookcase, and we both grabbed the shelf.

"Okay, on the count of three, we pull," I said.

Mel nodded.

"One, two, three," I said. Harold was right. It was heavy. We grunted and pulled, and with a little sweat one side yanked open. I got behind it and pushed it open as far as I could.

"Oh wow," Mel said.

"Well lookie there," Ma said. "A secret hiding place. Always wanted one a those."

"Incredible," I said.

Maya's mouth hung open, but she didn't make a sound.

In the wall was a small door with a combination lock built into it. "Harold, what's the combination?" I asked.

Maya came back from la la land. "Oh, he would have used the twin's birthday," she said.

I moved to the side. "Would you like to open it?

She walked over to the lock, and put in the combination. The door popped open. "Oh my," she said, and stepped back.

I counted seven shelves piled high with rows of money held together with rubber bands. Another four shelves above those were stuffed full of gold and silver coins. I gasped.

"Holy moly, she hit the jackpot," Ma said.

"Frick," Mel said.

Harold was relieved. "She'll be fine now. I'd completely forgotten about the coins. That will make things even easier."

"I'd think so," I said.

Maya didn't speak—she just stood there, and stared at the money.

"He wants you to keep the house," I said. "And he said if you invest the rest, you'll be fine."

Maya faced me. "He comes to Kyle, at night, in his dreams."

I nodded. "Yes, he told me."

She shook her head. "I didn't believe my son."

I placed my hand on her shoulder. "It's okay. You do now." I turned, and walked toward the foyer. Mel followed.

"Wait," Maya said. She bit her lower lip. "Is he still here?"

I nodded. "Yes. He can hear you, if you'd like to talk to him."

Tears fell from her eyes. "My love, I'm so lonely without you."

"I'm always with you," he said. "I'll never leave you."

My throat burned, and I had to swallow back a lump. I squeezed my eyes shut, and let the tears fall. "He's always with you, he said, and he'll never leave you." I glanced at Mel as she wiped tears from her eyes.

Maya looked at the wall full of money. "You promised you'd always take care of me," she said. She pointed to the money. "But I would give all of this away to have you back—just to see you one more time. All of it."

"We'll be together, my love. At night, while you sleep, I'll be there, and I'll come to you in your dreams."

It was hard to repeat that while bawling, but I did my best.

Maya pulled me to her, and hugged me. "I'm sorry about earlier," she said. "What you've given me is...is amazing. And I don't mean the money. I don't know how I can ever thank you."

"You could give her some of that cash," Ma said.

I hugged Maya again, mostly to hide my smile. "You don't have to repay me, Maya. It's what I do." I let go of the embrace and said, "I'm going to get out of your way now so you can do what you need to do to cancel this move, okay?"

She nodded. "Yes...yes, and thank you." She walked us to the door.

Before she walked out, Mel turned to Maya, tilted her head, and said, "Sorry about before."

Maya waved her off, shaking her head. "It's already forgotten."

Harold and I said our goodbyes outside. Mel made me ask him four times if he was sure he hadn't hidden money anywhere else, but he assured me he hadn't. She was bummed.

We got in the car, and Mel squealed. "Holy bundles of money Batman, that was freaking awesome." She used her hands to help her talk. "I can't believe you didn't want to do this stuff before." Her face contorted into an unfamiliar expression. "Oh, my God," she said, and then she cried.

"What's wrong?"

"That poor woman! Here I am pissed off at the world because my husband cheated on me. I don't want to be with Nick ever again, but Maya? Her husband is dead, and her heart is broken. How is she going to recover from that? The things they said to each other? My heart was breaking too, and I don't even know them." She wiped her nose with her hand. "It really puts my crappy life in perspective, you know?"

I opened the glove compartment, and handed her a tissue. "I know what you mean, but don't discount what you're going through because you think someone else is worse off than you. You're still allowed to feel what you feel."

"I know, but still. That was a real eye-opener. It was incredible."

I smirked. "It was pretty amazing, wasn't it? Did you like how I stuck my foot in the door?"

She laughed. "Where'd you learn that?"

"Ancient Chinese secret," I said, and started the car.

I dropped Mel off at Starbucks. She asked if I wanted to have another frappe, but I told her I had to get back, and deal with the Emily crisis.

"Oh, yeah. When you feel like talking about it, let me know."

"I will. Text or call later," I said.

I wasn't usually so closed mouthed about stuff with Mel, but I wasn't ready to talk about my daughter's virginity—or lack thereof—just then.

* * *

Jake and the kids were in the kitchen when I returned. Josh's eyes were glued to his phone, and Emily sat next to him at the kitchen table busying herself staring at her arm.

Jake had his laptop in front of him. "Was it there?" He asked.

"Yup."

"Was what where?" Emily tried to act normal, but her skittish expression gave her away.

"Long story," I said.

She took that as a brush off, hung her head, and got up from the table. "I'll be in my room."

"Hold on, honey," I said, grabbing her arm. "I'll go with you. We can chat a bit." I glanced at Jake, and mouthed, "Did you talk to her?"

He shook his head, and mouthed back, "Nope."

I raised an eyebrow at him. "Do you wanna come?" I asked in a normal voice.

"Ah, Josh asked me to help him with a game," he said.

Josh glanced up from his phone. "I did?"

I shook my head and mouthed, "Chicken."

"Mom, I like, really don't wanna be yelled at, okay?" Emily's voice shook, and her eyes, already swollen and red from crying, teared up.

"I'm not gonna yell at you, but we have to talk."

"Fine."

I wrapped my arm around her. "Come on."

Up in her room, we had a long about sex, boys, how to respect yourself, and how a boy should treat her. I wanted her to know I was there for her, and that even though she messed up big time, I didn't love her any less.

"Will I get to see Chandler again?"

I shook my head. "I don't think your dad's gonna allow that, kiddo."

"So it's really like, over? We're broken up?"

I nodded. "What happened last night wasn't just a big deal for you. It was a big deal for your dad and me, too." I bumped her with my shoulder. "You're his little girl. It's hard for him, you growing up like this."

"I'm not a kid anymore, Mom."

"Actually, you are, but you could be forty and he'll still see his little girl."

"He's, like, barely talking to me."

"Give him time, he'll come around."

"How long am I grounded for?" She asked.

"I'm not sure. We'll just see how things go, okay?" I kissed her on the forehead and got up. "And one more thing," I said.

She rolled her eyes, but I let it go.

"Sex in a car is cheap and sleazy, and is never, ever appropriate. You deserve better."

She bowed her head. "It wasn't that bad."

I laughed. "Honey, I'm gonna let you in on a little secret, okay?"

She nodded.

"No guy knows what he's doing until he's at least thirty."

"Really?"

"Yup."

"What about Dad?"

"According to him, he came out of the womb good at everything."

"Gross."

"Don't worry, he wasn't right."

CHAPTER ELEVEN

JAKE DIDN'T MENTION THE EMILY SITUATION all day. He played video games with Josh, worked a little, and watched TV. Emily—likely too scared to come downstairs again, stayed holed up in her room. I heard her crying, but decided she needed space. She didn't have access to her computer, the family iPad, or her cell phone, so I figured that was part of the reason for her tears, but mostly it was because of Chandler. I wasn't sure forcing them to break up was the right thing to do—in fact, I was pretty sure it would only drive her closer to the boy, but for the time being, I let sleeping dogs lie.

Mel sent a text. Since she'd decided against being a lesbian, she was now obsessed with marrying a millionaire. She'd done several calculations, and decided he needed to be at least seventy years old, and have about seven million dollars. She'd already decided exactly what she'd do with the cash.

"What if he wants you to sign a pre-nup?" I texted.

"He won't. I'll wow him with my incredible sexual skills."

"TMI."

"You could stand to listen. You might learn a thing or twenty."

"I'll have you know I'm a sexual dynamo. Ask Jake."

"Bahahahaha!"

"Rude." I wrote.

"Truth hurts."

Most of our texting was witty and casual, but there was an underlying tension in her comments. She neared her breaking point, and if we didn't get what she needed soon, I knew she'd explode.

I sat out on the deck. "Ma? Are you here?"

"Yup. Floating right in front of ya."

I focused hard in front of me, but all I could see was the fire pit. "I don't see you. Wave your arms or something."

"Well, you see anything? I'm getting tired flappin' my arms like a bird here."

"Meh, I got nothin'. Sorry."

"You gotta go see Linda. It's no fun sneaking up on ya anymore, anyway."

"I need to call her, and let her know what's going on."

"She knows. We've been talking for months now."

"Seriously?"

"Well yah. We've been trying to get your psychic radar working right. Besides, her spirit guides told her you were gonna start hearing me anyway, so she knew it was coming."

"Why don't my spirit guides talk to me instead of her?"

"The universe is funny like that. Lemme tell you how it works."

"Oh boy. Lessons from Fran."

"Don't get smart." There was an edge to my mother's voice, one I hadn't heard since she died.

"Yes, ma'am."

"I just finished a class about becoming a spirit guide, and I think I'm gonna apply to be one. I think I'd be good at guiding someone, ya know?"

"Good grief."

"Ah Madone, shut your spaghetti hole, and listen."

"Geesh, Ma. That's a great thing for a future spirit guide to say."

"Yah, I gotta work on my assertiveness. Dial it down a bit."

I laughed.

"So here's the thing. Spirit guides, they communicate all the time, you just don't know it. You gotta be open to hearing them, and you're a lotta things, but open-minded ain't one of them."

I couldn't argue that. "I pity the fool who gets you as their spirit guide, Mrs. Sensitivity."

"I'm working on it, geesh."

"Has Linda mentioned if I'll get my gift completely back?"

"Nope."

"Has she said anything about my gift?"

"Nope."

"Are you lying to me?"

"Yup."

"Can you tell me anything you talk about?"

"Yup."

I waited, but she didn't speak. "Well?"

"Mostly we make fun of you."

"Nice."

She laughed. "Nah, I'm kidding."

"So you *can* tell me what you guys said then, right?"

"Not about your gift, I can't, but don't worry, we both don't really know nothing about it now anyway. Lately we've just talked about Mel and the shuck."

"That's why I called for you, actually," I said.

"Oh, can ya make it quick? I was with Buddy and we're thinking of poppin' over to Italy. He's wants to go there 'cause that's where his daughter lives, and seeing as she's gonna die soon and all, it's kinda urgent."

"Wow, that's terrible. Is she ill? She can't be that old."

"She's fifty-five. She ain't no spring chicken, but yah, she's sick. The big C, like me. Smokes like a whore in a crack house."

"How do you know about crack houses, Ma?"

"Law and Order. I watch it with Josh on his computer."

"Josh watches Law and Order on his computer?"

"Uh oh. I wasn't supposed to say that."

"What else does Josh watch on his computer?"

"I dunno. I'm no narc. So about Mel."

"We gotta get moving on getting what she needs, Ma. She's gonna crack."

"Yah. You were right—what you said to her in the car at Harold's. I've been at her house, and she's losing it, all right. Her house is spotless. She's scrubbing stuff so hard, she's taking the finish off. That ain't right."

Mel was no slob, but like yours truly, she wasn't OCD about cleaning. "That's not good. Can you get the paperwork Jake mentioned?"

"Already did. Yah, I'm that good. Spirit Spy Fran, at your service."

"You already did? What'd you get? And when?"

"I popped over to the shuck's office after you finished with Harold, and he was there, with his baby mama.

Baby mama?

"After Carrie left, I stuck around—ya know, waiting to see what he'd do, and he got on his computer. He's got one of those fancy ones where you can touch the screen and stuff happens. So I touched it when he was touching it, and it wouldn't do what he wanted. Ah Madone, he was cursing up a storm, and I was cracking up. He's got a temper, that one. He was looking at something from the bank, so I memorized it."

"You memorized it?"

"Yah, and it was easy as pie."

"You always had a good memory, Ma."

"Yah but now it's supercharged."

"Okay, wait. How did you know it was bank stuff he was looking at?"

"'Cause it looked like my old bank statements that came in the mail, only the account balances were a hell of a lot bigger than mine. Your dad didn't pay me enough to take care of you, that's for sure."

"You saw his account balances?"

"Uh huh, and like, I said, I memorized it all, the numbers and balances. He's got a lotta money, too. One account's got 7,471 dollars and sixty-eight cents. Oh, wanna hear me say it backwards? It's a nifty trick I learned."

"I'll pass."

She did it anyway.

"That's creepy."

She did it again, and the hairs on my arms stood. "You sound like that demon on The Exorcist, Ma."

"That's rude."

I smiled. "Learned from the master."

The citronella candle on the fire pit flew up in the air, and then landed in the yard. I picked at my nails. "Put it back, please."

"Pfft."

The candle flew up and landed back on the fire pit.

"Thank you. Now, can we get back to Nick's bank information, please?"

A rock came from out of nowhere, and pelted me on the knee. I shot out of my chair. "Ouch! That hurt, Ma."

"It wasn't me."

I rubbed the red spot forming on my knee. I'd have to wear leggings for the next week. "Whatever."

Eek. I sounded like Emily.

"It wasn't me, Ang, I swear."

"Fine, then who was it?"

"Beats me. I don't see anyone."

"You're not gonna scare me, so knock it off."

"I'm not trying to scare you. I said it wasn't me because it wasn't me, and I don't know who it was 'cause I can't see no one around."

"You're serious? It's not you?"

"Yup."

"And you don't see anyone else?"

"Nope."

I stood still, focused my senses on the area around me, but didn't feel any energy other than my mother's. "This isn't right. I don't like that neither of us can see who's here."

"Sometimes that happens. The system ain't perfect."

"That's helpful."

"You're welcome."

I picked up the rock, examined it, and tossed it into the yard.

"Hey don't be throwing stuff at me. That isn't nice."

"How am I supposed to know where you are, Ma?"

"Oh, yah, I forgot."

"So much for the supercharged memory."

"That was rude."

"Back to the accounts." I said. "I need to write this down." I went inside and got a pen and paper and brought it back out to the deck. "Tell me what you know."

"I got a lot. I got his password, his user name, and his security question answers too, just in case."

The last computer she'd used was a terminal back in 1995. "How'd you know to get all of that?"

"When Nick was on the computer, I just started memorizing everything. When I came back here, I asked Josh what the stuff meant, and he Googled it for me. He's excellent with computers, that boy. He's gonna be the next Steve Jobs."

"He told you that, didn't he?"

"Yah."

"Do you even know who Steve Jobs was, Ma?"

"A computer genius."

"Josh told you that too?"

"Yup."

Ma said Nick had three accounts, and Mel's name wasn't on any of them. He had a joint account with Carrie Case. Carrie Case—and it had over 11,000 dollars in it. Between the three accounts his cash totaled about 20,000 dollars. Mel would flip.

"I gotta tell Jake."

"Yah, I gotta go. Buddy's here, and his daughter is getting close to coming to our side. I'll be back in a jiffy."

"Okay, Ma." I opened the door to the kitchen. "Oh, hey Buddy," I said.

"Hi Ang."

"I'm sorry about your daughter."

"Don't be. She's in a lot of pain, but she'll feel better when she gets here. I can't wait to hug her again."

"Come on Buddy, let's get a move on," Ma said.

Walking into the kitchen, I thought about what Buddy said, and how much I'd love to have another hug from my dad.

* * *

I sat in the chair in Jake's office. "Nick's got secret accounts totaling over 20,000 dollars."

"Jesus. Are you sure?"

I handed him the paper with the account information.

"Holy shit. How'd you get this?"

"Apparently our son is the next Steve Jobs."

"Huh?"

"Ma saw Nick on his computer at work. She realized it was a bank site because it looked similar to her bank statements, so she started memorizing everything he typed into the computer."

"Wow."

"I know, right? But since she's not up on security questions and stuff, she asked Josh to help her figure out what Nick was doing, so he Googled it. And then he told her he was the next Steve Jobs."

"That's wild."

"And he's watching TV on his computer at night."

"He takes after me."

"Unfortunately."

Jake read the paper again. "This is a lot of money," he said. "Have you shown this to Mel?"

I shook my head. "I just got it."

"She's gonna freak."

"You have no idea."

"He's got a joint account with Carrie Case. Who's that?"

"The girlfriend."

"Day'um."

"This is bad." I said.

"This isn't the Nick I knew."

"No one knows this one—except Carrie Case maybe."

He ran his hand through his hair, and it fell perfectly back into place. I hated that.

"Does Mel have an attorney?"

"Not that I know of."

He dug through a pile of business cards on his desk, and handed me one. "Have her call him. He's good."

I furrowed my eyebrows. "Why do you have a divorce attorney's card?"

He got up and came over to me. Bending down in front of me, he brushed the hair from my face, and said, "He sat next to me on the plane last week. Gave me his card, but I told him I didn't need it because I'm happily married to an amazing woman." He stood and kissed me, then walked back to his desk. "He said to keep the card, just in case."

"He's an ass."

"Probably."

"So how do you know he's good?"

"Because I Googled him. See where Josh gets it?"

I nodded. "I do."

"You gonna tell Mel?"

"Yes, but not tonight." I rubbed my temples.

"You okay?"

"Heavy head. Heavy heart."

"Need to talk?"

"No, but thanks. You do need to talk to Emily though. She's upset because you're upset—and because she can't see Chandler anymore."

"Damn straight she can't," he said. "And I know, I do have to talk to her."

"Restricting her from seeing Chandler is only going to make her want to be with him more, you know."

He nodded. "I know." He pointed at me. "You wanna tell me what happened with the two million dollar ghost?"

I shook my head. Tears stung my eyes, but I didn't know why. "Maybe later, okay? I'm gonna take a shower now, and crash. I just need some alone time."

"I'm here if you need me."

I walked over to my husband and kissed him. "I know, and I appreciate it."

"Love you," he said.

"Love you, too."

* * *

Upstairs, I tapped on Emily's door and said, "I'm heading to bed kiddo. Love you."

She responded, "Love you, too."

I turned on my shower, and walked into the closet to get my pajamas. I felt light-headed, and weak in the knees, and leaned against the back of the closet door. Buddy's words played in my head like a broken record. *I can't wait to hug her again. I can't wait to hug her again. I can't wait to hug her again.*

I covered my ears with my hands. My knees gave out, and I crumbled to the floor. A soft whimper escaped my lips.

I pulled my knees to my chest, bent my head into them, and sobbed.

Grief had a funny way of kicking the butt of those in mourning. Some days I was fine—almost normal. Those days were easy. It was the other days that did me in—the days when I felt a hole in my heart, missing my Dad and before, Ma, too. Sometimes it wasn't even a day—maybe just a few minutes or an hour, but when it hit, it hit hard, and it hurt.

I knew I had to come to terms with losing my father. My head understood that. It knew he'd probably never contact me, but my heart... my heart couldn't accept any of it. It was shattered into tiny pieces.

I gathered myself together, turned off the shower and collapsed in bed. Exhaustion beat out thinking, and I was out within seconds of my head hitting the pillow.

That night I dreamed I was sitting next to a campfire with an Indian named Alo. He told me he understood my sadness, but that it was time to move forward, that my father didn't want me to be sad. He said that maybe, from time to time, my father would make his presence known.

"I don't understand," I told the man. "I need him."

"It is his decision. He believes it is not in your best interests."

"But I miss him. Can't I just have one more visit? Just so I can tell him I love him?"

"He knows. He hears you. When you speak to him, he is near. He is in here." He placed his hand over his heart. "It is time for you to let go, and to move forward. Many great things lie ahead for you Angela, and you will be happy again."

Did I know this man? He seemed so familiar to me. So comforting. "Who are you? I feel like I know you."

"I am your Alo. I am with you always. Listen for me in the wind, and you will hear me," he said, and then he faded away.

* * *

Jake woke up and snuggled into me. "You planning to talk to Mel today?"

"Yeah, before I take our daughter to the gynecologist." I looked at the clock on my nightstand. "I gotta get up. Meeting her at Starbucks in thirty minutes."

"Sounds like a blast."

"Which part?"

"All of it."

"No so much, no." I got up to get dressed. "It's gonna be a great day," I said. "Between Mel and her potential freak out, and Emily and hers, I'm really not looking forward to the day."

"Come give me some sugar before you leave. It may be the last time I see you."

"That's not funny, Jake."

His cheeks flushed. "Yeah, I guess it's not. My bad."

I sat next to him on the bed. "Sorry. It's not you. It's me."

"Oh God. Are you breaking up with me?"

I hit him. "Nope. You're stuck with me."

"Good."

"I'm just dealing with some Daddy issues, that's all."

He pulled me into a hug. "I miss him, too, Ang."

A tear dropped onto his shoulder and I pulled away. "I can't do this now. I just need to move forward and focus on everyone else's crap so I don't have to deal with my own."

He nodded. "That always works."

"I could use a little support here."

"Sex is supportive. Want some?"

"Good Lord, you're a man whore."

"And proud of it."

"I'm going. You really need to talk to Em, and before I get home. I think it's best she hears what you have to say before she has her vagina examined by a stranger."

"I didn't need to hear that."

"Tough. Man up, dude."

He saluted me. "Yes, ma'am."

Before I left, I made a pit stop at Emily's room. "Appointment is in a few hours. Please be ready."

Her mouth dropped and her eyes widened. "Today?"

"Yup. Time to put your big girl panties on, kiddo. After all, you're a woman, now." I walked out giggling at my own wit.

Mel was late to Starbucks, so I got our drinks, and grabbed our table outside.

"Boo."

I didn't flinch. "I'm getting good at not being afraid of you, Ma."

"Party pooper."

I laughed. "Hey, how's Buddy's daughter?"

"She's passed last night. I was there with Buddy when it happened. She saw him before she died, too. Looked right at him and said, *I see you there, Daddy,* and then she croaked. It was beautiful."

"Ookay," I said, surprised by her choice of words. "So what's up?" I put my ear buds in my ears so it would look like I was talking on the phone, and not some crazy person talking to myself.

"We got another ghost, that's what's up."

"Where? Here? Now? Mel's on her way. I'm gonna tell her about Nick's account, and probably the baby, too."

"Yah, she's here. She was here yesterday too, but I told her to come back 'cause you were busy. So she did."

I was actually grateful for that. "Thanks." I shook my shoulders and hands, releasing stress. "So, hello?"

"Hi," a soft voice said.

"What's your name, and what can I do for you?"

"Brenda, and I need to get a message to my cousin, please."

"Okay," I said, feeling confident. "Shoot."

"It ain't gonna be that easy," Ma said.

I sipped my coffee, and leaned back in my chair. "*Of course* it's not." I waved my hand. "Go ahead. Tell me why."

"Brenda is Helen's cousin."

My heart raced, and acid rose in my throat. "Helen, as in Dad's Helen? My step mom?"

"That's what I'm sayin'," Ma said.

I leaned my head back, and shook it, and then I dropped the F-bomb.

Just then Mel pulled up, and honked. I straightened, and gave her a half smile and waved.

Mel sat and took a sip of her coffee. "Thanks, I needed this. Sorry I'm late. Nick was being an ass. He didn't pay the water bill last month, and the water was off this morning. How could he not pay the water bill? Then when I told him they'd shut it off for non-payment, he acted like it was my fault. I told him I wasn't responsible for paying the bills, and he said we didn't have any money because I spend it all of the time. Seriously? I barely ever shop for anything other than something the kids need." She took another drink from her cup. "He's such an ass."

When it rained, it poured.

I pounded my head on the plastic table.

"Ang?" Mel asked. "You okay?"

I looked up and said, "Ma's here." And then I whacked my head into the table again and left it there.

"Did I interrupt something?" Mel asked.

"Sort of," I said, my head still on the table.

"Does she have someone with her?"

I lifted my head. "Yup."

"Wow. Seems like Starbucks is the place for ghosts to hang, huh?"

"Yup."

"So what's the deal this time?" Mel was excited. Ghosts perked her up, at least the ones who didn't threaten her ability to climax.

"It's a woman who wants to connect with her cousin."

"Cool." She rubbed her hands together. "This'll help me forget about my jerk-of-an-almost-ex-husband."

I looked Mel in the eyes. "Her cousin is Helen."

It was Mel's turn to drop the F-bomb.

"That's what I said."

"She doesn't know, right?"

I shook my head.

"So what are you going to do?"

I moved my coffee from in front of me, and pounded my head on the table again, hoping to knock myself out, but I didn't.

Mel half laughed. "That helping?"

"Ah Madone, Angela. Stop that. You'll end up with brain damage."

"Ma says it'll give me brain damage." I pounded it again.

Mel giggled. "I love your mom."

"Uh huh."

"Is something wrong?" Brenda asked.

"Your cousin doesn't know Angela can talk to us spirits," Ma said.

"Oh," Brenda said.

"And I hadn't planned on telling her," I said.

"What's going on?" Mel asked.

I sighed. "Ma just told Brenda that Helen doesn't know I can talk to ghosts."

"Oh."

"Yeah, that's what Brenda said."

"So what're you gonna do?" Mel asked.

"This ain't about you, Ang," Ma said. "So you're gonna put on your big girl panties, and do what you're supposed to do, whether you like it or not."

Ma was right. It wasn't about me. I pressed my thumbs into my temples. "I'm gonna put on my big girl panties, and do what I'm supposed to do, whether I like it or not."

"That's my girl," my mother said.

Mel put her hand on my shoulder. "It's gonna be okay, Angela. I don't really know Helen, but I do know that you've changed the lives of everyone you've had these conversations with. You've given them something they needed more than anything."

"She's gonna want to know if I've talked to my dad. What do I say to her then?"

"You don't have to tell her you have this gift, you can just tell her you had a dream or something." She took a sip of her coffee. "You don't even have to mention your father."

"I don't know," I said.

"Has she mentioned her cousin recently? Does she know she's dead?" Mel asked.

"Yeah, she knows. Apparently there's been some questions about her death. She'd recently married a man much younger than her-what, fifteen years, Brenda?"

"Seventeen," Brenda said.

"Seventeen years younger than her, and then changed her life insurance policy to make him the beneficiary. Then she died, and he got everything. Her kids couldn't even pay for the funeral."

"Wow," Mel said. "Do they think the husband did it?"

"He didn't," Brenda said. "It was an accident. I tripped at the top of the stairs, and I fell. Brian—my husband—wasn't even home."

"She just told me he didn't. Said she tripped and fell down the stairs."

Mel sipped her coffee. "So maybe you tell Helen that you dreamed Brenda came to you, and told you that? She might be okay with that."

Mel had a point. "Brenda, I'm assuming that's what you want Helen to know. That is was really an accident?"

"Yes."

"What else?" Ma asked. "Do you got some cash hidden somewhere? We like to find cash. It's fun."

I shook my head.

"What?" Mel asked.

"Ma asked Brenda is she had cash hidden anywhere."

"I love your mom."

"I don't have any cash hidden anywhere, no."

"Drats," Ma said.

I asked Brenda why she'd want my stepmom to know what happened. "Don't you want to get a message to your kids?"

"I didn't have a relationship with my children," she said. "I hadn't for a long time, and I don't think they'd believe you if you talked to them."

I nodded. "But why Helen? I got the impression you two weren't all that close."

"Just before I died, I borrowed some money from her. I hadn't worked for some time, and Brian and I had separated—though nobody knew that, and I needed the money to pay my mortgage and attorney fees. I was in the middle of a lawsuit, and was expecting to win so I figured I could pay her back then."

"Oh, I see." I glanced at Mel, and then explained it to her.

"So she wants to apologize for not paying her back?" Mel asked.

"No, that's not it," Brenda said. "When she gave me the loan, I signed a loan agreement. It's an official document, and since the lawsuit was settled just before my fall, she can bring it to the lawyer and get a portion of her money back."

"So you want me to tell my stepmother—who doesn't know I can speak to the dead, and whose husband died recently—that her cousin did really trip and fall down the stairs, and oh, by the way, if you call her attorney, Mr. so and so, he's got some of that money she owes you?"

Mel nudged me. "Ang?"

"What?"

"Chill."

"Mel, Helen doesn't know."

"Maybe it's time she finds out."

I shook my head. "I'm not sure I can do this. I mean, if I could pass it off as a dream, maybe, but this is too much for just a dream."

"You can do it, Ang," Ma said.

"What if she doesn't believe me? What if she thinks I'm crazy?"

Mel placed her hand over mine. "She won't. Just give her the facts. Ask Brenda for specifics, and then have Helen call the attorney. She'll believe you then. She'll have to."

She was right, and I knew deep down Helen wouldn't think I was crazy, not anymore than she already thought, but that wasn't really my concern. "What about my dad?"

Mel nodded. "What about your dad?"

"She's going to want to know if I've seen or heard him Mel, and I'm gonna to have to tell her no. That's going to destroy her."

"She'll understand."

"I'm not sayin' me and Helen were best friends, but she's always done right by you, and I think you gotta tell her. I think Mel's right," Ma said.

"I can tell you everything in detail if you'd like," Brenda said.

The whole conversation made my stomach ache. I had no idea how I was going to talk to Helen. "Geesh, Dad, I really wish you'd say something right now."

"He ain't here," Ma said.

"Thanks, Ma. I kind of figured that."

"I'm just sayin'."

I held up my hand. "Let me just think this through for a minute."

No one said a peep. I dropped my head onto the table again. "This sucks."

"Quit that for cryin' out loud," Ma said.

I sat up, rolled my shoulders, took a few deep breaths, and said, "Okay, let's do this."

I grabbed a pen and note pad from my purse. "Brenda, I need everything. Lawyers contact information, details about the lawsuit, details about your fall, everything." I shifted my attention to Mel. "And you need to stay here. I've got stuff to tell you, too."

Her mouth dropped. "That doesn't sound good."

I didn't say anything, just half-smiled at her.

"Okay then, I'll get more coffee, and something with chocolate. You talk with Brenda." She pushed her chair back, and walked to the door. "I'm already getting pissed. This isn't going to be good." She pulled open the door and let it slam behind her.

"Oh boy," Ma said. "She's in for a shocker."

I nodded. "Okay Brenda," I said. "Shoot."

She gave me everything—from the events surrounding her death, to specifics about the lawsuit. Helen was going to get about 25,000 dollars.

I filled Mel in after she returned.

"Wow. That's a lot of money. You definitely need to tell Helen."

"Is that how much she loaned you?" I asked Brenda.

"It includes interest."

"I coulda used that kind of money when I was still kickin'," Ma said.

"Mother."

"What? All's I'm saying is it woulda been nice. Maybe I could a used it for a little vacation now and then. It would a done me some good. I mighta not got the big C."

"Smoking caused your cancer Ma, not lack of vacations."

"Well then maybe I could a used the money for one of those stop smoking classes they always got advertised on the TV. Then I could a gone on a nice vacation with the money I saved from not buying cigarettes."

"I'm consistently amazed by the way you think, Ma."

Mel asked what Ma said, and I repeated it to her.

"I'm with you on this one, Fran," she said.

"Lovely." I put the paper and pen away. "Okay. I need to prepare myself to make this call. I'll have Ma get in touch with you as soon as I'm ready, okay?"

"Yes, and thank you."

Ma said, "She's gone. Now let's get down to business."

I swirled the coffee in my cup, and contemplated how to tell Mel about Nick's bank accounts. "So, who do you think will win the super bowl this season?"

Mel groaned. "It's that bad, isn't it?"

I raised my eyebrows and nodded. "It's that bad."

She laughed nervously. "What are you gonna tell me, that Carrie's pregnant or something?"

"Ah Madone, she psychic?" Ma asked.

I dropped my head and stared at my coffee cup.

"Holy mother of God, she is, isn't she? That son-of-a-bitch, how could he?" Mel shot out of her chair, knocking it over in the process. "I'm gonna kick her ass." She grabbed her purse and went to leave, but I grabbed her arm.

"Wait," I said. "There's more." I pushed the chair closer to her. "Sit, so I can tell you."

She sat and shook her head. "How far along is she?" She pulled her hair out of its ponytail, twisted it around in her hands, and put it back up. Her beautiful Asian features morphed into a snarling, tomato red explosion of anger. "I'll kill him for doing this to my family." She pounded her hands on the table and our coffees fell over. "Son-of-a-bitch."

I winced, and grabbed our drinks before they emptied onto the ground. "Breathe," I said.

She exhaled and fanned her face, likely willing herself not to cry. "I'm fine. You said there's more, right?"

I nodded.

"Then spill it. It can't get any worse." She bit her lip. "Can it?"

I told Mel about the bank accounts and how Ma found them.

She leaned back in her chair. "That's over 20,000 dollars. No wonder he isn't paying the bills."

I nodded. "Yeah, I know."

"I'm sure they're not connected to our accounts. Did Fran get the passwords?"

I pulled out the paper with all of the account information and passwords on it. "Do you have an attorney?"

"No."

"Here." I handed her the attorney's business card Jake gave me. "Jake checked this guy out. He says he's good."

She took the card and nodded. "Thanks." She got up to leave.

"Call the attorney before you tell him anything. Please? Promise me."

She closed her eyes, and shook her head. "I'm not sure I can do that, I gotta go." Her eyes welled with tears.

"Okay, please call me, or come over, or whatever, if you need me. Please."

She nodded, and then turned and left.

I banged my head on the plastic table again, and then my cell phone alarm beeped. It was time to get Emily to the gynecologist. I got up, threw our cups out, and walked to the car.

Driving home Ma said, "Well that wasn't so bad. I thought she might go all Bruce Lee on you or something."

I laughed. "Did you ever watch Bruce Lee, Ma?"

"Sure did. Your dad loved him. I bet I could do some of those moves now, seeing as I'm more flexible in spirit form than I was as a human. I wonder if I could karate chop Nick for knocking that girl up? Hi-ya!"

"Good Lord. *In spirit form? As a human?* What's happening to you?"

"I'm evolving. It happens to all us celestial beings."

"No words, Ma. I have no words."

"That's a first."

"So Ma, why didn't you tell me about Brenda when she approached you before?"

"'Cause you mighta gone all Bruce Lee on me, and given me a hi-ya."

"I can't see you Ma, remember?"

"Oh yah."

"Well?"

"I was waitin' on Alo to have that talk with you, 'cause I didn't want you thinking or hoping your father would show up when you talked to Helen."

"Alo? Who's Alo?" And then I remembered, the Indian from my dream. "You mean the Indian from my dream? How do you know about my dream?"

"Me and Alo, we're tight," she said. "Thick as thieves, us two."

I shook my head. "I'm confused."

"Your spirit guide, Angela. Alo's your spirit guide."

I let that sink in, and then, for reasons I didn't even know, I asked my mother to stay away from my spirit guide.

"Fine, you want me to stay out of your life? I can do that," she said.

"That's not what I said, Ma." I rolled my eyes. "I don't understand this spirit guide stuff, but I guess I just don't want you, or even Linda, talking to him. If he's my spirit guide, then I should be the one talking to him. Okay?"

She didn't answer.

"Ma?"

She still didn't answer.

"Well, crap."

CHAPTER TWELVE

EVERY MOTHER SHOULD TAKE her teenage daughter to the gynecologist—not just because it's important—because it's a fantabulous mother payback moment. The complete and utter fear the girl feels before the exam is the greatest payback for teenage daughter angst known to mankind. I almost peed myself from holding back the laughter. Okay, so a few giggles may have snuck out, but I couldn't help it.

"Mom, it's not funny," Em whined.

"From this angle, it pretty much is, Em. Sorry."

"You're mean."

"You think I'm mean? Wait until you meet Dr. Sheila."

Her face paled. "Do I have to do this? I like, don't want to do this, Mom. Seriously. Can we just go? I can't, like, see Chandler anymore anyway so what's the point?"

I walked over to Emily and brushed her hair from her eyes. Her forehead was clammy. "Honey, seriously, this isn't as big of a deal as you think. The worst part is right now—the fear. I promise. The exam itself takes less than five minutes, okay? You'll survive." I hugged her, and she pulled the white paper robe tighter around her.

"Why don't guys have to go through this stuff?"

"Honey, if a man had to carry the burden for all the responsibilities of safe sex, we'd have billions more kids running around the world. Why do you think God made women the child bearers?"

"I dunno."

"Because we're the more responsible sex, that's why. As the saying goes, they think with the wrong head."

She laughed. "It's not fair."

"Yeah, I know. Blame it on Eve. Probably happened because she bit into that apple first, and God wanted to punish her."

"Probably."

Doctor Sheila walked in. "Well hello," she said, looking at Emily. "I'm Doctor Sheila, and you must be Emily."

"You know what? I'm going to leave you two alone for this," I said.

"No, Mom. Can you stay?"

"Don't sweat this Emily," Doctor Sheila said. "You'll be outta here in a flash."

"Okay," she said.

I kissed her forehead. "I'll be outside, kiddo."

Five minutes later Sheila came out, and filled me in on birth control options. "Emily said she'd prefer the shot, if that's okay with you?"

"Absolutely. I'd much rather she go that route, too."

We reviewed potential side effects, and then she wrote out the prescription. "Have her come back with the 'script, and we'll give her the shot." She ripped the prescription off of the pad. "She's getting dressed and will be out in a minute."

Emily walked out smiling. "That wasn't nearly as bad as I thought it would be."

"Pretty sure I said that too, didn't I?"

"Yeah, you did. Can we stop and get something to eat? I'm starving."

"Sure. We can drop off the prescription, too."

"Okay."

"Hey," I asked. "Did your dad and you talk at all?"

She nodded.

"Feel any better?"

She shrugged. "A little, I guess. He said I had to, like, ask you if I could have my phone back, but that I was, like, grounded for at least three weeks."

I was surprised Jake gave a time frame. Usually—because of his work schedule, he left that to me.

We got in the car. "I'm willing to give you your phone back, but if I find out you're texting or talking to Chandler, I'll take it back, and keep it indefinitely. Do you understand?"

She slid over to me and hugged me. "Yeah, and thanks, Mom."

* * *

I didn't hear from Mel the rest of the day. I sent her several texts, but she never responded. I talked to my mother too, but she was giving me the silent treatment. I worried about Mel, and felt bad about hurting my mother's feelings, but I tried to cut myself some slack. Truth was, I needed the breather to focus on what I'd say to Helen. I knew I needed to make the call, but I wasn't sure the words would come out.

I stood in my bathroom and practiced the call in front of the mirror. "Hi Helen, I know this is going to sound strange, but just hear me out, okay?"

I shook my head. "That was stupid."

I tried again. "Hey Helen, how's it hanging? You know your cousin Brenda? Yeah, her ghost came to me—with Ma, who's been hanging out with me since she bought the farm—and Brenda says you've got some cash waiting for you, so here's the attorney's number. K-thanks-bye." I stuck my tongue out at my reflection.

"Helen? Dude. It's me, your step kid. I was trippin' on acid this morning, and your cousin Brenda came to me, and said to call this number. Dude. It was awesome."

"Hey Helen. I'm crazy. Lock me up and throw away the key."

I plopped onto the bathroom floor, and lay down on my back. Maybe I could have Josh do it? He and Helen were close. Coming from him might make it sound less crazy, too. I shook my head.

Jake walked in. "Everything okay?"

"Yeah. No, not really." I reached out to him. "Help me up?"

He pulled me up, and we walked into the bedroom, and sat on the bed. "Tell me."

I burrowed my head into his chest. "I have a problem."

"You told Mel."

"Actually, I have two problems," I said.

He smirked. "You're welcome for the reminder."

"Thanks."

"So which problem do you want to talk about first?" He asked.

I raised my eyebrows and asked, "Is it selfish of me to say mine?"

"Nope. I think you're allowed."

I filled Jake in on the Brenda and Helen situation, and my fear of how Helen would react.

"Helen's a rational woman. Give her the facts, and ask her to follow up on them. Once she does, she'll believe you."

"That's what Mel said, too, but that's not the only thing I'm worried about."

He pressed his chin into the top of my head. "Then I'm missing something."

"What if she asks about my dad?"

"I'm sure she will."

"But I haven't heard from him."

"So you tell her that. You can't control who comes to you and who doesn't, and Helen will understand that."

"Mel said that too, I can't control who comes and who doesn't."

"We're both right again."

"I don't think my dad is going to come to me ever, Jake."

He sat up a little, and I moved to his side. "You can't be sure."

I nodded. "I can be pretty sure." I told him about Alo.

"Wow. You've just added another layer to the dip, huh?"

"Yup."

"I think Helen will be okay. You'll just have to explain it like the Indian dude did."

"Spirit guide," I said.

"Spirit guide. I wonder if they're all Indians because I'd like my spiritual guide to be Marilyn Monroe if that's at all possible."

"Of course you would, but I think yours is probably Granny from *The Beverly Hillbillies*."

"You're probably right."

Jake encouraged me to just lay it all out in my conversation with Helen, and then he asked about Mel, so I filled him in.

"She's what?" Jake said when I told him Carrie was pregnant. "Holy shit."

"Yup."

"She's not gonna be able to keep this quiet."

"I don't know. I'm not sure what I'd do if I was her."

"My guess is she's gonna nail Nick's balls to the wall," he said.

"As she should. Your balls would be in serious danger if you did that to me."

"What balls? The day we got married you hung those from your rearview mirror, and I haven't been allowed to touch them since."

"I let you have them back every so often. Like when you ride the Harley."

"A man has to have balls to ride a Harley."

"And a patient, understanding wife."

"And I have both."

"Okay, fine. We'll have sex tonight. Stop being so nice. It's making my stomach hurt."

We both laughed.

"Time to make that call, Ang."

He was right, but I stalled and changed the subject. "I know you talked to Emily already, and I want to know what happened."

"Later. This is more important."

"I knew you'd say that." I asked him to make sure no one interrupted me. He wished me good luck, and closed the bedroom door behind him.

I paced the length of my bedroom so many times I had to check the carpet for wear. I dialed Helen's phone, but clicked *end* before it rang. "Damn it," I mumbled. "You can do this, Angela. You can." I dialed again, and hung up again, too. My stomach flipped, and my mouth watered. I ran to the bathroom, and made it to the toilet just before I threw up.

I wiped my mouth, and splashed cold water on my face, sipped small handfuls, swished it around in my mouth, and then spit it out. I scrutinized my face in the mirror. "You can do this." I straightened my shoulders. "Yes, you can do this." I nodded at my image, then went and got my phone off the bed, and called my stepmom.

We made small talk before I dropped the bomb. "So have you heard anything more about your cousin, Brenda?"

"No. I've called her daughter, but she hasn't returned my calls. They weren't particularly close, so I'm not sure she'll have much to say."

I sat on the bed, crossed and uncrossed my legs, then got up and paced again. "I might have some information for you."

"About Brenda?"

"Yeah."

"Okay."

"Uh," I said, but couldn't find the next word anywhere in my head. I drew in a long breath, held it for a second, and then let it out.

"Hello? Angela?" Helen asked.

"I'm here, sorry."

"Oh, I thought maybe something happened to the call."

"Nope, just got distracted for a minute." My nerves were tingling. I rubbed my arms, hoping to make it stop.

"Are you okay?" She asked.

"Yeah, just tired. Hey, do you remember the dream Dad had about his grandfather? The one where he said his grandfather told him he'd be okay?"

"Yes, why?"

"Remember how Dad said he thought it was actually a visit from his grandfather?"

"Yes?"

"Well," I said, and that's when I completely chickened out. "I read an article recently that said there is evidence that kind of thing does happen. It said people who've reported having contact with their loved ones said that when they would go to bed, they'd ask the person they missed to visit them in a dream, and it would happen. I thought maybe you should give it a try with Brenda." I face-palmed myself in the forehead, and did a bad imitation of the chicken dance while I paced.

"I don't think so," she said, laughing. "I don't remember my dreams, but if I did, and that were possible, I'd ask your father and mine to visit before I'd ask Brenda."

I nodded. "Make sense. I always remember my dreams, so I figured I'd give it a try the other night. Told my parents to visit me while I slept, but I dreamed about an Indian." At least I said something truthful.

"Your father remembered his dreams too. He dream I did something mean to him, and he'd wake up mad at me the next day."

I laughed. "Like father, like daughter. I do that to Jake, too. Usually he breaks up with me, and ignores me. Mostly I dream that my teeth have fallen out, and I'm carrying them around in my hands, asking for someone to help me, but no one will."

"It must be genetic," she said. "Your dad dreamed about his teeth falling out, too."

I smiled, feeling a small connection to my dad.

After we hung up, I went back to the mirror, and chastised myself for being a chicken. "Now what are you gonna do?"

I lay on the bed, and examined the piece of paper with the contact information for Brenda's attorney. "Okay, Alo," I said. "If you're my

196   CAROLYN RIDDER ASPENSON

spirit guide like my mother says, here's your chance to guide me. How do I fix this?"

Alo must have been busy tending to his campfire because he didn't respond, so I texted my true sounding board, and asked him to come upstairs.

"For a quickie? Be right there." Jake wrote back.

He wasn't disappointed to find me sitting on the bed, fully clothed. "Okay," he said, closing and locking the door. "Let's get naked."

"I called Helen."

His expression changed from excited to concerned. "How'd it go?" He sat next to me on the bed.

"It didn't," I said, leaning my head on his shoulder. "I chickened out." I raised my eyes to his. "Bwok. Bwok."

He laughed. "It's okay, just call her tomorrow, and tell her."

I shook my head. "I can't. I made up some stupid story, and I'll look like a bigger idiot if I do that."

"Helen will understand, Ang."

I shook my head. "I can't tell her. I know I told Brenda I would, but I can't. I'm not ready."

He held my head in his hands, and kissed me gently. "It's okay."

I leaned my forehead into his. "No, it's not. What am I gonna do now?"

"We'll think of something," he said.

I fell back onto the bed. "What? Send her an email pretending to be the attorney, and tell her she's got money coming to her from a dead relative? I get those kinds of emails daily, and I'm sure she does, too."

"Maybe you could—"

I sat up, interrupting my husband. "Wait," I said. "I've got it." I grabbed the piece of paper, and showed it to Jake. "The number. I have the number." I waved the paper in the air. "I can call the attorney, and tell them I'm a family member, and say that Brenda told me about the lawsuit, and the loan with Helen. I'll ask them to contact her, but say I don't want to be involved or something, so Helen doesn't find out." I hugged Jake, and gave him a big, sloppy kiss. "You're so awesome, thank you for helping me." I leaned back, grabbed my phone and dialed the attorney's number.

He rolled his eyes. "That's what I'm here for."

"Don't leave," I said, holding the phone. "I want to know what you said to Emily, especially about her grounding."

I spoke with the attorney's assistant, and gave her the details, and asked her to keep me out of it. "I'd prefer to not be involved with please."

She didn't ask why, just said she'd have the attorney look into it, and if my information was correct, it would be taken care of.

"Great, thank you so much. I appreciate your help." I clicked *end*, and smiled at my husband. "So," I said, and lay down on top of the bed. "Tell me what happened with Emily, and then let's get naked."

The conversation was short, but the lovemaking was not.

* * *

The next morning, I got up before sunrise, fed the dog, and sat on the deck with a cup of coffee. I thought about what I'd done, and while I knew it wasn't exactly what Brenda had asked, it was something. My gift wasn't supposed to be about me, and I knew that by connecting me with Brenda, the universe was trying to teach me a lesson. I didn't expect an *A* for effort for handling the situation the way I did, but I hoped I didn't fail, either. Ma hadn't been around since our disagreement, and I feared my chickening out with Helen had broken my gift all over again.

"Ma, I think I screwed up. I didn't tell Helen, but I called the attorney, and they're gonna call her. I think it's a good compromise at least." I waited for her to say *boo*, but all I heard was the wind.

"I'm sorry about what I said before. Please, if you're mad at me—okay, but just let me know you're still around."

"Mom? You okay?"

I turned at the sound of Emily's voice, and quickly wiped my eyes with my hand. "Yeah, honey, I'm fine. Why are you up?"

She sat in the chair beside me. "I had to pee, and I heard you out here."

"I'm sorry. I didn't realize I was being loud."

"You weren't. My window's open."

"Oh, well go back to bed sweetie, it's early."

"I'm just gonna stay up. I have to work in like, two hours anyway." Her face was puffy, and her eyes were red.

"You've been crying again, huh?"

She nodded.

"I'm sorry."

She shrugged.

"After your shower, put some ice in a wash cloth, and hold it on your face. It'll help get rid of the puffiness."

"Do you think Dad's gonna, like, change his mind about Chandler?"

I didn't think he would, but saying that could open the floodgates again, and I didn't want her going to work a bigger emotional wreck than she already was. "I don't know, honey. We'll just have to wait it out, and see."

She handed me her phone. "Here."

I took it, and set it on the metal table. "Why? I said you could have it."

"I texted Chandler."

I raised my eyebrows, but didn't say anything.

"I told him I loved him. I, like, just wanted him to know." She wiped her eyes, and the floodgates opened anyway.

I nodded. I remembered that feeling, that intense need, and how it overwhelmed me, taking over my heart and my head, even though I couldn't quite understand it. "What did he say?"

"Nothing," she said, sobbing. "He never responded."

My heart ached for her. On the one hand, I thought Chandler was a jerk for not responding, but Jake's threat to bury him where no one could find him probably scared him enough to do as he was told. "Wanna know what I think?" I asked.

She sniffled and nodded.

"I think Chandler is a lousy jerk for not responding to you." I handed her back her phone. "I know you really care about this boy, Emily, but one thing is that people are consistent. Do you know what I mean?"

She scrunched her eyebrows and shook her head.

"I mean that you can look at how they've acted in other situations and get an idea about how they're going to react in the future."

She nodded.

"Think about the things he's said and done since you've been together and I suspect you'll find that maybe he doesn't care about you as much as you thought. I know that's hard to hear, but I don't want you sitting hear waiting for him to tell you he loves you when it's a good possibility he won't. Keep yourself busy and you'll begin to feel better, I promise."

She nodded and looked at her phone. "Maybe his phone's dead."

She didn't process a thing I said, but I was a fool to think she would. "Go get showered and take care of your face, okay?"

Emily hugged me, "Thanks, Mom," she said, and walked back inside.

I didn't know if she took what I said to mean she could continue to text Chandler or not. Truth be told, I didn't know if I meant that, either, but I really hoped she didn't.

I stayed on the deck to finish my coffee, and talk to my mother. "Ma? You here? Hello?"

I felt a light tap on my shoulder, and sat up straight. "Ma?"

Two more light taps brushed my shoulder. *Tap. Tap.*

I relaxed. "Nice try, but I'm not fallin' for it."

Tap. Tap.

I took a deep breath, closed my eyes, and focused my senses on the air around me. It didn't feel like Ma was there. I couldn't explain it, but it was different. I thought about how it felt when Bill made his appearance, and like then, I didn't feel threatened, so I relaxed.

"I don't know who you are," I said, "but in case you haven't heard, I'm having some communication issues, so I'm not sure I can help you."

I felt another tap on my shoulder, and laughed. "I don't know Morse Code, sorry." I felt two more taps, and had an epiphany of sorts. "Let's play a game. I'll ask you questions, and you tap once for yes, and twice for no, okay?

Tap.

I squealed. "All righty then. This is gonna be interesting. How about we start with the basics? We can totally do this."

Tap.

I rubbed my hands together, invigorated. "Are you female?"

Tap. Tap.

"Okay, you're a guy. Good to know. How old are you?"

Nothing.

"Oh, crap. Sorry. Yes or no questions only. Okay, when you died, were you over fifty?"

Tap. Tap.

I fist pumped the air. "Look at us, communicating without words. Is this awesome, or what?"

Tap.

I smirked. "Between twenty-five and fifty??"

Tap. Tap.

Oh boy. He was young. "Between fifteen and twenty-five?" I asked, my voice less excited.

Tap. Tap.

I sunk a little in my seat. The younger ones were always hard. "Oh, okay. Between five and fifteen?"

Tap.

I sighed. I wished we could just speak. I hated having to make this poor child struggle through my limited connection abilities. "I'm sorry we can't just communicate like normal. Were you younger than ten?"

Tap.

I was glad the universe hadn't taken back what little part of my gift I had left, but I was frustrated I couldn't make things easy for the boy. "Were you younger than five?"

Tap. Tap.

I leaned my head back in the chair. "So you were between five and ten. Okay." I didn't know anyone who'd lost a young child. "Do I know you?"

Tap. Tap.

I wasn't sure what to ask next. Thinking up yes or no answer questions wasn't easy. "I wish I could figure out how to communicate with you. I don't know what to ask or how to help you." I pressed on my right temple with the palm of my hand. "Give me a minute. We'll get this, okay?"

Tap.

I rubbed my neck. "Ma, I know you're mad at me right now, but can you put that aside for now? This little boy here needs our help."

Silence.

"Hello?"

Tap.

The right side of my mouth rose. "I know you're still there, buddy. That was for my mother. You don't happen to see anyone else around here, do you?"

Tap. Tap.

"That's what I figured." I ran my hand through my hair. I wasn't sure what to do. There were countless questions I could ask this spirit, but it would take hours. "I'm sorry, buddy. I'm trying, but I'm not sure this is going to work. I don't even know where to begin to help you."

From out of nowhere, a rock dropped, and hit me on the leg. I bent down, and picked it up. I rolled it between my hands. "A rock?"

Tap.

"A rock!" I said. "Of course! A rock! It was you, wasn't it? You're the one who hit me with the rocks."

Tap.

My heart beat faster. "Well, I'll be damned. And I blamed my mother." I felt a little bad for that.

Tap.

I bit my lower lip. "Let me think about this. What would rocks have to do with a boy your age? Aside from the fact that boys played with rocks, that is."

Tap.

"I didn't ask a question."

Another rock appeared on the deck railing. I picked it up. "Okay. Two rocks. What's that mean?"

Tap.

"Yes? Two rocks means yes?"

Tap. Tap.

I leaned back in my chair. "Cheese and rice, I'm confused."

Tap.

I rubbed my forehead. "Okay, lemme think." I held my hand up. "All right. So I know boys like to play with rocks. I have a son, and he did that a lot when he was younger. But they must me something more to you. Am I right?"

Tap.

"Did you collect them?"

Tap. Tap.

"Did you live by them?"

Tap.

My eyes widened. "You lived by them? That's good. Okay." I rubbed my chin, and then said, "Oh, around here? You lived around here?"

Tap.

"You lived near rocks. They're important to you. Are they important to you because you lived near them?"

Tap. Tap.

"I don't even know what the heck I'm talking about." I stood, and paced the deck. "Let's backtrack here. It was you who threw the rocks at me the day I ran at Central Park, right?"

Tap.

I nodded. I searched the recesses of my brain for a connection. After I lost my gift, I read as much about psychic mediums as I could, hoping it would spark something in me, and reignite my gift. It didn't, but I learned a lot. "Oh, I said. "I read somewhere that some spirits hold onto things related to their death. Do the rocks, or maybe Central Park even, have something to do with you dying?"

Tap.

I cheered myself, and gave the spirit a thumbs up, even though I couldn't see him. "Now we're getting somewhere."

Tap.

The back door opened and Jake came outside. "Hey, you're being kind of loud out here. What's going on?"

"The rocks," I said. "I figured out who's been throwing the rocks at me. It's a little boy, and it's got something to do with Central Park, but I don't know what yet, but we're communicating without Ma!" I was so excited I thought I'd peed a little.

"You can hear him?" Jake asked.

I shook my head. "No, but I'm asking him questions, and he's tapping me once for yes, and two for no."

"A little boy?"

I nodded.

"What about Central Park?"

"Like I said, I don't know, but it's got something to do with his death."

"Hold on." He walked back inside.

I shifted my head back and forth. "That's my husband, Jake," I said. "He'll be right back." I had no idea where he went, or why, but was too excited to care. "Okay, so you were at Central Park, and rocks mean something. So far, I'm on track, right?"

Tap.

"Okay. Let's see—"

Jake walked back out carrying his iPad, and interrupted me. "Ask him if he's Matthew Clough."

"Matthew Clough?" I asked, and then I remembered the name from the news. "The little boy they found in the park."

Tap.

I grabbed Jake's arm, and squeezed. "Oh God. He just tapped me."

Jake pressed his forehead into mine. "I'm sorry, babe."

"How'd you figure it out?"

He shrugged. "It sounded familiar, the rocks, the park, and a little boy. I can't believe we didn't think of it earlier."

A few months ago a five-year-old boy died at Central Park. He was playing in the woods, fell and hit his head on a rock. It took the police and volunteers three hours to find him because his babysitter said he'd run off. Initially there was speculation about her involvement, but the newspapers said it was determined an accident. It said he lived for a while after falling, and that if he'd been found sooner, he might have survived. It was a terrible tragedy.

"Matthew, I'm so sorry." I cried, tears dripping in a steady stream down my face. "I'm sorry I didn't figure it out sooner. Can you forgive me?"

Tap.

I turned toward Jake. "This whole time I was pissed about the rocks, and it was this poor child — this baby — trying to communicate with me. I'm such an idiot."

"You're not an idiot. You couldn't have known. You know now, and you can help him."

Tap.

I smiled. "Thanks, buddy, and you too, honey."

"What do you think he wants?" Jake asked.

I pressed my palm into my forehead, hoping to stop the headache I knew would come. "I don't know. I'm not even sure how to ask."

"Where's Fran?"

"Beats me. She didn't come when I called her before."

He burrowed his eyebrows. "That's odd."

"I think she's mad at me."

"Mad at you? As in truly mad at you or that bickering thing the two of you used to always do?" Jake asked.

I waved a hand in the air. "I don't know, but it'll be fine, I'm sure."

"Ah Madone, don't get your panties all up in a bunch, I'm not mad at you," Ma said.

I grabbed Jake's arm and squeezed again. "Ma! Finally! Where have you been? I have so much to tell you—"

She cut me off. "Such a *chiacchierone*—a talker—you are, but you're gonna have to wait. We got this little boy here—such a cutie patootie he is, too—and I'm guessin' he needs some help."

A soft, tiny voice spoke barely above a whisper. "Yuh huh."

I dug my nails into Jake's arm, not worrying that a bruise likely had begun to form. "I heard him."

Jake smiled, and then pulled his arm out of my death grip. He sat, and motioned for me to sit, too.

I did, and I took several deep breaths to calm myself. "Okay," I said. This is good. "Matthew honey, this will be a lot easier now that I can hear you, okay?"

"Yuh huh." His little voice trembled.

I wished I could give him physical comfort—a hug, or even a pat on the shoulder. "You probably want to see your mom and dad, don't you?"

"Yuh huh. Mommy's sad."

His voice didn't just tug at my heartstrings, it yanked those suckers right out. I wiped my eyes with my arm.

"You okay, babe?" Jake asked.

I nodded. "He said his mom is sad." I touched my hand to my heart. "She must be in so much pain. I can't even imagine. I need to tell her, Jake...I need to tell her he's okay."

Jake nodded, and wiped the tears on my cheeks. "You're amazing. I'm so proud of you."

I mouthed *thank you*, and then talked to Matthew. "Maybe we can go talk to your mommy, and she won't be so sad anymore. Would you like to do that?"

"I talk to her all the time, but she doesn't talk back."

"It's hard to explain, but if I go with you, I can talk to your mom for you. I can tell her what you're saying. Would you like that?"

"Yuh huh. That's what the nice man at the park told me. He told me to talk to you, but you didn't talk back either. So he helped me throw rocks at you because he said your psycho radio was broken. When my Daddy's phone was broken he took it to the store, and got a new one. You should take your radio to the store."

I giggled. If only it was that easy. "That nice man was right. My psycho radio *is* broken, but the old lady with us now? She makes it so I can hear you. She's got special powers or something, kind of like a superhero. Do you know what that is?"

"Yuh huh. *Power Rangers* are superheros. I like them."

Josh used to love the *Power Rangers* when he was that age, too. "Okay," I said, but Ma cut me off again.

"Hey, I'm not that old," she said. "And I stopped agin' too, when I bit the big one."

"You're wrinkly like my Nana, and gots a big tummy like her, too." Matthew said.

Oh boy.

"A big tummy? I don't have a big tummy. I'm skinny now, on account of the cancer and all."

"What's cancer?" He asked.

"Ma? Can we save that for later, please? Matthew needs us."

"Ah Madone. Fine."

"My mommy calls me Matty Bam Batty," he said.

Without trying, he'd just given me an important piece of validation for his mother. Kids never ceased to amaze me. "That's a good name. May I call you that, too?"

"My mommy said it's her special name for me. Will she be mad?"

"I don't think so but just in case, I'll stick with Matthew, okay?"

"Okay."

"Matthew," Ma said. "Do you know what Heaven is?"

"Yuh huh. It's God's and Grandpappy's house. They live on a cloud. That's what my mommy says."

"Your mommy's right, but there are a lot of people up in Heaven with your grandpa and God. It's a place where people go when they can't be here on earth anymore...when something happens to their bodies—people like me, and you, too. And everyone up there talks back when we talk to them."

"Mommy says talking back is sassin' and it's not good manners."

I covered my mouth, and giggled. Jake raised his eyebrows. "Hold on," I whispered.

"Well, your mommy's right about that, but I don't mean sass talkin'. I mean just regular talking—like you want your mom to do when you talk to her now," Ma said.

"Is my mommy mad at me?"

A lump rose in my throat. I swallowed it down, and spoke. "Oh honey, no. I'm sure your mom's not mad at you. That's not why she's not talking to you, I promise."

"You see," Ma said, "there's some people here that can still see and hear us—like Angela here—but most people can't—like your mom and dad. And that's kinda how we know we gotta go to Heaven. And Heaven is a whole lotta fun. They have some nifty stuff there. I bet you'll like it."

"The man at the park told me about Heaven, but I can't go 'cause I'm not 'posed to go anywhere without my mommy and daddy. That's why the man told me to talk to the lady with the frizzy hair."

I touched my hair.

"How about this?" Ma said. "Let's go see your mommy and daddy, and Angela will tell them anything you want. She'll even ask them if you can go up to Heaven, and if they say yes—which I bet they will—I'll take you up there myself, okay? You like that idea?"

I wiped my eyes. My mother was nothing short of amazing.

"Yuh huh."

I twisted toward Jake. "We're going to talk to his parents. Would you like to come?"

He held my hand. "And see you in action? Absolutely. I don't wanna miss any of these again if I don't have to."

"Matthew, do you think you can show us where your mommy and daddy live?" I asked.

"Yuh huh. I have a trampoline in my yard. You can jump on it if my mommy says it's okay."

Half of Georgia had a trampoline in their yard. I pressed my fingers into my cheekbone and then said, "That's okay. I'm a little too old for trampolines, buddy. Do you know the name of the street your house is on?" I asked.

"It's the blue house behind the park, Ang," Ma said. "I can get you there."

That was impressive. "It's amazing," I said. "How you can do that."

With all of the excitement, I'd totally forgotten about the time. Emily opened the back door, and said she needed a ride to work, her tone changing when she added, "Since I can't ever drive again."

"I need to feed the dog," I said. "Jake, can you run her there?"

He stood. "Yup."

We all walked inside, and I gave Emily an extra tight hug. "I love you so much," I said.

She pulled away, and nodded. "I know."

After they left, I told Matthew that I needed to take a shower before we went to talk to his parents.

"Pee-u," Ma said. "She sure does, doesn't she Matthew? She's stinky."

Matthew giggled. "You're funny."

I shook my head. "It's still early, and they're probably not even up yet, anyway."

"Mommy's in my room. She goes in there, and plays with my toys, and cries. I don't like it when she cries. Daddy sleeps in the chair all night with the TV on. Sometimes he has bad dreams, and screams. I told him it's okay to be scared, but he didn't hear me."

"I got an idea, Matthew. How 'bout me and you, we go to your house now, and I can show you some of my world famous trampoline moves? You like that idea?"

"You can jump on a trampoline?" He asked.

"You betcha I can. I got all these moves I learned from this man Bruce Lee. I can even teach ya a few if you'd like."

I held in a laugh. "You'll have to come back and get us though, you know."

"Yah, I know. You get rid of the stinkies, and we'll be back in a bit."

"Okay, but behave, Ma. You hear me?"

"Yah...yah, I hear ya."

CHAPTER THIRTEEN

JAKE CAME BACK, and jumped in the shower as I got out. We rushed to get ready, and I left a note for Josh next to the TV remotes, where I was sure he'd find it.

"You ready honey?" Jake asked.

"Yeah," I said. "I'm just sending Mel a quick text. I haven't heard from her, and I'm a little worried."

"We can stop there on the way home if you'd like," he said.

"That's okay. She probably just needs space, and a little time to think right now, I'm sure." I put my phone in my pocket. "Ma? We're ready."

"I'm here. I left the boy at his house," she said. "He's right about his mom. That woman's a wreck, and his dad? He don't do much but sit on the chair and stare at the TV."

I sighed. "I can't even imagine."

"Let's get a move on," Jake said, and walked into the garage.

In the car, I rubbed my hands on my Capri pants. They were shaky, and clammy. I couldn't put my finger on it, but something about this felt different. Maybe it was because Matthew was young, or maybe it was the publicity surrounding his death. It just felt different. "I need a coffee. Do you mind stopping at Starbucks?"

"You're having decaf," he said. "Your hands are shaking."

"It's nerves. I need caffeine to calm them."

He shook his head in defeat.

"Ah Madone. Coffee. Just one more time. Is that too much to ask?"

"Ma wants coffee too," I told Jake.

"It's got to be hell not having it," he said.

"You got that right," Ma said.

"Ma says you're right."

"Usually am."

"Good grief."

We got our coffee at a drive-thru Starbucks, and Ma gave us directions to Matthew's house.

"Amazing. It backs up right to the woods of the park," I said when we pulled up next to Matthew's house.

"Maybe that's why they got that crapzu vine growing all over," Ma said.

I laughed. "Kudzu, Ma. We went over this repeatedly before you died."

Jake shook his head, laughing.

She laughed, too. "I know, the Japanese brought it over, and it's good for wildlife—yada yada yada. But it ain't good for landscape. Jake ought a give Matthew's dad a few pointers on how to keep a yard looking nice."

"Aw, she just complimented you, honey."

"Me?" He asked.

"Yes, you. She said you keep a nice lawn."

"Well, I don't know how nice it would be if I had to deal with that crapzu stuff."

I laughed. "Okay," I said, and bit my bottom lip. "I'm scared shitless."

"You got this, honey."

"Yah, what he said, honey," Ma said.

I rolled my eyes. "It just feels different. I can't explain it."

"Just go in there, do what you do, and it'll be fine," Jake said.

I laid my head back on the seat. "You're right. I know you're right. I can totally do this." I took a gulp from my coffee. "Let's get this party started."

I got out of the car, marched up to the front door, and rang the bell.

Matthew's mother answered. Her hair, long, blond and curly, was frizzy and greasy and her face, swollen and puffy. She looked like she was pretty once, but death had taken her beauty when it took her son. "May I help you?" She asked.

I shook my head to break myself from stare mode. "My name is Angela Panther, and this," I pointed to Jake, "is my husband, Jake."

"Yes?"

"Mrs. Clough, right?" I asked.

She nodded.

"I'm sorry to disturb you, but I have some information for you. May we come in?"

Her eyes darted from me to Jake, and back again. "Information? Thank you, but I don't need any more grief pamphlets. They don't work anyway."

She went to close the door, but I put my foot in it. I needed to thank Mel for that move.

The door swung open, and a man holding a shotgun said, "You did not just stick your foot in my door. That right there is trespassing. I'd call the police, but they're useless. I'd be happy to use this though." He rubbed the gun.

"Well, ain't that crazy." Ma said. "That thing isn't even loaded. But nobody's gonna threaten my kid like that."

The gun flew out of the man's hands and landed at the front of the yard, next to the mailbox.

"What the—" the man said.

Matthew's mother's jaw dropped. "How did you do that?" She asked me.

I shrugged. "I didn't."

The man tried to close the door, but it wouldn't budge. He grunted. "Honey, help me out here, the door's stuck."

I glanced at Jake and whispered. "It's Ma."

He nodded, and whispered back. "I figured." He stepped an inch closer to the door. "Mrs. Clough, please, if you'll give us a moment, we can explain everything."

Matthew's mother studied me, her expression a mix of confusion and desperation. "It was Matthew, wasn't it?"

I shook my head. "No, it wasn't, but he's here, and he wants me to talk to you."

She stood in front of the door, blocking the man from closing it. "I'm letting them in Matt, and you're not going to stop me." Her posture stiffened, and I saw her push her back into the door.

Mr. Clough cleared his throat. "This is a bunch of bullshit, and you know it," he said.

"Matt, please," Mrs. Clough said.

He glared at me. "You're not the first opportunist to come knocking on our door."

I puffed out my chest, stood up straighter and said, "I am not an opportunist, Mr. Clough. I have nothing to gain from coming here. I'm only doing it because Matthew asked me to."

Jake got all puffy too, and started to speak, but I stopped him. "Jake, I've got this," I said, putting my hand on his arm. I spoke to Matthew's mother. "Matthew said you called him Matty Bam Batty. I call my son Little Man."

She blinked, and tears dropped down her cheeks. "Yes, I did." She moved aside and said, "Matt, the gun can't sit in the front yard like that. Please, go get it."

He didn't budge. "I don't want these kind of people in my house, Amanda."

"Matt, it's my house too. I have a say in who comes in and who doesn't, and they're coming in. Your gun flew out of your hands, and practically landed in the street. It flew out of your hands, Matt. Do you understand? They're different, and I'm going to listen to what she has to say, whether you like it or not. Now please, go get the damn gun."

Matt's mouth flattened into a thin line. His eyes narrowed, and I was worried he'd get the gun and shoot me. I turned and watched him walk toward it.

"Don't worry," his wife said. "I took out the shells last week, and threw them away. He knows. He's just hoping to scare you."

"Well, it worked," I said.

She shrugged. "He's harmless. Please, come in."

"Thank you, Mrs. Clough."

She wiped her eyes with her hand. "Please, call me Amanda."

"Amanda, okay."

We walked into the house, and sat in the living room.

"Hey Matthew," Ma said. "That was some pretty exciting stuff wasn't it?"

"Yuh huh. I'm scared."

"Aw, don't be little guy. It's all gonna be fine. I promise."

Mr. Clough walked in, glanced at us in the living room, and walked away, muttering, "I'm not gonna listen to that crap."

"I'm sorry," Amanda said.

"That's my mommy's other name," Matthew said. "But I get to call her the mommy, and she said I'm special 'cause no one else ever will."

Oh no. "Amanda, can you have any more children?"

Her eyes widened and she shook her head, but didn't speak.

"Ah, geez," Ma said. "That's terrible."

"I'm sorry," I said.

"Did he tell you that?" Amanda asked.

"Sort of. He said that you told him he was special because no one else could call you mommy."

"It's okay, Mommy," Matthew said. "You don't have to cry anymore. I don't like it when you're sad."

"Matthew doesn't want you to cry anymore. He doesn't like it when you're sad."

"Can he hear me?" She asked.

I nodded.

"Matty Bam Batty—my baby. Mommy misses you so much." She rubbed her hands together. "So much it hurts, and sometimes I cry. I'm sorry it makes you sad."

I served as messenger between the two for another thirty minutes. We laughed, and cried, and I watched Amanda's face gain color, watched her eyes come back to life. Jake sat silent, and I knew he was thinking about our kids.

Matt Clough had come back for a minute or two, but shook his head, and left again.

"Matthew," Amanda said. "Why were you alone in the woods? You know you're not supposed to leave Maria's side."

"But I didn't, Mommy. We went on a special walk so we could find pretty flowers for you. Maria said there were all kinds of pretty flowers in the woods."

Oh no. If what Matthew said was true, then why would the babysitter say she wasn't with him? "Matthew," I said. "Can you tell me what happened that day? Do you remember?"

"Yuh huh."

Amanda looked at me. "What's he saying?"

I swallowed hard, and shook my head. "I'm not exactly sure, but I'll tell you when he's finished."

She nodded.

"Okay, Matthew, go ahead," I said. "What do you remember from that day?"

"I remember playing catch with Maria at the park."

"That must have been fun," I said.

"She yelled at me 'cause I couldn't throw the ball good."

"That's okay Matthew, I can't do that either."

"I tried, but one time when I throwed it, it bounced, and it hit her in the knee. She got real mad, but then she was nice, and told me about the flowers."

"Is that when you went to get them?"

"Yuh huh."

"Did you go alone?"

"Uh huh. Mommy said not to go in the woods alone."

"Was Maria in the woods with him?" Amanda asked.

I bit my bottom lip. "Amanda, I think it's important for your husband to be here. Do you think you could talk to him?"

Her hands shook, and her face turned red. "Maria was in the woods with him, wasn't she?" She stood up. "I'll get Matt." As she walked into the hallway, she turned around, and said, "I knew she was lying. Matthew would never have gone into the woods alone."

"What's going on?" Jake asked.

I quickly explained what Matthew said.

"You think she had something to do with him falling?" He asked.

I shrugged. "I don't know."

"She did it, all right," Ma said. "And you gotta tell them, Ang."

"We don't know that for sure, Ma."

"You don't, but I do."

"What's that supposed to mean?" I asked, but she didn't answer because Amanda and Matt walked back into the living room.

"I'm only doing this for my wife," Matt said. "She can believe what she wants, but Matty's gone."

Matt Clough was a close-minded ass. Being a skeptic was one thing, but to not even consider the possibility that he son could be there was unacceptable to me. "Mr. Clough, have you sought help for your nightmares?"

"Excuse me?"

"Your nightmares. The ones you have in your chair in front of the TV."

"I don't have nightmares."

"Then why do you scream at night?" I asked.

His eyes shifted, searching the room. "How do you—." He stopped because a family photo dropped from the table next to him, and landed on the floor.

"Sorry about that," I said. "That's my mother. She's dead, too. When she gets mad, she knocks stuff down, and throws things—like your gun—don't you, Ma?"

The picture floated through the air and landed right on Matt Clough's lap. He jumped, and screamed, "Shit."

I got serious. "Mr. Clough, why don't you ask me something you think only Matthew could answer? Maybe that will help you believe."

He shook his head. "I...I don't..." His voice trailed off, and tears welled up in his eyes.

"Matty," Amanda said, "Remember that time Daddy went to the doctor? You were really worried about him then, weren't you?" Her eyes scanned the room.

"Do you remember that, Matthew?" I asked.

"Yuh huh," he said. "I was scared."

I nodded. "He remembers."

Matt Clough sat back down, but didn't speak.

"Matty, you gave Daddy something to take with him that day. Do you remember what it was?" Amanda asked.

"My Buzz Lightyear, because he projected Daddy."

Ma laughed.

"Thank you, Matthew," I said. "A Buzz Lightyear doll. He said it would project his dad."

Matt's eyes widened. "How is this possible?"

Jake laughed. "I was there once too, Matt," he said. "When Angela's mother came back."

"Now that was funny," Ma said.

I smirked. "It was." I turned to Matthew's parents. "Matthew said he and Maria went into the woods together, to pick flowers for Amanda. He said that before that, she was upset because he'd accidentally hit her in the leg with a ball."

Matt clenched his hands into fists, and pressed them into his thighs. He shook his head. "We told the police she was lying, but they didn't believe us."

"Amanda," Jake said. "May I have some paper and a pen?"

"Oh, yes. Let me get that. We'll need the details for the police." She got up and walked out of the room.

I shot Jake a look, and he said, "This could be important."

I took a deep breath. "I'm not going to the police, Jake. I can't do that."

He kneeled in front of me. "Angela, you need to find out the truth about what happened from Matthew. If it's what we think, then the Cloughs will need to tell the police. You know that."

I shook my head. "No, Jake. I can't. Do you know what that will do to our lives?" I shook my head again. "No." The scene played before my eyes. Reporters, police—I saw my house bombarded with them. I saw people staring at me at the grocery store, whispering behind my back. I saw Emily hiding in her room because her mother was the crazy woman who thought she talked to dead people. I knew it wasn't supposed to be about me but this was my life that could change and I was scared.

I pushed Jake away, and stood. "I'm done. I'm not doing this. I can't. It's my life that'll be changed, and yours, too, and God Jake, we have children. I can't do this to them." I was suddenly dizzy. I swayed, and grabbed onto the arms of the chair, sitting back down. The room spun in circles. I closed my eyes, but it didn't help. I dug my fingers into the arms for the chair. "Oh, God. Oh God. Oh God."

"It's okay, honey. It's gonna be okay." Jake kneeled before me again, his hands on my knees.

I pushed his hands away. "I can't do it, Jake. I can't." I fanned myself. "It's really hot in here. Is it hot in here?"

Jake shook his head.

"I'll get her a glass of water," Matt Clough said.

Amanda came back with the pen and paper. "Here—oh." She stood, staring at me.

"I can't breathe," I said. I clutched my chest. My mouth was dry, and my hands shook. I felt bile rise in my throat.

I tried to take big breaths, but couldn't get the air to go down. "I...I can't breathe."

The room spun again, and I pushed my back into the chair. I thought I was going to pass out, but instead the room filled with a bright light, and a burst of cold air sent an instant chill through my body. I looked at Jake, kneeling before me. His lips moved, but he sounded far away, like he was in a tunnel. I closed my eyes, and shook my head, and then a calm came over me, and I relaxed. When I opened my eyes, I understood why.

"You're okay, Sunshine."

Behind Jake, clear as the sun in a blue sky, was my dad. "You can do this," he said. "I won't let anything bad happen to you. I've got your six." And then he shimmered away.

I shook my head. "Dad?"

"No honey, it's me," Jake said. "Are you okay? You're scaring me, babe."

My heartbeat returned to normal, and I still felt the calm from seconds before. I smiled at Jake. "It's okay. I'm okay. Where's Ma?"

Jake shook his head. "Uh..."

"What? You see your father, but you can't see me? Pfft, Pauly's my favorite because your dad was always yours," Ma said.

I shifted toward my mother's voice, fully expecting to see my mother floating there in the blue gown she died in, but I didn't. I sunk back in the chair.

"It's all right Angela," Ma said. "He probably got special permission or something. Lord knows he's no advanced spirit like me."

"I'm sorry, Ma." I couldn't think of anything else to say.

"Don't be sorry, it ain't your fault," she said.

Amanda gave Jake the glass of water, and he handed it to me. "Here, drink this. It might help. Are you sure you're okay? We can come back later if need be."

Jake was giving me an out, offering me a chance to walk away, but I couldn't. My dad was right. I could do it, and I had to do it. It wasn't about me. It was about the Cloughs. They were devastated at the loss of their child, and if their babysitter was involved, they needed to know. The police needed to know. What I wanted didn't matter.

I took a sip of the water and nodded. "Yeah, I'm sure. I'm okay, honey." Jake lifted an eyebrow, and I smiled. "I promise," I said. "I'm sorry," I said to the Cloughs. "What I do isn't common knowledge, and I've really struggled with it. I'd like to finish talking with Matthew, and hopefully what he says will help you in some way."

They both nodded.

"Tell them I'm showing the lady my truck," Matthew said.

"That's a nice truck, Matthew," Ma said. "As a matter of fact, I just met a little boy the other day with one just like that."

"Is he in Heaven?" Matthew asked. "If my mommy and daddy let me go there, maybe I can play with him."

Those few words made me realize how blessed I was. My kids were safe and alive, and so was Jake, but two families I'd just met were grieving the loss of a father and a son. I'd helped one, and helping the other was just as important. "That's awesome, dude," I said, and told his parents about the truck.

"Did another boy pass?" Amanda asked.

I shook my head. "No, his father did. He was the man they found in the big lake."

"Oh, I heard about that on the news," Matt said. "He was fishing."

I nodded. I cracked my knuckles, and took a deep breath. "Okay, Matthew, can you finish telling me what happened that day at the park? Your parents might have some questions, too. Okay?"

"Yuh huh."

Matthew repeated how Maria had walked him into the woods. They'd gone off the path because she said the flowers were back farther away from the path. He said they'd got to the little creek where the flowers and rocks were, and he bent down to pick a flower, and then he showed it to Maria, and there were people everywhere, but nobody would talk to him except the nice, old man. He said the man asked him to come with him, but Matthew told him he couldn't because his mommy would be upset.

I told Matthew's parents the whole story. It wasn't definitive proof that Maria was involved with his death, but it did prove that she lied to the Cloughs, and the police, about the boy running off.

"Ask him if he remembers anything from just before he saw all of the people," Matt Clough said.

"He can hear you," I said.

"Oh." He spoke to his son, his voice unsteady. "Matty, think hard buddy. Can you remember right before you saw the people? Do you remember falling, and hitting your head?"

"Mommy and Daddy said to be careful by rocks because you could get a boo boo, so I was extra careful, and I didn't fall," Matthew said.

"Are you sure, Matthew?" Ma asked. "You're not in trouble, so don't be afraid to tell Angela what happened, okay?"

"I didn't fall. I was careful."

I shook my head. "He says he didn't fall, and that he was being careful." I looked at his parents. "Okay buddy, you're doing great. Your parents are really proud of you right now."

Amanda wiped her eyes. "Oh, Matty Bam Batty, I am so proud of you," she said. "You're such a good boy. But it's really important that you remember how you got hurt. Do you think you can do that? Think extra hard, okay? Like how you used to think when you were trying to read a word in your *Goodnight Gorilla* book. Remember?" She let out a sob, and Matt rubbed her back.

"That's my favorite book Mommy, and I can read it all by myself now."

"Matthew, I'm gonna tell your mom that, and while I do, do you think you can think real hard for her?" I asked.

"Yuh huh."

I told them that Matthew could read the book on his own now, and Amanda cried harder.

Ma giggled. "He's scrunchin' his face like he's gotta poop."

I giggled, too, and when Matt curled the side of his upper lip, I explained why. "My mother says he looks like he's got to go to the bathroom."

Both Matt and Amanda laughed. "That's what he did when he was thinking hard," Amanda said. "It was precious." She cried more, but it sounded less sad. It was progress.

"I don't remember," Matthew said.

My shoulders sank. "He doesn't remember."

"Tell them I'm sorry. I shouldn't a gone to the woods, and I did."

My heart ached for Matthew. "He wants you to know how sorry he is for going in the woods."

Amanda's eyes searched the room. "Matty, I want you to listen to me, okay? You did not do a thing wrong. You don't have to be sorry. Do you understand? You're a good, good boy, baby."

"But I don't want them to be sad anymore," he said. "I want them to be happy, and to go for walks again."

Even in death Matthew carried the weight of the world on his shoulders. "He doesn't want you to be sad. He wants you to go for walks again, and to be happy."

"Mommy and Daddy used to laugh a lot, but they don't laugh anymore."

"He said you don't laugh like you used to."

Amanda sobbed. "I know baby. I'm so sorry. We just miss you so much."

"I think the old man at the park wanted to take Matthew to Heaven," I said. "My mother's told me that our loved ones come to guide us when it's our time, but Matthew didn't know the man, and like he said, he didn't want to go without your okay. He told me his grandpa lived on a cloud with God, and I think that might be the man. Do you have a picture of him?" I asked. "He said the man helped him contact me so he could talk with you."

"It's my dad," Amanda said. "He died when I was fifteen." She got up. "I have a picture of him in the family room. I'll get it."

"I'm going to the police," Matt Clough said. "They need to know Maria lied. When they hear this, they'll have to do something. I'll force them to do something. She did it, I know she did it."

I cringed. I knew he was right, he should go to the police, but I wasn't prepared for what that would mean for my family and me.

Ma spoke. "He's right Ang. She did it, and she's gonna confess. All's the cops gotta do is put a little pressure on her, you know, like they do on Law & Order, and she'll pop."

That didn't make me feel any better. "Are you sure?"

"Yah, I'm sure. It's my super spirit powers, they're tellin' me."

I pictured my father's spirit telling me it would be okay, and took a deep breath. "It will be okay, like Dad said, right Ma?"

"It will be okay, like he said."

Amanda came back with the picture, and handed it to me. "This is my father, Charles Platt."

"That's what the old man said his name was," Matthew said. "And that's him, but who's the girl?"

"Matthew said that's the man he saw after he died." I pointed to the girl in the photo. "Is this you?"

Amanda nodded, tears pouring down her face. "My daddy came for him. Oh, Matty, you can go with Grandpa. It's okay."

"Can he find him again? What if it's too late?" Matt Clough asked.

"It's not too late," Ma said. "He's here now. Us celestial beings, we got it together."

"Hi," Matthew said. "Mommy says you're my grampa."

I smiled at Amanda. "Your father is here."

Amanda reached her hand to her mouth, and gasped.

"Hi Matthew," he said. "Your mommy's right. She's is my baby girl, and that makes you my grandson."

"She's not a baby, silly. She's a mommy," Matthew said.

"Yes, she is," Charles said. "Angela, I'm glad you can hear us now. My apologies for the rocks, but it was all I could think to do."

"I understand."

"Please, would you tell my daughter that I'm so very proud of the woman she's become?"

I nodded, and wiped the tears pooling in my eyes. "Your dad said he's so proud of the woman you've become."

Amanda nodded, but didn't speak.

"We should go now, Matthew," Charles said. "There are a lot of little children waiting to meet you."

"Okay," Matthew said. "I'm gonna go now."

I choked back a lump. "He's going now," I said.

Matty's parents sobbed, and Matt pulled his wife into an embrace. As I watched them hug Matthew appeared with them, his arms wrapped around his parents. I gasped.

"You can see him, can't you, Ang?" Ma said.

I nodded.

"Well what about me? Can you see me?"

I froze, afraid to turn for fear that if I did, she wouldn't be there—that I still couldn't see her. I wasn't sure I could handle that disappointment again.

"Ah Madone," Ma said, and then, in the blue nightgown she died in, my mother appeared in front of me. "Boo."

I covered my mouth with my hand, and nodded as tears fell down my cheeks.

"I'm gonna go now," Matthew said, getting my attention.

I smiled at my mom, and gathered my composure, which was hard because Ma was so pumped, she wouldn't shut up. "Finally, for cyin' out loud! That took forever!"

I didn't let anyone in on my secret, but Matthew knew. He saw me look him in the eye, and smiled. I smiled too. As he held his grandfather's hand, he said his last goodbye, and then he and Charles shimmered away.

"They're gone," I said.

The Clough's both had tears in their eyes, but Matt's face was stern. "We need to get to the police," he said.

Amanda nodded.

I turned to Jake. "We should go."

Jake nodded, and handed Matt Clough the notes he'd taken. "I'm not sure what this will do, but hopefully it helps."

"Thank you," Matt said, and then he approached me. "I'm sorry."

I shook my head, and hugged him. "It's okay. People threaten me with guns on a daily basis."

He nodded. "What you've done for us? I don't know how to thank you."

"It's okay, honest."

"I know you're worried about the police," he said. "I promise you, Amanda and I will do our best to leave you out of it."

"I'm not sure that's gonna be possible, Matt," I said. "You need to be honest with them, or I'm worried they won't pursue Maria."

"They may not if we tell them our son told us information through you."

I nodded. "There is that, but you have to find a way to get them to talk to Maria. My mother assured me she was involved in Matthew's death. She said Maria would confess if they push on her."

Amanda gasped and Matt's eyes light up. He hugged me again. "Thank you, Angela." He turned to Jake, and shook his hand. "And thank you, too. Thank you both so much."

*   *   *

"Well I'll be damned, Ang. You did it. Who'd a thunk?" Ma said outside.

"Talk about having no faith, Ma. Thanks."

"Oh, I had faith. I knew it was coming. That's why I had to stay away, on account of I didn't wanna get myself in trouble by blabbing. Sometimes I get a little excited, and I can't keep it in."

"You *knew*?"

She smirked, and pointed to the top of her head. "Course I knew. Super spirit powers, remember? I knew you'd get your gift back all along, I just wasn't sure when. You had to learn some lessons first, and I was a little worried that would take forever, seeing as you're so hard-headed and all."

I gave her the stink eye.

She spun in circles like a little girl trying on a new dress for the first time. "So, how do I look? Haven't aged a bit have I?"

"I don't know," I said, scrutinizing her slightly transparent face. "I think I see a few more age spots, and a couple more wrinkles around your eyes."

Her mouth dropped open, and I could see the grass behind her through it. "What? You're kidding me, right? That ain't right, agin' in the afterlife. They said it don't happen."

"You can see Fran?" Jake asked.

"Yup," I said, and waved it off. "Just another day in the life of a medium." I clicked the key fob to unlock the door. "You drive," I said. "I've got a lot to tell you."

He smiled. "I can only imagine."

CHAPTER FOURTEEN

I FILLED JAKE IN ON EVERYTHING.

He smiled, and the laugh lines around his eyes spread to his hairline. It was one of the sexiest things about him. "Your dad always had impeccable timing."

"And apparently he still does." I leaned back in the seat, and my body relaxed.

"What about the police?" Jake asked. "You okay with the Cloughs going to them?"

I tensed, and sat up straight. "I don't really have an option, do I?" I ran my hand through my hair. "If they tell them about me, what's gonna happen?"

"I don't know, honey, but get through it. Look at everything else we've been through. We'll just add it to the list." He smiled, but his hands gripped the steering wheel so tight, his knuckles were white. He was scared, too.

But he was right. We'd been through so much together, and we'd always ended up better, stronger. From job layoffs, to medical issues, the deaths of my parents, and of course Emily's drama, we'd been through a lot together. If we could make it through all of that, we could make it through anything. "Emily, Jake. You know this could really screw her up."

"You mean, *would really screw her up more.*"

I pressed my thumbs into my temples. "Oh, God. If this gets out— that I can talk to dead people—Emily's going to end up institutionalized. It'll send her over the top."

"Let's just take this one step at a time, honey. We don't even know if the Cloughs will mention you to the cops. If they do, we'll figure out what to do next. It'll be fine."

* * *

Josh was sitting at the kitchen counter, holding a shattered frame of a picture of Emily and Chandler. "Mom, Emily's upstairs crying again. I tried to see if she was okay, but she threw this at me, and slammed the door shut," he said.

I pushed the threat of my gift being discovered to the back of my mind, but kept close the possibility of Emily being institutionalized, just for a different reason. "You're a good brother, Josh. Thank you," I said, and took the picture from him. "Wish me luck, I'm going up."

Jake didn't offer to come, scaredy cat.

I knocked on Emily's door. "Go away Josh," she yelled, her voice nasally sounding.

"It's me, honey. Can I come in? Just don't throw anything at me, okay?"

Emily pulled the door open, sighed, then turned, and flung herself onto her bed, crying. I shut the door, grabbed the box of tissues off her desk, and sat next to her. "Here," I said, holding a tissue out. "Blow your nose."

She turned, took the tissue, blew, and handed it back to me, then plopped her face right back into her pillow, and sobbed some more.

I wanted to be patient and understanding, but the drama got old, fast. "Aren't you supposed to be at work?" I checked the clock on her nightstand, unsure of how long we'd been gone. The clock was dark. She'd probably unplugged it, and used the alarm on her cell phone. She hadn't responded. "Emily?"

"He broke up with me. Are you happy? He, like, totally said it was because of you and Dad." Her voice was muffled by the pillow.

"Em, sit up honey, I can't understand you."

She flopped over, her face red and puffy, and her eyes bloodshot, as if she'd been out partying all night.

"I thought your dad had already done that for him," I said. "So I'm a little confused."

She pulled another tissue from the box, and blew her nose again.

"He said you and Dad were too strict, and...and that he, like, tried to love me, but, like, I just wasn't loveable. He said I was still a stupid baby that, like, had to do what her parents said, and he needed a real woman."

Oh boy. Chandler was a tool.

I lay down next to her. "You've got a boogie hangin'," I said. That got a half smile from her. "Come here." I put my arm around her, and pulled her close, her head on my chest. "Honey, I'm sorry. But the truth is, Chandler's an idiot. I know you're going to want to defend him, but hear me out first, okay?"

She nodded into my chest.

"If a man—a boy in this case—truly loves a girl, he doesn't say things like that. He doesn't call you stupid, and he doesn't say you're not loveable. Real love isn't like that, honey."

"But he's right, Mom. You and Dad are too strict. He said it's stupid to, like, get into our business like that. And he's right, Mom. I'm not a kid anymore. I'm not a baby."

Was stupid the only adjective teenagers knew? Everything was always stupid to them. School was stupid. Rules were stupid. Cleaning their rooms was stupid. Personally, I thought they were stupid, but I didn't say that.

"Emily, you're seventeen, so by law, yes, you're still a child. Are you a baby? No, of course not, but let's be honest, sometimes you act like one." I pushed her hair from her eyes. "The other night, what happened? It was wrong. If Chandler loved you like he said, he wouldn't have put you in that position. He wouldn't have parked in a barely lit parking lot, and had sex with you—for the first time mind you, which is a pretty big deal—in the back seat of a car. That's just all sorts of wrong, kiddo. And let's not forget that you were grounded. I'm sure he knew that. If he loved you, he wouldn't have wanted you to get into more trouble by going out."

"But I wanted to Mom, that's not his fault."

"It might not be entirely his fault, but whose idea was it?"

She looked away. "His."

"Uh huh. Emily, you deserve better than him. You're a smart, funny, beautiful girl. Don't aim so low in the boyfriend department. There are plenty of boys out there who would love to call you their girlfriend. Be pickier, and show them you deserve to be treated well, because you do."

"I'm never going to find someone to love me, Mom." She cried into my chest.

"I don't believe that for a minute. And you know what? If Chandler had any balls, he could have come here, apologized to your father and me, talked with us about how we expect our daughter to be treated, and things may have worked out."

"But I didn't know that, so I didn't tell him."

"That's kind of the point. You shouldn't have to tell him. If you meant as much to him as he means to you, he would have done it on his own, but it didn't even come to mind. I'm sorry, sweetie."

"Things are different now, Mom, and you don't know Chandler. Maybe I should tell him."

I leaned back, and grabbed her phone from the nightstand. "I don't think so, honey. I'm gonna keep this for a bit. If Chandler changes his mind, and contacts you, then let me know, and we'll go from there. But for now, I think it's best you back off, give him some space, and try to move on."

"I don't want to. I want to be with him."

I told Emily about my first serious boyfriend, and how hard it was when we broke up. How sad I was, and how much it hurt, but that eventually, a little each day, things got better. And how one day I realized he wasn't the first thing I thought about when I woke up, and he wasn't constantly on my mind. I told her it would happen that way for her, too, but she just needed to give it time.

"I don't think I'll ever forget him," she said.

I nodded. "Probably not, but remembering someone, and still having feelings for him aren't the same thing."

"I should have listened to you. I shouldn't have had sex with him."

I nodded again, but didn't say anything, fearful the dreaded, *I told you so* would sneak out.

* * *

I sat on the deck with Jake, and filled him in on the latest Emily crisis. It took a bit of convincing, but he finally changed his mind about finding Chandler, and fulfilling his promise.

Josh escaped the drama, and went to Turner's for a sleepover again. He was pretty good at that escape thing.

Jake picked at the wood in the fire pit, even though there was no fire. "Have you heard from Mel?"

"Nope, and I'm really starting to worry, too." I grabbed my phone from my pocket and sent her a text. "Worried. Please call or text me. XOXO."

"I'm sure she's okay."

"I don't know, Jake. Her husband is having an affair, and the girl is pregnant. That's not an easy thing to be okay with."

"Are we going to talk about my testicles again?"

"Ew. I really hate that word."

"What do you want me to call them?"

"Nuggies."

"That's what we called Josh's balls when he was a baby."

I grimaced. "That word's worse than testicles."

He shook his head, and laughed. "I'm not physically capable of referring to my own balls as nuggies. Sorry."

I got up, and sat on his lap. "Whadda ya mean yours? Those things became mine when we got married."

"Doesn't matter. They're still attached."

"You know what? You can keep them. They've been closed for business for a long time anyway."

He laughed. "Maybe Mel just needs some time, but I hope she's at least called that attorney."

"Time's the last thing she needs. She needs to be divorced, and get on with her life, or it's gonna go on without her."

"Okay, Fran. Whatever you say."

I laughed. "Good Lord, I'm becoming her, aren't I?"

He pushed me away a little, and his eyes scanned my body. "Your chest is significantly smaller."

I smacked him on the shoulder. "You're a tool."

"But you love me."

"Lucky for you." I leaned my head onto his shoulder, and sighed. "Today was intense. I'm exhausted."

"Me too, and you did all the work. I was just the secretary."

I laughed. "A hot secretary, too. Do you think my dad will come around again?"

"I don't know, babe, but I wouldn't expect him to. It doesn't seem to be his thing."

I took a sip of my wine. "I know." I exhaled.

We sat on the deck, and talked for a long time. Jake brought up burying Chandler again, and I finally convinced him it was a bad idea.

"Seriously. I can see dead people. He'd probably haunt us."

He frowned. "That would be bad, huh?"

"Yes, Jake. That would be bad."

I limited my wine to only two glasses, but that was still enough to give me a buzz, and I was frisky. "If we don't go to bed now, your window of opportunity might close."

He was up and inside in two steps.

I stumbled upstairs a little slower, and checked on Emily, who was sound asleep in her bed. I pulled the covers over her, and kissed her on the forehead. Jake had jumped in the shower, and by the time he was done, I was undressed, and passed out on the bed. His window had closed, after all.

* * *

The next morning didn't call for a greasy breakfast, and I was thankful. I checked my messages, but still hadn't received anything from Mel. Jake was up and out, spending the day in Atlanta, visiting clients, and Emily was up, getting ready for work.

"You feeling any better, kiddo?"

"Not really, but I have to work," she said as she pushed on her face, still puffy from crying.

"Actually, working is good. It makes the time go by faster, and keeps you distracted."

"Yeah, I know."

"Well, I'm going for a run," I said. "Call me if you need me, okay?"

"You have my phone."

"Oh, right." I rushed to my room, and grabbed it from my drawer. "Here, but please, don't text him. Just trust me on this, okay?"

She nodded. "Mom?"

I played with her hair in the mirror. "Yeah?"

"Thanks for what you said yesterday."

I wrapped my arms around her, and leaned my head on her shoulder. Our faces were close, and I could see my features in her in the mirror. "You're welcome."

"I'll be home before dinner, okay?"

"Okay, I'll make something yummy," I said. "Love you, Em."

"Love you, too."

I jogged down the stairs, feeling like everything would be okay. As I drove to the park, Mel texted.

"I'm okay. Don't worry. Will call you soon."

I wasn't sure I believed her, but I didn't push.

At the park I ran the same path where Matthew and Charles had first tried to communicate with me. It was where he died. "Oh, Matthew," I said. "I wish I'd have figured it out sooner, little guy. I'm sorry." I picked up my pace, and eased into a run.

"Boo," Ma said, as she appeared in front of me.

I jumped.

She bellowed, snorting at the end. "Ah Madone. I love that."

"You're a pain in my butt," I said, laughing. "You gonna run with me or something?"

"Pfft. Celestial beings don't run, Ang. We float. I'm gonna float while you run, 'cause we gotta talk."

It was never good when someone said, *we gotta talk*. "Please, let it be about something minor, like Hershey Bars." I slowed my pace to a jog so I could keep talking.

"Don't get me started on my Hershey Bars again. I'm still mad at you about those."

"Ma, it was over thirty years ago. Build a bridge and get over it."

"No. Those were my Hershey Bars. I worked my butt off every day so you could have your *Sassoon* Jeans, and umpteen bottles of hairspray a week, and treated myself to a little something every now and then, only for you to get your grubby little hands on them."

I flicked my hand. "Good grief."

"It's your father's fault, too, so I'm still mad at him."

"How's it his fault? You were divorced already."

"That's how it's his fault. If we didn't get divorced, I could a used his money to get me my Hershey Bars, and maybe bought a safe to hide them in."

I shook my head. "It's amazing how you do that."

"Do what?"

"Forget it. I'm sure I'm gonna regret this, but tell me what we need to talk about."

"The Cloughs, they told the police about you."

I stopped. "Are you sure?"

She nodded. "Yup. I was there."

"What did they say?" I leaned my back against a tree and dropped the F-bomb.

"And you get on me when I curse."

"Ma, no jokes, please. This is serious. What's gonna happen now? What am I gonna do?" I sunk to the ground. "Oh God, what are people gonna say? This is gonna be bad, Ma. Real bad."

"Angela, you gotta stop worrying about what other people think. It ain't about you anymore, and you don't know what's gonna happen, so don't get all upset and have another one of those anxiety attacks like yesterday."

"I don't care what other people think of me, Ma. This isn't about me. It's about my family."

She threw her hands in the air. "Ah for cryin' out loud, Ang. You're all, *I don't want people to think I'm a whack job because I see dead people,* and *I gotta wear my ear plugs, so people don't think I'm a crazy person talking to myself.* Sure, you care about your family, but this here? It's completely about you."

"It's ear buds, and seeing dead people is a big thing, Mother. It's not like I'm afraid to go to Starbucks without makeup or anything."

"You don't need makeup. You look like me."

The places my mother could go in a conversation always fascinated me. "Yes, Ma, I look like you, but that's not the point. The point is, I do not care what people think of me."

"You keep thinkin' that. I hear there's some oceanfront property for sale in California, too."

I shook my head. "It's Arizona, Ma. California really is next to the ocean."

She tilted her head. "Oh, yah." She flipped her hand in the air. "You know what I mean. You're full of crap if you think you don't care what other people think about you."

I got pissy. "Fine, Ma. Whatever. It's not true, but whatever." I took off running, but Ma stayed behind. "Ma? You comin'?"

She held up her index finger. "Oh crap," she said. "This ain't good. We gotta go." She shot up in the air, and disappeared.

I looked up, equally impressed and freaked. "Ma? What's going on? Come back!"

She popped back in front of me. "Get to the car. It's Mel. She's at Carrie's apartment. The poop's gonna hit the fan. Meet me there."

I dropped the F-bomb again, and sprinted back to the car, which thankfully, was less than a mile away.

I called Mel on the way to Carrie's apartment, but she didn't answer. "I'm on my way. Please, please don't do anything. Just wait for me."

Just then Ma popped back in. "Nick's there."

"Crap. What's going on?" I took the back roads, hoping to bypass the construction on the regular route.

"A lotta yelling, that's what."

"Who's yelling?" I figured it was Mel, but hoped Ma would say someone else.

"Who do you think? She's gonna get all Bruce Lee on them. Put the pedal to the medal."

"Ma, you gotta go back. Make Mel calm down. Distract her. I don't care what you do, but make her stop before she makes things worse."

"I'm on it," she said, and shimmered away.

I texted Jake through the talk to text option on my phone. " Mel's cracked. Will keep you posted."

When I pulled into the apartment parking lot, I remembered I needed to be buzzed in. "Dammit," I mumbled, and then pressed buttons until someone finally beeped back. "Can I help you?"

"Yes, I'm here to deliver flowers, but they're not answering. Would you mind buzzing me in?"

I screeched through the gates, and pulled up alongside Mel's car. I knocked on Carrie's door, and heard Mel inside. "Fran, I know that's you. Knock it off." Something fell to the ground and shattered.

"Shit." I knocked harder.

A young, Asian woman—I assume Carrie— answered. "What?"

Oh boy. She had an attitude like Emily.

"I'm Mel's friend. May I come in?"

Carrie snarled, and moved to the side. I walked through as she said, "Be my guest. That woman is gonna lose it."

I flipped around, and only inches from her face, sneered, and said, "You're pregnant with her husband's kid, Carrie. You're lucky she hasn't nailed your slutty ass to the wall already."

Her jaw dropped. Mel probably hadn't dropped that bomb yet. "How...how do you know that? I haven't even told Nick."

I scanned the inside of her townhouse, but the main area was down a hall, and I couldn't see Mel, but I could hear her. "My guess is Mel will handle that for you."

I walked through the hallway into the main area, and saw Mel's hands flying through the air as she yelled at Nick. He stood there, stone-faced, and quiet. Pieces of a glass picture frame covered the area between them. Ma stood next to the couch. I pointed my index finger at the glass, and raised an eyebrow. She winked, and we both smiled.

I walked over to Mel. "Hey, you okay?"

Her hands were clenched in fists. She turned to me, and the whites of her eyes were bigger than I'd ever seen them. She had spit in the corner of her mouth. She didn't say anything.

"Mel."

She held a hand up to my face. "I've got this," she said. "You don't need to be here."

"Maybe we should get outta here? Get a coffee, or something?"

Mel shook her head. "I've got exciting news for Nick, here." She paused, and then a jabbed a finger in his face. "You're gonna be a daddy again."

Nick's eyes widened, and he stepped back. "You're pregnant?"

Mel straightened her shoulders, and laughed. "No jackass. Your little girlfriend is. Congratulations."

Nick's head shifted toward Carrie, and I watched his mouth soften. He loved her. "Carrie?" He asked.

Carrie nodded once. Nick walked over to her, and touched her stomach.

"Ah Madone. That ain't good," Ma said.

I held Mel's arm, feeling it tense in my hand. "You son of a bitch," she yelled. She tried to pull away, but I held her back.

"Mel, let's go."

"I'm not done yet."

Nick's face hardened again. "You need to leave, Mel."

Mel's arm tensed again, and I let go. I thought she'd rush him, but she didn't. She turned toward the door, and then turned around again, and said, "Your stuff will be on the front lawn. If it's not gone by tomorrow morning, it's going to Goodwill." She turned back around and walked out.

I glared at Nick.

"I'm sorry you had to see this, Ang," he said.

I pointed to Carrie, but kept my eyes focused on Nick. "Sure hope she's worth losing your family over." Then I turned around and walked out, too.

Outside, Mel leaned against her car. Her head was back, and her eyes were closed. I leaned up against it, and closed my eyes, too.

"I didn't lose it in there."

"No," I said. "You didn't."

"You thought I would."

"Not for a minute."

"Liar."

"Absolutely."

"He loves her."

"I know," I said.

"I wish I didn't still love him."

"I know."

"I hired that attorney."

"That's good."

"I'm gonna be all right."

"Better than ever," I said.

"I hope you're right."

"I'm always right."

"There is that."

* * *

I made sure Mel left, and then decided I needed caffeine, and headed to Starbucks.

"You did good, Angela," Ma said. "And Mel, too. I thought she was gonna have a stroke, she was so red, but she handled it good."

I yawned. "I think she's gonna be okay. She hired an attorney, and I think she's ready." I yawned again.

"She'll be fine. It ain't gonna be easy, but the hardest part is over."

I yawned again. "I hope so."

"You need a nap or something?" Ma asked.

"I'm just beat, Ma. A lot's happened in the past couple days."

"You shouldn't be pushing yourself like you do with the exercise. You're getting too old for that."

"I'm not getting old, Ma. And I'm not exercising too much. I've barely done anything lately, which is probably part of the reason why I'm tired. And I got a triple whammy of drama dropped on me in the span of a day, you know."

"I'm just sayin'."

"Well, you just say it to someone else. I'm not getting old."

"Yup, that's what I said when I was goin' through the change, too."

I pulled into the Starbucks parking lot, and parked the car. I shifted in the seat, and gave my mother the stink eye. "I am not going through the change."

"Bahaha! That's a joke, right? 'Cause it's funny, I tell ya. You're smack dab in the middle of the change, Ang."

I stared at the steering wheel. "Oh, God, Ma, I think you're right. What's happening to me?"

"You're becoming your dad, that's what's happening."

I shook my head. "What the hell's that supposed to mean?"

"You know, growin' facial hair and all. You're looking more like your dad, and less like me."

"Well, at least Dad was an attractive man."

"To some, I guess."

"Nice, Ma."

"What?"

I shook my head. "When I couldn't hear you, I had all of these questions about stuff, like when you went through menopause, and how long it lasted. But right now, I just want to get a cup of coffee, go home, and take a shower, and think about nothing."

"Enjoy that while it lasts," Ma said.

"Why? What do you know?"

She shook her head. "My lips are sealed," she said, and then shimmered away.

"I still hate when you do that!" I yelled.

* * *

Josh was home, holed up in the den, playing his game. I peeked in, told him I was going to shower, then nap.

"You sick?"

"No, just tired."

"Yeah, Emily does that to me, too."

I laughed. "I bet."

I took a long, hot shower, then snuggled under my covers. Gracie jumped up, found her favorite position on Jake's pillow, and went right to sleep. I ran my hand down her back. "I wish I could sleep like you, Gracie."

My cell phone rang. When I looked to see who it was, it said, "Dad". I'd never taken his name off of my contacts list. It just seemed too permanent.

"Hello?" I answered.

"Angela? It's Helen."

"Hey, how are you?"

"I'm good," she said. "I thought you'd like to know, I received some information about my cousin."

I smiled. "Oh? Did her daughter call you?"

"No, but an attorney did."

"Oh, really? About what?"

Helen told me all about the lawsuit, the money, and how a family member, who wished to remain anonymous, called the attorney and gave them her number. She was thrilled to have the money returned, and I felt like less of a heel for not being honest.

After we disconnected, I spoke to Brenda. "I know it's not what you asked, but I just couldn't tell her about my gift."

Brenda appeared in front of my bed. "I understand," she said. "Thank you for helping me."

I nodded. "If you see my father, can you tell him to come and visit me some time?"

Brenda nodded, and then she shimmered away.

* * *

Jake was still in the city, so when Emily called to see if she could hang out with Hayden, I let her.

She needed to get out, and have some fun, and I needed to trust her to make the right decisions. They were going to the water park, and she promised she'd be back by eleven.

I made myself a ham sandwich with extra mayo, poured a big glass of water, and sat at the table. I scarfed the sandwich down in milliseconds, and made another one. I didn't realize I was that hungry.

"Wish I could have one of those," Ma said.

I chewed with my mouth open, and made *num num num* sounds. "It's so good."

"You got some horrible manners, Ang." She smirked. "And you're rude, throwing that sandwich in my face like that."

"It's a gift."

"Hi Grandma," Josh said as he walked into the kitchen.

"Tell your Ma she's being rude eatin' in front of me like that."

"I can't. I'm gonna be rude in a minute, too. I'm hungry."

"Pfft. You got manners just like your Ma."

I held the last bite of my sandwich out to my mom. "Here. Want this?"

Josh did a double take. "Mama, can you see Grandma?"

I'd completely forgotten that Josh didn't know. "Yup. Make yourself something to eat and I'll fill you in."

"Okay."

I filled him in on what happened with Matthew, and warned him about the possibility of our lives changing. He didn't appear at all concerned.

"Told you I wasn't leaving rocks in the house," he said. He finished eating his sandwich and retreated back to the den.

I shook my head. "He amazes me."

"He's like my side of the family," Ma said.

I ignored that. "What's gonna happen, Ma?"

She busied herself looking at my counter. "I would have picked a lighter top if I was you," she said. "What kind of stone is this anyway? Back in my day, we used Formica. That stuff was easy to clean. This stuff here, all them colors?" She shook her head. "Too much work."

"What aren't you telling me, Ma?"

"Angela, you know I got rules."

"Again? You're using that again?"

"Whadda ya mean, usin' that again? I ain't usin' nothing. It's the truth. There are things I can't tell you."

"Yeah, like you couldn't tell me my father was going to die. Stupid rule if you ask me."

"If you couldn't talk to the dead, you wouldn't have known anyway." She flicked her hand in the air. "That's how it works. It's not my place to disrupt the natural order of things. Besides, I'll get in trouble, and I'm almost ready to be a spirit guide, and I don't wanna mess that up."

I sympathized with the person who had Ma for a spirit guide. "So instead of coming right out and breaking the rules, you figure it's okay to drop hints? That doesn't get you in trouble?"

She shrugged. "Not as much."

"Good grief."

"What am I gonna do if it gets out?"

"You're gonna do what you always do—deal with it. You're strong. You're made of good stock. This won't break you."

"I'm not sure that's true."

"Well I am, and I gave birth to you, so I know."

I sat at the table, my head in my hands, picturing reporters, and people crowding my yard. I pictured Emily embarrassed, and hiding in her room for being labeled *that girl with the crazy mother.* "Ugh. I'm screwed. We're gonna have to move."

"Nah, you don't gotta move. Things have a way of working themselves out."

I studied my mother's expression. It wasn't easy, because of her transparency. She knew things I didn't know, and wouldn't steer me in the wrong direction. She'd already told me the Cloughs told the police, so if it was going to get ugly, she'd drop hints about it. She wouldn't be able to stop herself. But she hadn't, so I had to believe everything would be okay. "Okay Ma. I trust you, and I'm not gonna worry anymore," I said.

"Well it's about time."

"Oh geez."

"Do me a favor, change outta those pajamas and put on something presentable. While you're at it, pull your hair up in a bun or something. You oughta get it cut. You're too old for long hair. You look like a floozy."

"Here we go again," I said, and got up.

"What?" She asked.

I shook my head. "Why do I need to get dressed, Ma? It's almost seven o'clock. I'm not going anywhere."

"It ain't good manners to receive guests in your pajamas, Angela. Now scoot."

That, I took as a hint.

CHAPTER FIFTEEN

I WAS SITTING ON THE COUCH when Jake walked in. "What are you all dressed for? It's almost eight."

The doorbell rang.

"For that," I said.

He raised an eyebrow, and moved to answer it.

"I'll get it," I said. "I know who it is."

I rested my head against the front door, took two deep breaths, and then plastered a big smile on my face, and opened it. Jake stood behind me.

A man stood on the front step. He flipped open his wallet, and said. "Angela Panther?"

I nodded.

"Detective Aaron Banner. May I come in?"

Jake stepped toward the detective, but I touched his arm. "Honey, it's okay."

I opened the door wide enough for him to enter. "Come on in, Detective. I was expecting you."

Jake shot me a look, and I mouthed. "Ma."

He nodded, but furrowed his brow.

We passed the den, and Josh looked up, but didn't flinch. Jake noticed, too.

I held my hand toward the chair. "Have a seat, Detective."

Jake and I sat on the couch.

The detective sat. "I'd like to ask you a few questions about the Clough family," he said.

I nodded. "I figured."

I watched as my mother appeared behind the Detective. She smirked and said, "Knock 'em dead."

"Where did you get your information about Maria?" The detective asked.

I pressed my lips together, and then nodded. "Detective, I'm going to assume, since you're here, you know the answer to that."

"I'd like to hear it from you, Mrs. Panther."

"Their son Matthew told me."

He didn't flinch. "Their dead son, Matthew."

I nodded.

He didn't say anything.

"Is that it, Detective?" I asked.

"Can you explain to me what happened? How you were able to talk to their dead son, Mrs. Panther?"

I leaned forward, and rested my forearms on my legs. "I have a gift, Detective."

He pulled out a notepad. "How long have you had this uh, gift?"

"Apparently I had it as a child, but it just went dormant or something until my mother died. And then I lost it again when my father died."

He looked at me, but didn't speak.

"But now it's back again, so it's all good." I smiled.

"I see. Continue."

The detective had no sense of humor.

"The Cloughs' son Matthew came to me, and asked me to give his parents a message. I didn't realize who he was at first, but my husband did some research, and found out. I felt like I owed it to his parents to give them closure."

"And what did you tell them?"

Just then the TV remote scooted across the table, and fell to the ground. I covered my mouth to hide a giggle, and looked at my mother, who just shrugged. Jake smirked.

The detective, visibly uncomfortable, shifted in his seat. "Uh..."

"I'm sorry. My mother's got a strange sense of humor. You were saying?"

"Your mother?" He shook his head. "I uh...I asked...oh, what did you tell the Clough boy's parents? Just tell me exactly what happened when you went to them, okay?"

He'd recouped well. I laid out the details, giving the detective as much information as possible.

"So you actually saw their little boy, Matthew?"

I shook my head. "Not at first. No. I couldn't even hear him at first. Like I said, I had lost my gift when my father died, but that hasn't stopped the dead from trying to connect."

"I don't understand," he said.

Jake intervened. "You're not the first to say that. I still don't understand any of it, but my wife is telling you the truth. She can communicate with the dead, Detective. I've seen it for myself."

"There are many people who profess to have that ability," Banner said. "But that doesn't mean they do."

Jake turned to him. "Look, with all due respect, officer—"

"It's detective."

"My apologies. With all due respect, Detective, I don't appreciate your tone. My wife isn't professing to anything. She's telling you the truth. Why are you here? Is my wife in some kind of trouble?"

I hadn't thought about that. I wondered if they could arrest me for something. I glance at my mother, who was laughing, so I figured I was going to be okay.

"No, sir. This case is closed. I'm just doing my due diligence, and following up for the Cloughs. They've been through a lot, and I don't want them being hurt further."

That softened both my husband and me. This man must have cared about the family.

"Were you the detective who helped them originally?" I asked.

Ma nodded in unison with Banner.

"Oh, well, I'm sorry if we're being rude, but I've kept my ability private—as much as possible at least—and I'd like to keep it that way. I had idea that what Matthew said would implicate the babysitter. I just wanted to help him speak with his parents."

"Did you charge them anything for the information?"

My face contorted. "Good God, no. I don't do it for money. I do it because otherwise the damn ghosts won't leave me alone." I paused, and then said, "And because it's the right thing to do."

He actually laughed, and his face softened a bit. Maybe he did have a sense of humor after all. "I don't believe people can communicate with the dead, ma'am. I'm sorry."

"Yeah, well, there was a time I would have said that same thing, but now I know better."

Jake laughed. "Me too, but she convinced me."

I rubbed his knee. "Get hit on by any granny hookers lately, babe?"

"Thankfully, no."

"I don't believe it's possible," Banner said. "And I'd like the Cloughs to be able to move forward, not wait and hope that we'll reopen the case, and arrest the babysitter. They don't need to have any more pain."

"Detective Banner," I said. "I have it on good authority that if you question the babysitter, she'll tell you the truth."

"The case is closed ma'am. It was ruled an accident. The boy fell, and that's all there is to it."

"But what if it's not? What if you were to talk to Maria again, and she confessed? What if I'm not lying, but you do nothing, and then later, she does confess? How will that make you feel? How will it make you look, knowing you could have done something, but didn't? I think *that* would cause the Cloughs more pain, Detective."

"Yah, Ang. That's good. Real good," Ma said.

From the expression on Banner's face, it seemed he was leaning toward questioning Maria, so I pushed harder. "Have you ever lost anyone close to you, Detective?"

"Yes, ma'am."

"I'm sorry for that, but do you think, if you had any question about how that person died, you'd be able to just let it go, and move on? Do you think the Cloughs can do that, knowing what they know? And Matt, he's a loose cannon. He came to the door with a shotgun. God only knows what he'll do if he decides to confront Maria."

Ma snorted.

Banner stewed on that for a bit, and then said, "He brought his shotgun to the door?"

I nodded. "Apparently I'm not the first medium to approach them, but I am the first real one."

He closed his notebook. "You're right. Matt's had a hard time with this, and I don't want him risking jail time by confronting the babysitter. I'll tell you what I'm going to do. I'll talk to her again, tell her we've discovered some new information, and ask her to reiterate one more time, what happened. If you're right, and she confesses, I'll come back and apologize for not believing you. If she doesn't, then I'm going to be watching you like a hawk, Mrs. Panther."

I nodded. Jake bowed up, but I put my hand on his knee again and squeezed. "That works for me, Detective Banner."

We walked him out, and after closing the door, Jake lit up. "What a piece of crap," he said.

I walked over to the couch and sat. Shaking, I said, "He's not a piece of crap, Jake. He just doesn't believe."

"He's gonna believe, Ang. You just wait," Ma said. "Want I should go with him? You know, toss a few cups or somethin' if need be?"

"Ma, I think it's best we let this play out on its own. I don't want to make it any worse than it might get, okay?"

"Drats. You're no fun."

"So I hear."

Jake was staring at me. "It's always odd, watching you talk to yourself like that. I mean, I know you're talking to Fran, but it looks like you're talking to yourself."

"Thanks hon, that's exactly what I want to hear right now. *Honey, you look crazy, can't wait for this to be public.*"

He sat next to me. "That's not what I meant. I'm sorry."

"'S okay. I'm just preparing for the worst. Do you have any connections to any witness protection people?"

He shook his head. "Not that I'm aware of."

"Pfft. Good for nothing but sex, huh?"

"I'm handy around the house, too."

"There is that. I guess I'll keep you. Too bad you're not younger."

"Thanks."

I laughed. "Let's go to bed. I'm tired."

"Me, too, but first you owe me for last night."

Ma said, "Ew, I'm outta here."

"That window, honey, closed hours ago. I'm exhausted."

"I need to figure out a way to lock that window in the open position."

* * *

The next morning, Josh and Emily both got up, ate breakfast and left. Emily graciously offered to take Josh and Turner to the water park. Jake thought it was sweet of her, but I suspected there was a cute lifeguard or someone there who Emily had her eye on. As they left, I caught Emily's eye and winked. She winked back.

I texted Mel and asked how things had gone the night before.

"Don't know. I went to bed, and when I got up, his stuff was gone."

"Probably best," I wrote back.

"Meeting with the attorney in an hour. Then looking online for a job."

"One thing at a time."

"I'm in survival mode," she wrote.

"Get through the hard stuff and then aim toward the future, Mel. You don't need the added stress."

"I feel sick to my stomach."

"I'm sorry." I hadn't told Mel anything about what'd been happening with me, and I wasn't going to for the time being. She needed to focus on her own problems, not mine. "Text me when you can."

"Always do. Thanks for being my best friend."

"No one else wanted the job."

"Bite me."

"You're not my type. Love you."

"Ditto."

Jake offered to cancel his trip. He was heading back to New York for meetings, but I told him no. "If Banner comes back, I'll be okay. It's not like he can arrest me, or anything. I haven't done anything illegal. I don't think."

"I don't think he's going to arrest you. I'm just offering my support."

"I know, and thank you, but it's okay. I'm a big girl. I'll be fine. Besides, we don't even know if he went to Maria's already, or not."

"I have a feeling he went straight there."

I did too. Jake didn't need to miss work because of my stuff. "Go, please. Make me miss you. I'm tired of seeing your face. You're becoming old cow, so scoot." I pushed him toward the stairs. "Get in the shower. You've got man smell."

He sniffed himself. "I do not."

"Uh huh. Seriously honey, I'll be fine."

He went up and showered, and was out the door with a kiss and a hug thirty minutes later.

Relieved to be alone, I pulled open the fridge to grab another Diet Coke, only to find there were none left. "Crap. Who drank the last one?"

"It wasn't me," Ma said.

"Funny, Ma."

"Me and Buddy are going on a quick trip to Italy again. I wanted to let you know I'm gonna be gone for a bit."

"How long?"

"In your time? Maybe a day, two, tops."

My heart beat faster. "But what about Detective Banner, Ma?"

"What about him, Ang? I told you, it's all gonna be okay."

Buddy appeared, and smiled. "Hello, Angela."

"Hi buddy." I shook my head. "This is gonna take a lot of getting used to."

"Okay, well, we're outta here," Ma said.

"But Ma—"

It was too late. They'd both shimmered away.

"Dammit."

I sat at the kitchen table, sipping on a glass of ice water instead of Diet Coke, and prepared for the worst. I thought of where we could move, and how I'd survive without Mel. Maybe I could convince her to come, too?

I stilled myself, and focused my senses. I hoped to feel my father, but I didn't. "Dad? I don't know if you can hear me or not, but I know why you came to me, and I just wanted to say thank you."

I drank the rest of the water. "I might need you again though, so don't stop checking on me. I'll always be daddy's little girl." I rubbed the tears from my eyes.

My life had shifted. I realized the importance of my gift. It wasn't about me, and I didn't want it back for myself, but I'd be lying if I said I wasn't glad to see my mother, and wished I could see my dad. It wasn't about them, or me, and helping Matthew and his parents made that clear. I just wish I knew what would happen next.

I sat on the couch, enjoying the peace and quiet. I enjoyed it so much, I'd fallen asleep. When the doorbell rang, I shot up, and squealed.

It was Detective Banner, and he wasn't smiling. I ran my fingers through my hair, smiled, and let him in. "Have a seat," I said. "Can I get you anything to drink?"

"No, ma'am, but thank you."

I stood for a second, and then sat, too. I stuffed my hands under my legs because I didn't want to fidget, and appear nervous. "So..."

He started to speak and then stopped, and looked at the TV. "Can you turn that on?" He nodded toward the TV.

"Uh, sure." I grabbed the remote, and flipped it on. "What channel?"

"Local news would be good. There's something I want you to see."

"News? What time is it?" I looked at the clock. It was after six in the evening. "Oh, wow. I slept through the whole day." I shook my head. "Sorry, I'm babbling." I changed the channel to an evening news program, and asked, "How's this?"

"That's fine," he said.

We watched the end of a commercial, and when the news came back on, Matthew's picture appeared on the screen. Next to it was the photo of a woman. I assumed it was Maria.

"Local authorities made an arrest today in the recently reopened case of Matthew Clough, the five-year-old who police thought hit his head at an Atlanta suburb park. The babysitter, Maria Alverez, who was with Matthew Clough the day he died, was arrested for first degree murder," the reporter said. "Sources say an anonymous tip led Detective Aaron Banner to question the babysitter again. Alverez confessed to pushing the boy, and leaving him there to die. She's currently being held without bond."

I clicked off the TV, and raised an eyebrow at the detective. "An anonymous tip?"

He smiled. "That comes with a price, Mrs. Panther."

"I'm not sure I understand."

He leaned forward. "I don't know if you can do what you say, but I do know you told me Alverez would confess, and she did. Now whether you knew that because of a dead person or not remains to be seen, but whatever the case, I'd like to use you to help me with current, future and maybe even cold, unsolved cases."

I was speechless, and as an Italian woman, that was rare.

"Did you hear me, Mrs. Panther?"

"Please, call me Angela, and yes, I heard you."

"Well?"

"Uh, I...I don't know what to say. To be honest, this was the last thing I expected. I'm not sure what to think."

"Believe me, I'm not sure what to think, either. All I know is you told me something that ended up being true, and I can't discount that. Do I think you can talk to the dead? No, but you can do something, and I believe that something would be beneficial to people in law enforcement."

"I really don't want people to know what I can do."

"Of course, and we'll do everything to maintain your anonymity," he said. "In fact, everything you do will be completely off the record, and unfortunately, without pay."

"I told you, I don't accept payment for helping people, Detective."

"Call me Aaron, and that's great because the department doesn't have a budget for psychics."

"I'm not a psychic. I'm a psychic medium. There's a difference."

"Well, you knew Alverez would confess."

"Yes, but only because my mother told me."

"Your dead mother."

I nodded. "Yup, that one."

He shook his head. "This is definitely going to take some getting used to. I don't think I'll ever be a believer, but we'll see."

Just then an older woman with silky white hair, wearing a beautiful red and gold dress appeared next to Banner. "My grandbaby boy," she said, and then she winked at me. "I have something to tell him."

I smiled, and said, "Aaron, there's someone here who wants to talk to you."

The End

ACKNOWLEDGMENTS

There are far too many people to thank when it comes to this book. Had reviews for Unfinished Business not been so good, I don't know if I would have had the nerve to ever write again, so first and foremost, thank you to everyone who read Unfinished Business. You all made me feel like I could actually write and that's pretty darn awesome!

Of course I have to say a big thank you to my wonderful friend Karyn 'Cupcake' Clough, who read every chapter of this book repeatedly and offered wonderful ideas. She is the best unofficial editor ever!

For all of the advanced readers who took the chance to read this and didn't throw it in my face screaming about how horrible it was, ya'll rock!

And most importantly, to my 'hottie hubby' Jack, the biggest thank you of all. I do not deserve such a great guy. Okay, wait, maybe I do.

Keep in touch with Carolyn:

carolynridderaspenson.com

carolynridderaspenson@gmail.com

ALSO BY CAROLYN RIDDER ASPENSON

Unfinished Business
(Book 1 in the Angela Panther Series)

MORE GREAT READS FROM BOOKTROPE

Joe Vampire **by Steven Luna** (Paranormal/Humor) Hey, folks. I'm Joe, and I'm a vampire – not by choice, mind you, but by accident…a fate-twisting, fang-creating, blood lust-inducing misunderstanding.

Touched **by A.J. Aalto** (Paranormal) The media has a nickname for Marnie Baranuik, though she'd rather they didn't; they call her the Great White Shark. A forensic psychic twice-touched by the Blue Sense, which gives her the ability to feel the emotions of others and read impressions left behind on objects, Marnie is too mean to die young, backed up by friends in cold places, and has a mouth as demure as a cannon's blast.

The Collection **by T.K. Lasser** (Paranormal Romance) A human lie detector and an immortal art thief are thrust together in a ruthless plot of high stakes acquisition and murder by a black market art buyer.

Haunted **by Eileen Maksym** (Fiction) The Society for Paranormal Researchers, a group of college friends, get involved in a dangerous investigation of a local haunted house.

Discover more books and learn about our
new approach to publishing at **booktrope.com**.

CPSIA information can be obtained at www.ICGtesting.com
Printed in the USA
LVOW13s0704290614

392137LV00001B/4/P